EVERYMAN'S LIBRARY

EVERYMAN,
I WILL GO WITH THEE,
AND BE THY GUIDE,
IN THY MOST NEED
TO GO BY THY SIDE

JANE AUSTEN

Northanger Abbey

with an Introduction by
Claudia L. Johnson

———

EVERYMAN'S LIBRARY

109

First included in Everyman's Library, 1906
Introduction, Bibliography and Chronology © David Campbell
Publishers Ltd., 1992
Typography by Peter B. Willberg

ISBN 1-85715-109-7

A CIP catalogue record for this book is available from the
British Library

Published by David Campbell Publishers Ltd., 79 Berwick Street,
London W1V 3PF

Distributed by Random House (UK) Ltd.,
20 Vauxhall Bridge Road, London SW1V 2SA

NORTHANGER ABBEY

INTRODUCTION

Northanger Abbey is at once Jane Austen's first and last complete
novel. Drafted in 1798–9, the novel (then called _Susan_ and
later _Catherine_) was revised, sold for ten pounds to Crosby &
Co., and advertised for publication in 1803. Crosby & Co.,
however, never printed the manuscript, and although Austen
bought it back in 1809, it was not to appear until 1817, five
months after her death.[1] Clearly, the editor who decided not
to publish Austen's first novel made a mistake for which
literary history can hardly forgive him. But mistakes can be
instructive, and his invites us to consider how this little novel –
once considered no more than a fledgling effort of limited
interest – not merely encompasses but in a sense also inspires
Austen's canon. Abounding in youthful hilarity, _Northanger
Abbey_ is, among other things, a parody of gothic fiction, and as
such it is obviously affiliated with the exuberant literary
parodies among Austen's 'juvenile' productions, such as _Love
and Freindship_ [sic] (1790). But the accident of its publication
alongside _Persuasion_ alerts us to how much _Northanger Abbey_ has
in common with Austen's late work as well, especially with the
unfinished _Sanditon_, which shares not only its determination to
detach a heroine from her home, its depiction of resort life, and
its bluntness of tone, but also its conspicuous preoccupation
with reading.[2] It is this last feature which I consider particularly significant. _Northanger Abbey_ narrates a young heroine's
'entrée into life', but it also constitutes a young author's
'entrée' into literature. In 1803, Austen could have made this
entrance with a number of other works in manuscript: she
could have revised _First Impressions_ (the early version of _Pride
and Prejudice_, which she had already tried and failed to get
published six years earlier); she could have turned to _Lady
Susan_ or to _Elinor and Marianne_ (later, _Sense and Sensibility_). It is
tempting to argue – though this is, after all, only speculation –
that faced with a choice among all these estimable, now-lost
manuscripts, Austen opted to initiate her career with _North-
anger Abbey_ because in addition to being a good novel it alone

was also a manifesto of her artistic program, one which was to retain its pertinence for years to come.

As recently as a generation ago, this claim would have struck many as rather strained. Austen seemed to be the most demure of novelists, a homely songbird indifferent to her art, as Henry James described her, with a mixture of querulousness and condescension.[3] Most appreciations dwelled with evident satisfaction on Austen's supposed modesty about her art, as if inviting us to reward her with our admiration in part because she herself had no pretensions to greatness: Austen was archly ironic, to be sure, but never would she exhibit anything so unladylike or so unseemly as ambition or a sense of artistic self-importance. In an oft-quoted section of *A Memoir of Jane Austen* (1870), J. E. Austen-Leigh recollects how Austen quickly put away or hid her drafts whenever the creaky door announced that visitors were coming. According to his representation, Austen is the good aunt, cheerfully surrendering herself to the casual interruptions that beset her as she worked in the common sitting-room. She naturally considered the entertainment of children such as himself of greater importance than artistic application.

Some of Austen's own statements would appear to support this view. Austen defended her niece's youthful attempts at composition by averring, reportedly, that 'writing stories was a great amusement, and *she* thought a harmless one, though many people, she was aware, thought otherwise', encouragement which sounds painfully uncomfortable to modern ears.[4] Finally, Austen's famous characterization of her fiction as a 'little bit (two inches wide) of Ivory' – even granting that it reads ironically in context – retreats from the grand and ambitious to the diminutive and the unassuming. This retreat implies an awareness that the imperative of female modesty did not cease to apply at the edge of a lady's writing table.[5] But *Northanger Abbey* gives us quite another picture. Far from being self-deprecatory about her compositions, Austen was plainly aggrieved by the novel's non-appearance. The 'Advertisement' to *Northanger Abbey*, written in 1816 in order to account for its belatedness, makes no attempt to conceal her lingering mortification. 'That any bookseller should think it worth while to purchase what he did not think it worth while to publish seems extraordinary,' Austen writes irritably, and that the book 'was even advertised' only later to be unaccountably withdrawn adds insult to injury.

If the neglect of thirteen years could not diminish the author's concern for *Northanger Abbey*, the reason has much to do with the fact that the novel itself is a spirited defense of novels. 'Yes, novels,' the narrator taunts towards its outset, daring the glib insults of reviewers who make a profession out of disparaging the novelist's art. In light of *Northanger Abbey*'s inaugurating position in Austen's career, we would do well to consider this bravura vindication of fiction that occupies its fifth chapter. Not for Austen the professions of diffidence contemporary novelists often employed in order to conciliate the critics: 'I will not adopt that ungenerous and impolitic custom so common with novel writers, of degrading by their contemptuous censure the very performances, to the number of which they are themselves adding'. Scorning such self-censure, she, on the contrary, goes on the offensive. It is reviewers, not novelists, who are the 'threadbare' ones, so warped by 'pride, ignorance, or fashion' that they 'eulogize' with 'a thousand pens' the 'nine-hundredth abridger of the History of England', to say nothing of the umpteenth anthologist of the same dozen lines from 'Milton, Pope, and Prior' along with a 'paper from the Spectator, and a chapter from Sterne', while pooh-poohing with 'common cant' the labours of novelists which have 'only genius, wit, and taste to recommend them'. That unobtrusive little word 'only' packs the power of Austen's ironic punch.

With the benefit of some two hundred years of literary history behind us, the most recent of which have illuminated as well as challenged the very foundations on which cultural study itself is usually placed, we can now see that Austen is engaging in canon-reformation. When what we now call the novel emerged in England at the end of the seventeenth century, it was decried as a vulgar and potentially revolutionary form with no entitlement to the name literature, written and largely read by persons of both sexes without a classical education. The debate about the value of novels relative to other literary forms had not stopped by Austen's time, though its terms changed somewhat as novels themselves came increasingly to be considered a feminine medium. At stake in Austen's high-spirited defense – and its playful humor does not qualify its underlying seriousness – is not only the artistic dignity of novels, which had been assailed by cultural arbiters who refuse to recognize such 'labours' as literature at all, but also the legitimacy of the social vision of people who wrote them, people formerly excluded from the ranks of authorship and denied the distinction and the privilege of authority. The debate in which Austen is engaging is not essentially different from the controversy occurring on both sides of the Atlantic today in the press, in politics, and in the academy, as to whether the works of women, so-called 'minorities', and non-western peoples can be considered great literature in the same sense that the works of Homer and Shakespeare are.

Writing at the dawning of liberal feminism, and a generation after figures such as Mary Wollstonecraft and Catherine Macaulay, Austen does not make a theoretical issue of the way in which sexual bias *per se* motivates the exclusion of works by women from the dignified ranks of great literature. Nevertheless, all the examples she cites indicate her awareness that the writing, reading and assessing of literature are gendered activities, and that women's activities on all these fronts are unfairly devalued. When reviewers, novelists, and novelistic characters themselves throw their books aside and sigh ' "Oh! it is only a novel!" ', Austen (lingering ironically once again on 'only') paraphrases their disclaimer in a way that both explodes its legitimacy and shows her own hand:

"It is only Cecilia, or Camilla, or Belinda;" or, in short, only some work in which the greatest powers of the mind are displayed, in which the most thorough knowledge of human nature, the happiest delineation of its varieties, the liveliest effusions of wit and humour are conveyed to the world in the best chosen language.

It is not just the novel in general, but the emergent female tradition of the novel in particular that the narrator touts here with stunning superlatives. No reader will fail to catch the astonishingly self-assured implication that *Northanger Abbey* belongs to the tradition represented by sister-novelists Frances Burney and Maria Edgeworth. Novels of manners like Burney's *Evelina* (1778), *Cecilia* (1782), *Camilla* (1796), and Edgeworth's *Belinda* (1801) dramatize an intelligent, unaffected, and sheltered girl's first encounters with the perplexing and often brutal realities of the contemporary social world. Catherine Morland's 'entrée into life' at Bath, her attempts to learn about its rituals, to fathom its mysteries, to account for its contradictions, and finally to face its corruptions, are unquestionably modelled on the experiences of these earlier fictional counterparts.

But what about Ann Radcliffe, the most eminent author of the kind of fiction spoofed in *Northanger Abbey*? Do her novels – which typically narrate outlandishly extreme and vaguely supernatural goings-on in far-away places long ago – have a place in the tradition Austen champions? Or does *Northanger Abbey* engage in the same degrading attempt at advancement through negation that the narrator explicitly deplores, scapegoating gothic novelists like Radcliffe in order to spare novelists of manners like Edgeworth, Burney, and – by implication of course – Austen herself? The majority of scholars have maintained the latter, characterizing *Northanger Abbey* as an anti-gothic novel, which establishes its norms of sanity, moderation, and civility by ridiculing and reversing the excesses of books such as Radcliffe's *The Mysteries of Udolpho* (1794) and *The Italian* (1797). Superficially, there is much to support this view. By the late 1790s, the gothic novel had already become a conspicuously formulaic genre, and as such was often the butt of critical satire. The *Magasin encyclopédique* of 1797, for example, listed the following as a '*Recipe*' for a gothic novel:

An old castle, half of it crumbling down,
A long corridor, with numerous doors many of which must be hidden,
Three corpses weltering in their blood,
Three skeletons carefully wrapped up,
An old woman hanged, stabbed several times in her throat,
Robbers and ruffians galore,
A sufficient dose of whispers, stifled moan and frightful din.[6]

This list of 'ingredients', which is to be 'well mixed and

divided into three parts or volumes' by the cook/novelist, is manifestly similar in mood to much of the parody in *Northanger Abbey*. Catherine, for example, can't get her mind off the skeleton of Laurentini in *Mysteries of Udolpho*. When she learns that she is to journey to Northanger Abbey, she is overcome with the thrilling expectation of encountering its 'long, damp passages, its narrow cells and ruined chapel'. She even goes so far as to hope to discover there 'some awful memorials to an injured and ill-fated nun'. Henry Tilney, himself a parodist of sorts, jokingly encourages the gullible young Catherine to look for other 'horrors that a building such as "what one reads about" may produce' – such as 'peals of thunder' and 'frightful gusts of wind'; remote and dimly lit bedchambers walled with 'sliding pannels and tapestry'; hidden doors 'secured by massy bars and a padlock'; ponderous chests and cabinets 'which no efforts can open'; heart-stopping excursions through secret subterraneous corridors disclosing the obligatory 'dagger ... drops of blood ... [and] instrument of torture'.

Austen appears bent on satirizing the conventions of Radcliffean fiction by inciting her heroine to gothic expectations with the sole purpose of disappointing them. Northanger Abbey, for example, far from moldering into a sublime pile, is fully modernized, 'improved', and spruce, its pointed windows repaned with transparent glass admitting the reassuring brilliance of sunlight. The bedchamber into which Catherine is ushered is comfortable and cheery, with no lurid tapestries or mouldy velvet drapery in sight. The large chest she discovers there contains neatly folded hats and bonnets rather than the human remains of murder most foul, and the black cabinet is impossible to pry open only because Catherine herself had locked rather than unlocked it to begin with. Once open, it is discovered to contain a roll of manuscript pages comprising not the memoirs of a mysterious sufferer, but a laundry list and a farrier's bill.

But Austen's joke is not on Catherine's supposed obsession with gothic paraphenalia alone. *Our* gothic expectations about her are thoroughly mocked well before poor Catherine has the foggiest notion what gothic novels are, her library evidently containing nothing more modern than *Sir Charles Grandison*.

The very first line of the novel – 'No one who had ever seen Catherine Morland in her infancy, would have supposed her born to be an heroine' – thus calls attention to our gothic preconceptions, not to hers. The haplessly ordinary Catherine is not, we discover, a poor orphan; she is plain, rather than lovely; dull rather than precocious; and far from exhibiting any incipient symptoms of heroic femininity – such as a fondness for nursing dolls, animals and flowers – she is a tomboy, hating 'confinement and cleanliness', and loving 'nothing so well in the world as rolling down the green slope at the back of the house'. Even after Catherine grows into young womanhood, she fails to exhibit that proclivity towards heroic inanition we (still) expect in heroines – in Radcliffe's novels, for example, only servants express solicitude for their bellies. Indeed, she returns home after a disappointing ball most unheroically to appease her 'extraordinary hunger' and consign herself not to a sleepless and tear-drenched pillow, but to a 'sound sleep' of nine refreshing hours. As the foregoing amply shows, it is not for nothing that so many readers have concluded that Austen's agenda in *Northanger Abbey* was to sweep aside the extravagant claptrap of gothic fiction and to replace them with her own circumscribed but also fresher and more realistic art.

But *Northanger Abbey* does not ultimately repudiate the gothic novel, and to mistake Austen on this point is to miss the richness, not to mention the joke, of *Northanger Abbey*. It is also to misapprehend Austen's celebrated irony in general. The opening chapter describes how Catherine 'fell miserably short of the true heroic height' only to assert that this 'young lady is to be a heroine' anyway. Austen makes no fast distinction between the gothic novel and the novel of manners. After all, Edgeworth and Burney were thoroughly imbued with Radcliffe's novels, and Austen launches into her encomium on the female novelistic tradition when Catherine retires to read Radcliffe's fiction – not theirs. Establishing a sense of artistic solidarity in a hostile critical climate – 'Let us not desert one another,' she declares, 'we are an injured body' – the narrator hoists the Augustan male literary establishment on its own petard by upbraiding works already regarded as veritable classics of Augustan prose: the *Spectator* essays. Austen was surely aware that the *Spectator* was celebrated for its polish, 'always equable,' as Samuel Johnson had put it in the *Life of Addison*, 'and always easy ... always luminous ... familiar but not coarse, and elegant but not ostentatious'. But her attack on the *Spectator*, which might seem to be purely gratuitous censure, is actually a strategically brilliant turn, for she proceeds to assail the very model of stylistic moderation on precisely the same grounds that gothic novels were – and still are – routinely attacked. Catherine herself later observes that respectable 'Mr. Allen had been used to call [gothic novels] unnatural and overdrawn'. But as the narrator would have it here, it is the *Spectator*, not *The Mysteries of Udolpho*, that is gross and exaggerated, saturated with 'improbable circumstances, unnatural characters' and language so 'coarse as to give no very favourable idea of the age that could endure it'. *Northanger Abbey* will go on to show that novels – and this includes gothic novels – actually give a clear, if unfavorable, picture of the age, accurately reflecting the way things are as she and novelists like her saw them.

This lengthy and sophisticated tribute to the feminine fictional tradition is no casual or momentary intrusion, to be indulged and then promptly forgotten. Rather, it states in a detached and self-conscious way the central contention of the novel: readers' different senses of propriety and plausibility, of the strange, the probable, the natural, the linguistically coarse or appropriate – and with all of these, of course, their different assessments of literary value – depend on their own authority, that is, on their relationship to established power. How one reads novels, Austen's novel will show, depends then on how one reads one's culture and one's place within it.

Northanger Abbey is a gothic novel about novels – about writing them, as we have seen above, but just as importantly about reading them. It dramatizes a heroine's encounters with the uncanny not by reversing but rather by rejuvenating and ultimately reaffirming gothic conventions. Despite what the narrator, adopting gothic discourse, describes as Catherine's 'strange' ordinariness, and despite the unaccountable 'perverseness' of her neighbourhood in failing to supply her with a hero-sweetheart, both she and we will learn to recognize the gothic outlines of her story as we learn how to read properly. Catherine, of course, seems a wholly naive reader, of both her world and her novels. She is comically endearing in part because she is as haunted and perplexed by the mysteries of Bath as she is by those of *Udolpho*. She starts out as a reader content with surfaces: Isabella professes a lofty disdain for the maneuvers of men, and Catherine, believing her older and wiser friend, simply overlooks her coquettish and transparently mercenary pursuit of them; her brother declares that rattles like John Thorpe are favored by women, and so Catherine suppresses her own irritation in his company; General Tilney professes an indifference to money, so Catherine does not believe he will object to Isabella's poverty.

More than inexperience is at issue in Catherine's readiness to take people at their word, for Catherine is rather trustful than merely credulous. In other words, 'with all the civility and deference of the youthful female mind', Catherine has faith in the truthfulness, the wisdom and the goodwill of persons who stand in a relationship of authority to her. If such a person is a 'self-assured man', she is especially 'fearful of hazarding an opinion of her own' in opposition to him, no matter how ludicrous or offensive he may be; if he represents the 'high authority' of an eldest brother, his views will be hard to resist, no matter how blinkered and selfish; and if he is a father and a general to boot, his being 'perfectly agreeable and good-natured, and altogether a very charming man, did not admit of a doubt', no matter how oppressive his company. No proto-revolutionary, Catherine relies wholly on her elders and betters – 'he could not propose any thing improper for her', she remarks of General Tilney with a girlish trust that seems painfully pathetic in light of his eventual viciousness towards her.

Catherine may be trustful – from the start we are told that her mind is marked by 'youth and diffidence' – but she is not stupid. Before long her confidence ruptures. Once the disparity between profession and fact becomes too conspicuous for her to overlook, she begins to experience her world as a troubling and baffling place, and to become, in short, a gothic heroine beset by mysteries. She cannot 'avoid a little suspicion' of Isabella's duplicity; she feels 'astonishment' – which along with awe and terror are mandatory gothic sentiments – at Thorpe's exaggerations and contradictions; she is 'distressed, but not subdued' by the heartless and unprincipled attempts of her brother and friends to pressure her into breaking her engagement with the Tilneys; and she is 'puzzled' by the constraint Henry and Eleanor seem to suffer in their father's company. The gothic novel is before all else devoted to dramatizing the intuition of horrible truths concealed beneath imposing surfaces, to exposing how persons and institutions ostensibly devoted to the protection of the powerless instead coerce and betray them in the interests of greed and dominion. These examples – along with the novel's pervasive and entirely non-parodic use of gothic keywords relative to agony, captivity, torment, violence, submission – show how carefully Austen has used the language of gothic fiction to expose a horrible truth about daily life in Regency England.

Catherine experiences greed, betrayal, and dominion aplenty in Bath. But one of the novel's least appreciated jokes is the fact that even though she sometimes verges on connecting the world of gothic novels and the world of Bath – meditating 'by turns, on broken promises and broken arches, phaetons and false hangings, Tilneys and trap doors' – she does *not* see herself as the budding gothic heroine she is. Unlike characters in other novels written at least in part to mock the extravagancies of fiction and its female readers – one thinks of Lady Arabella in Charlotte Lennox's *The Female Quixote* (1752) and Cherubina in Eaton Stannard Barrett's exceptionally nasty *The Heroine* (1813) – Catherine is unable to imagine herself a gothic heroine until she is placed squarely and quite literally within a gothic abbey. *We* are able to perceive John Thorpe's boorish and brutal determination to force Catherine on a carriage ride with him despite her vociferous refusal – a refusal which prompts him merely to laugh and smack his whip – as a genuinely oppressive variant on the standard gothic abduction scene. *We* can discern in the neglect Catherine experiences at the Allens' hands a distant relative to the profound and haunting isolation endured by

gothic heroines. And *we* can recognize the corporeal as well
psychological violence to which James and the Thorpes resort
to force her compliance with their schemes as a transposition
of the gothic scene of torture which the heroine virtuously
withstands.

The gothic frame established from the outset of the novel –
to which Catherine, of course, has no access – invites us to
conclude that gothic modulations may intensify the horror of
daily life, but they do not distort it beyond all recognition.
Until the conclusion of the novel, Catherine, by contrast,
cannot realize this, and for the same reason that she is
dumbfounded by Henry Tilney's comparison of dancing and
marriage. A literalist through and through, she refuses Henry
Tilney's simile because marriage and dancing 'are so very
different', and no amount of elaboration on his part will make
her budge. Similarly, mistaking gothic conventions for unme-
diated representation, she concludes that gothicism is something that happens only on stormy nights in medieval abbeys
rather than ballrooms at Bath; that fierce ruffians cannot be
the good friends of trusted brothers; that gothic villainy consists
of nothing less than the imprisonment and murder of women.

For Henry Tilney the case stands quite differently. He
regards gothic novels as nothing but an inventory of machi-
nery. Henry is just as jaded about Bath chit-chat, considering
the discourse of ordinary life and gothic fiction similarly stale
and risible. Because Henry Tilney is often taken for Austen's
surrogate, it is important to examine his attitudes on this
score. When Catherine first meets Henry, he forms 'his features into a set smile ... affectedly softening his voice ... with a
simpering air' and delivers himself of a brief dramatic parody
of banal Bath prattle. Yet when Catherine and Eleanor later
meet, they exchange civilities identical to the chatter Henry
ridicules: 'not an observation was made, nor an expression
used by either which had not been made and used some
thousands of times before, under that roof, in every Bath
season'. Inasmuch as the narrator specifically praises Catherine and Eleanor's conversation for its 'simplicity, and truth',
we must conclude that even clichéd, hyper-conventionalized
discourse can be worthwhile, productive, and dignified – a

conclusion which says as much about small-talk as it does about gothic novels.

Clearly, Henry Tilney is no authority on language, as pertains to life or literature, even though he presents himself as such. Despite his general benignity and good-humour, he is at times dangerously Thorpe-like in his presumption upon the authority attributable to his education, his age, his calling as a clergymen, and his sex. Men in *Northanger Abbey*, like Sir Thomas and Edmund in *Mansfield Park*, have a real mania for measurement, for determining the precise boundaries of time, of space, or – in Henry's case – of words. Having in his first conversation with Catherine not only caricatured Bath conversation but also chided women's letters for a 'general deficiency of subject, a total inattention to stops, and a very frequent ignorance of grammar', Henry immediately establishes himself as a stickler for words, bristling at every verbal transgression. Redundance (as in 'promised so faithfully', exaggeration (as in 'amazement'), semantic flattening (as in 'nice'), and definitional blurring (as in teachers 'tormenting' rather than 'instructing') turn Tilney into a linguistic despot of sorts, bent on 'overpower[ing]' offenders – the word is not without a gothic resonance – with the law of lexicographers and rhetoricians, in particular 'Johnson and Blair'.

Henry's patrol over proper usage culminates as Catherine and his sister, Eleanor, misunderstand each other when Catherine alludes to 'something very shocking' about to 'come out in London', something including 'murder and every thing of the kind'. Catherine of course is referring to the latest gothic novel, but Eleanor thinks only of the London riots which government troops – including her brother, Captain Frederick Tilney – may be called in to suppress. For Tilney, this *malentendu* demonstrates a typically feminine carelessness of thought and language, a carelessness at once regrettable and amusing. 'Perhaps,' he observes, 'the abilities of women are neither sound nor acute – neither vigorous nor keen.' Gallantly stepping in to assist woman in her weakness, and vaunting his manliness and his lucidity in such a way as to imply their intrinsic connection he asserts that: 'I will prove myself a man, no less by the generosity of my soul than the clearness of my head.' The playful solemnity of his tone notwithstanding, Henry is authorized to consider feminine discourse – in conversation, and in books – mistaken or absurd, and thus ever in need of his watchful arbitration.

But in linking political and literary unrest – the riotous crowds of London and the riotous pages of gothic novels – Catherine and Eleanor's unruly language has actually served them quite well, for both forms of excess are responses to unacceptable rule. The abusiveness of rule is, of course, the very premise of the gothic world. The linguistic regulations Tilney observes have no relevance in the gothic world, where words have been wrenched from their customary moorings, alas; where promises are not faithful, exaggerations are not excessive, and education is torment. The illegitimacy of rule, however, is exactly what Henry cannot imagine. His own position of authority – indeed his very clarity of and capacity for speech – depend on accepting the fitness of the prescribed order. This is why Henry is so appalled to learn that Catherine – her gothicizing imagination licensed by Northanger Abbey itself – suspects his father of murdering his mother:

"If I understand you rightly, you had formed a surmise of such horror as I have hardly words to – Dear Miss Morland, consider the dreadful nature of the suspicions you have entertained. What have you been judging from? Remember the country and the age in which we live. Remember that we are English, that we are Christians. Consult your own understanding, your own sense of the probable, your own observation of what is passing around you – Does our education prepare us for such atrocities? Do our laws connive at them? Could they be perpetrated without being known, in a country like this, where social and literary intercourse is on such a footing; where every man is surrounded by a neighbourhood of voluntary spies, and where roads and newspapers lay every thing open? Dearest Miss Morland, what ideas have you been admitting?"

For a moment, Henry, that master of words, is stupefied. Not all the words of Johnson and Blair can help him utter the 'horror' that gothic novels have invited Catherine to believe with such breezy nonchalance: that a modern Englishman, a law-abiding Christian living in full view of neighbours whose esteem he values, could nevertheless be plausibly suspected of killing his wife. The terms of Henry's indignation recapitulate the charges against gothic fiction – improbable circumstances, unnatural characters, and coarse language – that Austen deftly turned back on the Augustan masters in Chapter Five. They force us to recognize that people on the outside of ostensibly civilizing institutions he trusts may have different ideas about what is natural, probable, or overstated; that figureheads of domestic as well as political order can present a menacingly double image to girls like Catherine. Catherine herself, for the moment still caught up in the literalness of murder, will soon be brought to an appreciation of the figurative and moral truth of her suspicion. Cold-hearted, rapacious, mean-spirited, unprincipled and tyrannical, General Tilney *is* a gothic villain. He did in some legitimate sense of the term 'kill' his unhappy wife, not by locking her up and starving her to death, but rather by quashing her voice – note that General Tilney is a great interrupter, forcing opposition into silence – and stifling her vitality, much as he visibly crushes the spirits of his children. His subsequent behavior bears out Catherine's suspicion.

At the climax of *Northanger Abbey*, General Tilney banishes Catherine unprotected into the night solely because she is discovered not to be as rich as he had foolishly imagined. This act falls short of the grandeur of murder, to be sure. But to underrate its seriousness is to imply that important gentlemen are not to be judged by their treatment of poor girls, a devaluation which the female tradition of the novel gothically protests. Judged in historical terms, General Tilney's expulsion of Catherine is grossly uncivil in the deepest sense, exhibiting insolence towards inferiors, indifference to the good opinion of neighbours, and a contempt for the rules of hospitality, gentlemanliness, and decency, particularly towards women. When Catherine sees General Tilney working in his study at night, furrowing his brow and pondering the interests of national security in a dangerously unstable time, her mind leaps to Radcliffe's arch-villain, Montoni. Catherine does not ponder the conjunction gothic literature prompts her to sense. But we must, for it is perceptive. In addition to being the heroine's guardian and persecutor,

Montoni is the chief of a savage band of *condottieri* carving up
the countryside of Italy during the civil wars. In associating
General Tilney with Montoni, Catherine is sensing his doubleness, for he is a figure of order as well as the agent of
lawlessness. By the novel's end, Catherine concludes that
gothic novels taught her what no one and nothing else would.
They have brought her to the essential, though not the literal,
truth about a figure who represents national as well as
domestic order: 'in suspecting General Tilney of either murdering or shutting up his wife, she had scarcely sinned against
his character, or magnified his cruelty'.

To Henry, as we have seen, the haunting doubleness of
gothic fiction is semantically and politically impossible. Hence
his dismissal of gothic novels as shallow if entertaining artifice,
devoid of any claim to verisimilitude. Catherine's vision of
General Tilney as a respectable father *and* as a gothic villain is
to him as inadmissable as her linkage of the verbs 'to torment'
and 'to instruct' is absurd. But Catherine's final appraisal of
General Tilney is allowed to stand as correct, unqualified by
the narrator, unchallenged by Henry himself. This ultimately
pro-gothic conclusion shows that, ironically enough, it is not
Catherine, but Henry Tilney who turns out to have been the
naive reader, blinded by his own privilege to the unsettling
truths gothic novels made visible to Catherine. The major
purpose of Austen's prefatory 'Advertisement' is to apologize
for 'those parts of the work which thirteen years have made
comparatively obsolete', thus obscuring her design: 'The
public are entreated to bear in mind that thirteen years have
passed since it was finished, many more since it was begun,
and that during that period, places, manners, books, and
opinions have undergone considerable changes.' As several
scholars have demonstrated, Austen carefully accumulates
details about contemporary England – there are more in this
novel than in any other – which darken the portrait of General
Tilney and his household: General Tilney's hothouses devoted
to the cultivation of pineapples for the rich; his practice of
enclosure, with its infamously disastrous effects on the rural
poor; his arrogantly high-handed treatment of servants; the
family's references to riots caused by food shortages and

political unrest, together with vague suggestions about the General's involvement in 'the affairs of the nation'; and Henry's satisfied allusion to the Treasonable Practices Act of 1794 which permitted a 'neighbourhood of voluntary spies' to report anyone for seditious speech.[7] Informed readers of Austen's day would recognize in these details symptoms of social ills endemic to the ruling class. The docile Catherine, chastened by Henry's scolding, had made us smile when she opined that Radcliffe's characters are not to be found in 'the central part of England' – though, 'if hard pressed, she would have yielded the northern and western extremities' along with Italy and the south of France. But surely Henry's call-down, itself a version of it-can't-happen-here, is less sophisticated and more wrong, and it is not merely the outcome of the plot, but the evidence of his own household – evidence which he cannot 'read' – that proves this.

Yet Henry Tilney was destined from the first chapter to be the 'hero' of this novel, and he does not disappoint us. Defying his father's wrath, he keeps faith with Catherine, journeying to Fullerton to ask her hand in a marriage his father will not allow. In her final *homage* to the gothic, Austen brings her novel out of this unhappy impasse by flaunting gothic conventions. Reminding us that the 'tell-tale compression of the pages' means 'that we are all hastening together to perfect felicity', she appeases the General's worldly vanity by marrying Eleanor off to a fabulously wealthy Viscount, non-existent till the eleventh hour. ('My own joy on the occasion is very sincere,' the narrator remarks, garrulously.) She affirms the 'rules of composition' by assigning to his ownership the washing-bills Catherine had mistaken for a woeful memoir. She enlarges the income of the Morlands' estate enough to satisfy the General's 'greedy speculation'. And, most importantly of all, she establishes a happy ending by deliberately fudging the novel's central problem, ironically averring that the General's 'unjust interference' actually helped rather than hindered Catherine and Tilney. The stylized excess of these quintessentially gothic gestures of closure – where all the strings are tied up, where all the problems are solved, where villains turn out to be nice guys, where all the characters retire to conjugal bliss – reminds us that we are in the never-never-land of comedy rather than the 'midland counties of England'. The obviously hasty, extravagant, and overdetermined felicity of the conclusion suggests that comic resolutions may be more fictive than gothic terrors, that fantasies about happiness may be less credible than fantasies about suffering and persecution.

Northanger Abbey is, then, a delightful novel, but also a serious one, and the first completely to master the stylistic method that would become the hallmark of its author's art: irony. Austenian irony is no mere matter of sarcastically saying x while meaning y. On the contrary, it is two-sided, functioning somewhat like a Mobius strip, where two apparently discrete and opposite planes are manipulated into a mind-bending coextensiveness. Consider, for example, the following exchanges in *Northanger Abbey*:

Mrs. Allen was one of that numerous class of females, whose society can raise no other emotion than surprise at there being any men in the world who could like them well enough to marry them. She had neither beauty, genius, accomplishment, nor manner. The air of a gentlewoman, a great deal of quiet, inactive good temper, and a trifling turn of mind, were all that could account for her being the choice of a sensible, intelligent man, like Mr. Allen.

The advantages of natural folly in a beautiful girl have been already set forth by the capital pen of a sister author [Burney]; – and to her treatment of the subject I will only add in justice to men, that though to the larger and more trifling part of the sex, imbecility in females is a great enhancement of their personal charms, there is a portion of them too reasonable and too well informed themselves to desire any thing more in woman than ignorance.

Brain-twisters of sorts, these examples both turn on and turn against the very persons we expected them to champion, prompting us to do a double-take just when we thought we had caught the drift and slackened our concentration. In a passage which seems devoted to satirizing Mrs Allen's stupidity, it is the sensible and intelligent Mr Allen who ends up looking decidedly more like his wife in having chosen her for her very weaknesses; and 'reasonable and well-informed men' men, far from being morally and intellectually segregated from their trifling brethren, are brought into disturbing juxtaposition with them for preferring merely ignorant rather than downright stupid women.

Northanger Abbey accomplishes as a whole what these passages do in a smaller compass. Opposing the 'alarms of romance' to the 'anxieties of common life', and to all appearances siding artistically with the latter, the novel finally brings them into an illuminating and troubling conjunction. The gothic novel itself was devoted to defamiliarizing the common so as to bring its alarming strangeness into view. But by the time Austen took up her pen, its strangeness itself had become so familiar as to be dismissed as convention alone. Gothic strangeness itself had to be defamiliarized, and the only way to do so was to make it ordinary. In adapting the fictional norms of gothic to Regency England, Austen was thus rehabilitating them. Even Henry Tilney, of course, enjoyed gothic novels: 'The Mysteries of Udolpho, when once I had begun it, I could not lay down again.' But Austen's claims for Radcliffe's fiction, as for Edgeworth's, Burney's and her own, go well beyond the pleasure of a good 'read'. She reclaims a fictional tradition the better to examine 'strange' truths about familiar life, sharpening our discernment and enlarging our understanding by obliging us to be attentive readers of books and worlds that we, like Henry Tilney, erroneously think we already understand. In so doing, *Northanger Abbey* makes good its assertion that novels are works 'in which the greatest powers of the mind are displayed ... in the best chosen language'. It was an awesome beginning.

Claudia L. Johnson

NOTES

1. The chronology of Austen's early work has been a matter of controversy. For an explanation, see A. Walton Litz, *Jane Austen: A Study of her Artistic Development*, Oxford University Press, New York, 1965, pp. 171–80; and B. C. Southam, 'Mrs. Leavis and Miss Austen: The "Critical Theory" Reconsidered', *Nineteenth-Century Fiction*, 17, 1961, 21–32. Six years before selling *Northanger Abbey* to Crosby & Co. Austen had taken steps to attract the publisher Cadell in *First Impressions*, but Cadell was not interested.

2. Although Austen's 'Advertisement' of 1816 suggests an intention to publish, in 1817 Austen wrote that 'Miss Catherine is put upon the Shelve for the present, and I do not know that she will ever come out' in a letter to Fanny Knight, 13 March 1817. Scholars opine that Austen suspended publication plans because she feared the literary and political allusions of *Northanger Abbey* would not wear well. This decision may have made Austen freer to let the mood of *Northanger Abbey* rub off on *Sanditon*.

3. See B. C. Southam, ed., *Jane Austen: The Critical Heritage*, Routledge & Kegan Paul, London, 1968, Vol. 2, pp. 229–30.

4. *Persuasion, with a Memoir of Jane Austen*, ed. D. W. Harding, Penguin Books, Baltimore, 1965, p. 187.

5. Letter to J. Edward Austen, 16 December 1816. For a discussion of female modesty as it both enabled and limited women writers, see Mary Poovey, *The Proper Lady and the Woman Writer*, University of Chicago Press, Chicago, 1984.

6. I am indebted to Litz, p. 60, for this brilliant gothic parody, which as he notes, employs a translation from D. P. Varma, *The Gothic Flame*, London, 1957, pp. 179–80.

7. For these insights into the political allusions in *Northanger Abbey*, I am indebted to B. C. Southam's seminal, 'General Tilney's Hot-Houses', *Ariel*, 2, 1971, 52–62, and to Robert Hopkin's still indispensable 'General Tilney and Affairs of State: The Political Gothic of *Northanger Abbey*', *Philological Quarterly* 57, 1978, 213–24. For a fuller discussion of the political character of *Northanger Abbey*, see my *Jane Austen: Women, Politics, and the Novel*, Chicago and London, 1988.

SELECT BIBLIOGRAPHY

Jane Austen has attracted massive and sometimes uncritical attention since the pioneer work of R. W. Chapman in the 1920s. The brief selection below covers texts, interest in her life and time, letters, and general critical appraisals which include *Northanger Abbey*; some of these have specific sections or chapters devoted to the novel.

Texts There are three good annotated editions. The first is the Chapman edition (begun in 1923), in five volumes to which a sixth was subsequently added. These were revised by Mary Lascelles (1965–7) and became the Oxford Illustrated edition. Derived from this is the World's Classics edition, edited and with new notes and introductions (1990). There is also the Penguin English Library edition, which began with *Persuasion* in 1965. Of the Jane Austen companions, easily the best and most up to date is *The Jane Austen Handbook*, Athlone Press, 1986, edited by J. David Grey. The range is impressive: it is a detailed filling in of Jane Austen's background and foreground. The standard edition of *Jane Austen's Letters* is that by R. W. Chapman, Oxford University Press, 1952. The third edition, edited by Deirdre Le Faye, was published in 1995.

Biographies which merit attention begin with *A Memoir of Jane Austen* by her nephew J. E. Austen-Leigh, Richard Bentley, 1870, expanded 1871 (ed. R. W. Chapman, Oxford University Press, 1926); it is elegant, charming, pious, and just avoids being cloying. His son William and R. A. Austen-Leigh published *Jane Austen, Her Life and Letters: A Family Record*, 1913 (reprinted Russell, New York, 1965), a responsible, scholarly work. Elizabeth Jenkins' *Jane Austen: A Biography*, Gollancz, 1938, is an intelligent, perceptive commentary on the period and tells a convincing, graphic story. Lord David Cecil's *Portrait of Jane Austen*, Penguin, 1978, is a balanced account, comfortable and comforting. Park Honan's *Jane Austen: Her Life*, Weidenfeld, 1987, is excellent, the result of dedicated and sympathetic research. It is particularly strong on family background.

Criticism Jane Austen criticism has changed immensely over the past two hundred years. B. C. Southam's *Jane Austen: The Critical Heritage*, 2 vols., Routledge, 1968–87, anthologizes every important commentary that appeared from Austen's own time through the first part of our century, and also provides an extensive analysis of how appraisals have changed. Most full-length studies of Jane Austen devote a separate chapter to *Northanger Abbey*. For some excellent discussions of Austen's stylistic development and formal mastery, see Mary Lascelles, *Jane Austen and Her Art*, Oxford University Press, 1939; A. Walton Litz, *Jane Austen: A Study of Her Artistic Development*, Oxford University Press, 1965, and Joseph Wiesenfarth, *The Errand of Form: An Assay of Jane Austen's Art*, Fordham University Press, 1967. Book-length studies considering Austen's novels in relation to the political controversies of her time include Marilyn Butler, *Jane Austen and the War of Ideas*, Oxford University Press, 1975, rev. 1987, which argues for Austen's sternly Tory sympathies; and Claudia L. Johnson, *Jane Austen: Women, Politics, and the Novel*, University of Chicago Press, 1988, which emphasizes Austen's progressive stances, particularly as regards women. Other studies focusing on Austen's representation of women's experience include Mary Poovey's important *The Proper Lady and the Woman Writer*, University of Chicago Press, 1984, which analyses the ideology of female propriety; Alison Sulloway, *Jane Austen and the Province of Womanhood*, University of Pennsylvania Press, 1989, which places Austen's novels in the context of contemporary debates about women, concluding that she was a moderate feminist. Marvin Mudrick's *Jane Austen: Irony as Defense and Discovery*, Princeton University Press, 1952, still sets the terms for many discussions of Jane Austen and her ostensibly cold irony, and Michael Sadleir's *The Northanger Novels*, English Association Pamphlet No. 68, 1927, is still useful in acquainting the general reader to the reading-list of gothic thrillers alluded to in *Northanger Abbey*.

A NOTE ON THE TEXT

The text is based on that of the first edition of *Northanger Abbey* which was published, together with *Persuasion*, posthumously in 1818.

CHRONOLOGY

Readers wishing to know more of Jane Austen's family background and the achievements of her brothers should consult Park Honan's *Jane Austen: Her Life* (1987).

DATE	AUTHOR'S LIFE	LITERARY CONTEXT
1770		Wordsworth born.
1771		Sir Walter Scott born.
		Smollett: *Sir Humphrey Clinker*.
		Death of Gray.
1772		Coleridge born.
1773		Earl of Chesterfield dies.
1774		Death of Goldsmith.
		Dr Johnson: *A Journey to the Western Isles*.
		Goethe: *Werther*.
1775	Born at Steventon, Hampshire, on 16 December (five brothers, one sister, Cassandra).	Charles Lamb, J. M. W. Turner born.
		Beaumarchais: *The Barber of Seville*.
1776		Gibbon: *Decline and Fall of the Roman Empire*.
		Rousseau: *Reveries of a Solitary Walker*.
		Death of Hume.
1777		
1778		Hazlitt born.
		Deaths of Voltaire and Rousseau.
		Burney: *Evelina*.
1779		Johnson: *Lives of the Poets* (completed 1781).
		Hume: *Dialogues Concerning Natural Religion*.
1780		
1781		Rousseau: *Confessions*.
		Kant: *Critique of Pure Reason*.
1782		John and Charles Wesley: *Hymns for the Nation*.
		Laclos: *Les Liaisons dangereuses*.
		Burney: *Cecilia*.
1783		Crabbe: *The Village*.

HISTORICAL EVENTS

Lord North's ministry (to 1782).

Boston Tea Party.
Priestly discovers oxygen.

American War of Independence – Battle of Bunker Hill. Washington in command of American army.

Adam Smith's *Wealth of Nations*. American Declaration of Independence (4 July).

Burgoyne surrenders to American forces at Saratoga.
The Roman Catholic Bill passed, repealing the most repressive anti-Catholic laws.

The Gordon Riots.
Franco–American victory at Yorktown.

Resignation of Lord North. Ministries of Rockingham and Shelburne.

Treaty of Versailles (3 September). England formally recognizes American Independence. Fox-North ministry.

DATE	AUTHOR'S LIFE	LITERARY CONTEXT
1784-5	At Abbey School, Reading, with Cassandra.	Beaumarchais: *The Marriage of Figaro*. Deaths of Diderot and Johnson.
1785		Cowper: *The Task*.
1787		Schiller: *Don Carlos*. Goethe: *Iphigenia, Egmont*. Sade: *The Misfortunes of Virtue*.
1786	Leaves Abbey School (December).	Burns' first poems.
1788	Visits Sevenoaks (July).	Byron born.
1789		Blake: *Songs of Innocence*. De Staël: *Letters about Rousseau*.
1790		Burke: *Reflections on the Revolution in France*. Kant: *The Critique of Judgment*.
1791		Boswell: *Life of Johnson*. Chateaubriand: *Essay on Revolutions*. John Wesley dies. Paine: *The Rights of Man*.
1792		Shelley born. Wollstonecraft: *A Vindication of the Rights of Woman*. Goethe: *Roman Elegies*.
1793		Godwin: *Political Justice*.
1794	Comte de Feuillide, husband of her father's niece Eliza, executed (February) in the Terror in Paris.	Radcliffe: *The Mysteries of Udolpho*.
1795	Writes *Elinor and Marianne* in the form of letters.	Keats born. Matthew Gregory Lewis: *The Monk*.
1796	*First Impressions* (later *Pride and Prejudice*) begun (October).	Burney: *Camilla*. Goethe: *Wilhelm Meister's Apprenticeship*. Burns dies.
1797	Visits Bath (November). Begins *Sense and Sensibility* (November). *First Impressions* offered to Cadell.	Burke, Horace Walpole and Wollstonecraft die. Radcliffe: *The Italian*. Hölderlin: *Hyperion*. Schelling: *Ideas towards a Philosophy of Nature*.
1798	*Susan*, later *Northanger Abbey*, written. Visits Godmersham with Cassandra.	Wordsworth and Coleridge: *Lyrical Ballads*. Malthus: *Essay on the Principles of Population*.

HISTORICAL EVENTS

Pitt the Younger becomes Prime Minister (19 December).

Cartwright invents power weaving.
Mozart: *Don Giovanni*.

Regency crisis. Impeachment of Warren Hastings (acquitted 1795).
French Revolution – storming of the Bastille.

Anti-Jacobin riots at Birmingham (July).

France is declared a republic.

Britain goes to war with France. Louis XVI executed (21 January).
Suspension of the Habeas Corpus Act. French relieve Toulon (artillery
commanded by young Napoleon Bonaparte). In England, a run of bad
harvests, financial crises, and loss of continental markets make for social unrest.
Josiah Wedgwood dies (3 January). Bonaparte disperses Paris mob
(5 October). Treason and Convention Bills introduced (6 November).
Spain declares war on England.
Catherine the Great of Russia dies. Jenner performs first smallpox
vaccinations.

Naval mutinies at the Nore and Spithead.

Pitt introduces income tax. Nelson defeats French at Aboukir Bay. Irish
rebellion.

DATE	AUTHOR'S LIFE	LITERARY CONTEXT
1799	Stays in Bath (May–June) with her mother.	Lewis: *Tales of Terror*. Schiller: *Wallenstein*.
1800		Cowper dies. Maria Edgeworth: *Castle Rackrent*. Wordsworth: *Preface to Lyrical Ballads*. De Staël: *On Literature*. Schiller: *Mary Stuart*.
1801	Again visits Bath (May) with her family. Family settles (autumn) in Bath.	Lewis: *Tales of Wonder*. Chateaubriand: *Atala*.
1802	Visits (summer) to Dawlish and Sidmouth.	Scott: *Minstrelsy of the Scottish Border*. Chateaubriand: *The Genius of Christianity*. Paley: *Natural Theology*.
1803	*Susan* (*Northanger Abbey*) sold to Crosby (spring).	
1804	Visits Lyme (September). Death of Mrs Lefroy (16 December).	Death of Kant. Schiller: *William Tell*.
1805	Father dies (21 June). *Lady Susan*/ *The Watsons* probably written.	Scott: *The Lay of the Last Minstrel*. Death of Schiller. Hazlitt: *Principles of Human Action*.
1806	Family move to Southampton (autumn).	
1807	Family settled in Castle Square, Southampton. With mother and Cassandra at Chawton (September).	Wordsworth: *Poems*. Crabbe: *The Parish Register*. Hegel: *Phenomenology of Spirit*.
1808	Idea of moving to Chawton (October).	Scott: *Marmion*. Goethe: *Faust*, part 1. Kleist: *Penthesilea*.
1809	Settled happily at Chawton (July).	Byron: *English Bards and Scotch Reviewers*. Goethe: *Elective Affinities*.
1810		Scott: *The Lady of the Lake*. Goethe: *Theory of Colours*.
1811	*Mansfield Park* begun (February, finished summer 1813). *Sense and Sensibility* published (November) by Egerton.	
1812	*Pride and Prejudice* sold to Egerton (November).	Byron: *Childe Harold* (to 1818). Crabbe: *Tales in Verse*. Dickens born.

CHRONOLOGY

Repressive acts against radicalism passed. Napoleon appointed First Consul.

Napoleon defeats the Austrians at Marengo. Peace negotiations between France, England and Austria.

First census taken. Defeat of Pitt. Assassination of Paul I; Alexander I becomes Tsar of Russia.

Peace of Amiens with France. Bonaparte appointed 1st consul for life.

War resumed with France. In Rome, first excavation of the Forum.

Return of Pitt as Prime Minister. French invasion of England planned.

Napoleon Emperor of France. Anglo–Russian Alliance (joined by Austria 1805).

French fleet defeated by Nelson at Trafalgar (Austro–Russians defeated at Austerlitz).

Blockade of Britain. Death of Pitt.

Franco–Russian alliance against England. Abolition of the slave trade.

Napoleon captures Madrid.

Wellesley defeats the French at Talavera. French victory over English at Walcheren. Moore's defence of Corunna.

French cleared out of Portugal. George III declared insane; Prince Regent takes over. First Luddite riots.

Madrid recaptured. War with the United States. End of Napoleon's Russian campaign – retreat from Moscow.

DATE	AUTHOR'S LIFE	LITERARY CONTEXT
1813	*Pride and Prejudice* published (January). Visits London (September). Second edition of *Pride and Prejudice* (November). Second edition of *Sense and Sensibility* (November).	Byron: *The Giaour*.
1814	*Emma* begun (21 January; finished 29 March 1815). *Mansfield Park* published (May) by Egerton.	Scott: *Waverley*. Cary's *Dante* completed.
1815	*Persuasion* begun (summer; finished August 1816). *Emma* published (December) by John Murray.	Trollope born. Scott: *Guy Mannering*. Byron: *Hebrew Melodies*. Wordsworth: *The White Doe of Rylstone*, poems.
1816	*Quarterly Review* – Scott's laudatory notice of *Emma* (March). Second edition of *Mansfield Park*.	Scott: *The Antiquary* and *Old Mortality*. Constant: *Adolphe*. Peacock: *Headlong Hall*. Coleridge: *Christabel* and *Kubla Khan*. Shelley: *Alastor*.
1817	Writes *Sanditon* (January–March). Dies at Winchester (18 July). *Northanger Abbey* and *Persuasion*, with a Biographical Notice of the Author published (December?) by John Murray (dated 1818).	Byron: *Tasso* and *Manfred*. Coleridge: *Biographia Literaria* and *Sibylline Leaves*. Keats: *Poems*.
1818		Scott: *Heart of Midlothian*. Mary Shelley: *Frankenstein*. Peacock: *Nightmare Abbey*.
1819		Byron: *Don Juan* (completed 1824). Wordsworth: *Peter Bell*.
1820		Shelley: *Prometheus Unbound* and *The Cenci*. Keats: *Lamia, Isabella, The Eve of St Agnes* and the *Odes*. Clare: *Poems Descriptive of Rural Life and Scenery*. Scott: *Ivanhoe*. Southey: *Life of Wesley*.
1821		Keats dies. Shelley: *Adonais*.

CHRONOLOGY

HISTORICAL EVENTS

Robert Owen: *A New View of Society*. Wellington successfully concludes the Peninsular War.

Peace with America. The Allies take Paris.

Napoleon returns from Elba. Allies defeat Napoleon at Waterloo. Peace of Vienna. Restoration of the French monarchy (Louis XVIII). Corn Law passed.

Spa Fields riot. Economic depression. Holy alliance between Russia, Prussia and Austria, to preserve European status quo.

Princess Charlotte dies. David Ricardo: *Principles of Political Economy and Taxation*.

Congress of Aix-La-Chapelle. Church Building Society founded: Parliament votes £1,000,000 to support it.

Peterloo Massacre. Birth of Queen Victoria. Factory Act restricts child labour.
Death of George III; accession of Prince Regent as George IV. Cato Street conspiracy. Trial of Queen Caroline.

NORTHANGER ABBEY

THIS LITTLE work was finished in the year 1803, and intended for immediate publication. It was disposed of to a bookseller, it was even advertised, and why the business proceeded no farther, the author has never been able to learn. That any bookseller should think it worth while to purchase what he did not think it worth while to publish seems extraordinary. But with this, neither the author nor the public have any other concern than as some observation is necessary upon those parts of the work which thirteen years have made comparatively obsolete. The public are entreated to bear in mind that thirteen years have passed since it was finished, many more since it was begun, and that during that period, places, manners, books, and opinions have undergone considerable changes.

VOLUME I

NORTHANGER ABBEY

CHAPTER I

No one who had ever seen Catherine Morland in her infancy, would have supposed her born to be an heroine. Her situation in life, the character of her father and mother, her own person and disposition, were all equally against her. Her father was a clergyman, without being neglected, or poor, and a very respectable man, though his name was Richard – and he had never been handsome. He had a considerable independence, besides two good livings – and he was not in the least addicted to locking up his daughters. Her mother was a woman of useful plain sense, with a good temper, and, what is more remarkable, with a good constitution. She had three sons before Catherine was born; and instead of dying in bringing the latter into the world, as any body might expect, she still lived on – lived to have six children more – to see them growing up around her, and to enjoy excellent health herself. A family of ten children will be always called a fine family, where there are heads and arms and legs enough for the number; but the Morlands had little other right to the word, for they were in general very plain, and Catherine, for many years of her life, as plain as any. She had a thin awkward figure, a sallow skin without colour, dark lank hair, and strong features; – so much for her person; – and not less unpropitious for heroism seemed her mind. She was fond of all boys' plays, and greatly preferred cricket not merely to dolls, but to the more heroic enjoyments of infancy, nursing a dormouse, feeding a canary-bird, or watering a rose-bush. Indeed she had no taste for a garden; and if she gathered flowers at all, it was chiefly for the pleasure of mischief – at least so it was conjectured from her always preferring those which she was forbidden to take. – Such were her propensities – her abilities were quite as extraordinary. She never could learn or understand any thing before she was taught; and sometimes not even then, for she was often inattentive, and occasionally stupid. Her mother was three months in teaching her only to repeat the 'Beggar's Petition;' and after all, her next sister, Sally, could say it better than she did. Not that Catherine was always stupid, – by no means; she learnt the fable of 'The Hare and many Friends,' as quickly as any girl in England. Her mother wished her to learn music; and Catherine was sure she should like it, for she was very fond of tinkling the keys of the old forlorn spinnet; so, at eight years old she began. She learnt a year, and could not bear it; – and Mrs. Morland, who did not insist on her daughters being accomplished in spite of incapacity or distaste, allowed her to leave off. The day which dismissed the music-master was one of the happiest of Catherine's life. Her taste for drawing was not superior; though whenever she could obtain the outside of a letter from her mother, or seize upon any other odd piece of paper, she did what she could in that way, by drawing houses and trees, hens and chickens, all very much like one another. – Writing and accounts she was taught by her father; French by her mother: her proficiency in ther was not remarkable, and she shirked her lessons in both whenever she could. What a strange, unaccountable character! – for with all these symptoms of profligacy at ten years old, she had neither a bad heart nor a bad temper; was seldom stubborn, scarcely ever quarrelsome, and very kind to the little ones, with few interruptions of tyranny; she was moreover noisy and wild, hated confinement and cleanliness, and loved nothing so well in the world as rolling down the green slope at the back of the house.

Such was Catherine Morland at ten. At fifteen, appearances were mending; she began to curl her hair and long for balls; her complexion improved, her features were softened by plumpness and colour, her eyes gained more animation, and her figure more consequence. Her love of dirt gave way to an inclination for finery, and she grew clean as she grew smart; she had now the pleasure of sometimes hearing her father and mother remark on her personal improvement. 'Catherine grows quite a good-looking girl, – she is almost pretty to-day,' were words which caught her ears now and then; and how welcome were the sounds! To look *almost* pretty, is an acquisition of higher delight to a girl who has been looking plain the first fifteen years of her life, than a beauty from her cradle can ever receive.

Mrs. Morland was a very good woman, and wished to see her children every thing they ought to be; but her time was so much occupied in lying-in and teaching the little ones, that her elder daughters were inevitably left to shift for themselves; and it was not very wonderful that Catherine, who had by nature nothing heroic about her, should prefer cricket, base ball, riding on horseback, and running about the country at the age of fourteen, to books – or at least books of information – for, provided that nothing like useful knowledge could be gained from them, provided they were all story and no reflection, she had never any objection to books at all. But from fifteen to seventeen she was in training for a heroine; she read all such works as heroines must read to supply their memories with those quotations which are so serviceable and so soothing in the vicissitudes of their eventful lives.

From Pope, she learnt to censure those who

'bear about the mockery of woe.'

From Gray, that

> 'Many a flower is born to blush unseen,
> 'And waste its fragrance on the desert air.'

From Thompson, that

> —— 'It is a delightful task
> 'To teach the young idea how to shoot.'

And from Shakespeare she gained a great store of information – amongst the rest, that

> —— 'Trifles light as air,
> 'Are, to the jealous, confirmation strong,
> 'As proofs of Holy Writ.'

That

> 'The poor beetle, which we tread upon,
> 'In corporal sufferance feels a pang as great
> 'As when a giant dies.'

And that a young woman in love always looks

> —— 'like Patience on a monument
> 'Smiling at Grief.'

So far her improvement was sufficient – and in many other points she came on exceedingly well; for though she could not write sonnets, she brought herself to read them; and though there seemed no chance of her throwing a whole party into raptures by a prelude on the pianoforte, of her own composition, she could listen to other people's performance with very little fatigue. Her greatest deficiency was in the pencil – she had no notion of drawing – not enough even to attempt a sketch of her lover's profile, that she might be detected in the design. There she fell miserably short of the true heroic height. At present she did not know her own poverty, for she had no lover to portray. She had reached the age of seventeen, without having seen one amiable youth who could call forth her sensibility; without having inspired one real passion, and without having excited even any admiration but what was very moderate and very transient. This was strange indeed! But strange things may be generally accounted for if their cause be fairly searched out. There was not one lord in the neighbourhood; no – not even a baronet. There was not one family among their acquaintance who had reared and supported a boy accidentally found at their door – not one young man whose origin was unknown. Her father had no ward, and the squire of the parish no children.

But when a young lady is to be a heroine, the perverseness of forty surrounding families cannot prevent her. Something must and will happen to throw a hero in her way.

Mr. Allen, who owned the chief of the property about Fullerton, the village in Wiltshire where the Morlands lived, was ordered to Bath for the benefit of a gouty constitution; – and his lady, a good-humoured woman, fond of Miss Morland, and probably aware that if adventures will not befall a young lady in her own village, she must seek them abroad, invited her to go with them. Mr. and Mrs. Morland were all compliance, and Catherine all happiness.

CHAPTER II

IN ADDITION to what has been already said of Catherine Morland's personal and mental endowments, when about to be launched into all the difficulties and dangers of a six weeks' residence in Bath, it may be stated, for the reader's more certain information, lest the following pages should otherwise fail of giving any idea of what her character is meant to be; that her heart was affectionate, her disposition cheerful and open, without conceit or affectation of any kind –

her manners just removed from the awkwardness and shyness of a girl; her person pleasing, and, when in good looks, pretty – and her mind about as ignorant and uninformed as the female mind at seventeen usually is.

When the hour of departure drew near, the maternal anxiety of Mrs. Morland will be naturally supposed to be most severe. A thousand alarming presentiments of evil to her beloved Catherine from this terrific separation must oppress her heart with sadness, and drown her in tears for the last day or two of their being together; and advice of the most important and applicable nature must of course flow from her wise lips in their parting conference in her closet. Cautions against the violence of such noblemen and baronets as delight in forcing young ladies away to some remote farmhouse, must, at such a moment, relieve the fullness of her heart. Who would not think so? But Mrs. Morland knew so little of lords and baronets, that she entertained no notion of their general mischievousness, and was wholly unsuspicious of danger to her daughter from their machinations. Her cautions were confined to the following points. 'I beg, Catherine, you will always wrap yourself up very warm about the throat, when you come from the Rooms at night; and I wish you would try to keep some account of the money you spend; – I will give you this little book on purpose.'

Sally, or rather Sarah, (for what young lady of common gentility will reach the age of sixteen without altering her name as far as she can?) must from situation be at this time the intimate friend and confidante of her sister. It is remarkable, however, that she neither insisted on Catherine's writing by every post, nor exacted her promise of transmitting the character of every new acquaintance, nor a detail of every interesting conversation that Bath might produce. Every thing indeed relative to this important journey was done, on the part of the Morlands, with a degree of moderation and composure, which seemed rather consistent with the common feelings of common life, than with the refined susceptibilities, the tender emotions which the first separation of a heroine from her family ought always to excite. Her father, instead of giving her an unlimited order on his banker, or even putting an hundred pounds bank-bill into her hands, gave her only ten guineas, and promised her more when she wanted it.

Under these unpromising auspices, the parting took place, and the journey began. It was performed with suitable quietness and uneventful safety. Neither robbers nor tempests befriended them, nor one lucky overturn to introduce them to the hero. Nothing more alarming occurred than a fear on Mrs. Allen's side, of having once left her clogs behind her at an inn, and that fortunately proved to be groundless.

They arrived at Bath. Catherine was all eager delight; – her eyes were here, there, every where, as they approached its fine and striking environs, and afterwards drove through those streets which conducted them to the hotel. She was come to be happy, and she felt happy already.

They were soon settled in comfortable lodgings in Pulteney-street.

It is now expedient to give some description of Mrs. Allen, that the reader may be able to judge, in what manner her actions will hereafter tend to promote the general distress of the work, and how she will, probably, contribute to reduce poor Catherine to all the desperate wretchedness of which a last volume is capable – whether by her imprudence, vulgarity, or jealousy – whether by intercepting her letters, ruining her character, or turning her out of doors.

Mrs. Allen was one of that numerous class of females, whose society can raise no other emotion than surprise at there being any men in the world who could like them well enough to marry them. She had neither beauty, genius, accomplishment, nor manner. The air of a gentlewoman, a great deal of quiet, inactive good temper, and a trifling turn of mind, were all that could account for her being the choice of a sensible, intelligent man, like Mr. Allen. In one respect she was admirably fitted to introduce a young lady into public, being as fond of going every where and seeing every thing herself as any young lady could be. Dress was her passion. She had a most harmless delight in being fine; and our heroine's entrée into life could not take place till after three or four days had been spent in learning what was mostly worn, and her chaperon was provided with a dress of the newest fashion. Catherine too made some purchases herself, and when all these matters were arranged, the important evening came which was to usher her into the Upper Rooms. Her hair was cut and dressed by the best hand, her clothes put on with care, and both Mrs. Allen and her maid declared she looked quite as she should do. With such encouragement, Catherine hoped at least to pass uncensured through the crowd. As for admiration, it was always very welcome when it came, but she did not depend on it.

Mrs. Allen was so long in dressing, that they did not enter the ball-room till late. The season was full, the room crowded, and the two ladies squeezed in as well as they could. As for Mr. Allen, he repaired directly to the card-room, and left them to enjoy a mob by themselves. With more care for the safety of her new gown than for the comfort of her protegée, Mrs. Allen made her way through the throng of men by the door, as swiftly as the necessary caution would allow; Catherine, however, kept close at her side, and linked her arm too firmly within her friend's to be torn asunder by any common effort of a struggling assembly. But to her utter amazement she found that to proceed along the

room was by no means the way to disengage themselves from the crowd; it seemed rather to increase as
they went on, whereas she had imagined that when
once fairly within the door, they should easily find seats
and be able to watch the dances with perfect convenience. But this was far from being the case, and though
by unwearied diligence they gained even the top of the
room, their situation was just the same; they saw nothing of the dancers but the high feathers of some of the
ladies. Still they moved on – something better was yet
in view; and by a continued exertion of strength and
ingenuity they found themselves at last in the passage
behind the highest bench. Here there was something
less of crowd than below; and hence Miss Morland had
a comprehensive view of all the company beneath her,
and of all the dangers of her late passage through them.
It was a splendid sight, and she began, for the first time
that evening, to feel herself at a ball: she longed to
dance, but she had not an acquaintance in the room.
Mrs. Allen did all that she could do in such a case by
saying very placidly, every now and then, 'I wish you
could dance, my dear, – I wish you could get a partner.'
For some time her young friend felt obliged to her for
these wishes; but they were repeated so often, and
proved so totally ineffectual, that Catherine grew tired
at last, and would thank her no more.

They were not long able, however, to enjoy the
repose of the eminence they had so laboriously gained.
– Every body was shortly in motion for tea, and they
must squeeze out like the rest. Catherine began to feel
something of disappointment – she was tired of being
continually pressed against by people, the generality of
whose faces possessed nothing to interest, and with all
of whom she was so wholly unacquainted, that she
could not relieve the irksomeness of imprisonment by
the exchange of a syllable with any of her fellow cap-
tives; and when at last arrived in the tea-room, she felt

yet more the awkwardness of having no party to join, no acquaintance to claim, no gentleman to assist them. – They saw nothing of Mr. Allen; and after looking about them in vain for a more eligible situation, were obliged to sit down at the end of a table, at which a large party were already placed, without having any thing to do there, or any body to speak to, except each other.

Mrs. Allen congratulated herself, as soon as they were seated, on having preserved her gown from injury. 'It would have been very shocking to have it torn,' said she, 'would not it? – It is such a delicate muslin. – For my part I have not seen any thing I like so well in the whole room, I assure you.'

'How uncomfortable it is,' whispered Catherine, 'not to have a single acquaintance here!'

'Yes, my dear,' replied Mrs. Allen, with perfect serenity, 'it is very uncomfortable indeed.'

'What shall we do? – The gentlemen and ladies at this table look as if they wondered why we came here – we seem forcing ourselves into their party.'

'Aye, so we do. – That is very disagreeable. I wish we had a large acquaintance here.'

'I wish we had *any*; – it would be somebody to go to.'

'Very true, my dear; and if we knew anybody we would join them directly. The Skinners were here last year – I wish they were here now.'

'Had not we better go away as it is? – Here are no tea things for us, you see.'

'No more there are, indeed. – How very provoking! But I think we had better sit still, for one gets so tumbled in such a crowd! How is my head, my dear? – Somebody gave me a push that has hurt it I am afraid.'

'No, indeed, it looks very nice. – But, dear Mrs. Allen, are you sure there is nobody you know in all this multitude of people? I think you *must* know somebody.'

'I don't upon my word – I wish I did. I wish I had
a large acquaintance here with all my heart, and then I
should get you a partner. – I should be so glad to have
you dance. There goes a strange-looking woman! What
an odd gown she has got on! – How old fashioned it
is! Look at the back.'

After some time they received an offer of tea from
one of their neighbours; it was thankfully accepted, and
this introduced a light conversation with the gentleman
who offered it, which was the only time that any body
spoke to them during the evening, till they were discovered and joined by Mr. Allen when the dance was
over.

'Well, Miss Morland,' said he, directly, 'I hope you
have had an agreeable ball.'

'Very agreeable indeed,' she replied, vainly endeavouring to hide a great yawn.

'I wish she had been able to dance,' said his wife, 'I
wish we could have got a partner for her. – I have been
saying how glad I should be if the Skinners were
here this winter instead of last; or if the Parrys had
come, as they talked of once, she might have danced
with George Parry. I am so sorry she has not had a
partner!'

'We shall do better another evening I hope,' was Mr.
Allen's consolation.

The company began to disperse when the dancing
was over – enough to leave space for the remainder to
walk about in some comfort; and now was the time for
a heroine, who had not yet played a very distinguished
part in the events of the evening, to be noticed and
admired. Every five minutes, by removing some of the
crowd, gave greater openings for her charms. She was
now seen by many young men who had not been near
her before. Not one, however, started with rapturous
wonder on beholding her, no whisper of eager inquiry
ran round the room, nor was she once called a divinity

by any body. Yet Catherine was in very good looks, and had the company only seen her three years before, they would *now* have thought her exceedingly handsome.

She *was* looked at however, and with some admiration; for, in her own hearing, two gentlemen pronounced her to be a pretty girl. Such words had their due effect; she immediately thought the evening pleasanter than she had found it before – her humble vanity was contented – she felt more obliged to the two young men for this simple praise than a true quality heroine would have been for fifteen sonnets in celebration of her charms, and went to her chair in good humour with every body, and perfectly satisfied with her share of public attention.

CHAPTER III

EVERY MORNING now brought its regular duties; – shops were to be visited; some new part of the town to be looked at; and the Pump-room to be attended, where they paraded up and down for an hour, looking at every body and speaking to no one. The wish of a numerous acquaintance in Bath was still uppermost with Mrs. Allen, and she repeated it after every fresh proof, which every morning brought, of her knowing nobody at all.

They made their appearance in the Lower Rooms; and here fortune was more favourable to our heroine. The master of the ceremonies introduced to her a very gentlemanlike young man as a partner; – his name was Tilney. He seemed to be about four or five and twenty, was rather tall, had a pleasing countenance, a very intelligent and lively eye, and, if not quite handsome, was very near it. His address was good, and Catherine felt herself in high luck. There was little leisure for speaking while they danced; but when they were seated at tea, she found him as agreeable as she had already given him credit for being. He talked with fluency and spirit – and there was an archness and pleasantry in his manner which interested, though it was hardly understood by her. After chatting some time on such matters as naturally arose from the objects around them, he suddenly addressed her with – 'I have hitherto been very remiss, madam, in the proper attentions of a partner here; I have not yet asked you how long you have been in Bath; whether you were ever here before; whether you have been at the Upper Rooms, the theatre, and the concert; and how you like the place altogether. I have been very negligent – but are you now at leisure to satisfy me in these particulars? If you are I will begin directly.'

'You need not give yourself that trouble, sir.'

'No trouble I assure you, madam.' Then forming his features into a set smile, and affectedly softening his voice, he added, with a simpering air, 'Have you been long in Bath, madam?'

'About a week, sir,' replied Catherine, trying not to laugh.

'Really!' with affected astonishment.

'Why should you be surprised, sir?'

'Why, indeed!' said he, in his natural tone – 'but some emotion must appear to be raised by your reply, and surprise is more easily assumed, and not less reasonable than any other. – Now let us go on. Were you never here before, madam?'

'Never, sir.'

'Indeed! Have you yet honoured the Upper Rooms?'

'Yes, sir, I was there last Monday.'

'Have you been to the theatre?'

'Yes, sir, I was at the play on Tuesday.'

'To the concert?'

'Yes, sir, on Wednesday.'

'And are you altogether pleased with Bath?'

'Yes – I like it very well.'

'Now I must give one smirk, and then we may be rational again.'

Catherine turned away her head, not knowing whether she might venture to laugh.

'I see what you think of me,' said he gravely – 'I shall make but a poor figure in your journal to-morrow.'

'My journal!'

'Yes, I know exactly what you will say: Friday, went to the Lower Rooms; wore my sprigged muslin robe with blue trimmings – plain black shoes – appeared to much advantage; but was strangely harassed by a queer, half-witted man, who would make me dance with him, and distressed me by his nonsense.'

'Indeed I shall say no such thing.'

'Shall I tell you what you ought to say?'

'If you please.'

'I danced with a very agreeable young man, introduced by Mr. King; had a great deal of conversation with him – seems a most extraordinary genius – hope I may know more of him. *That*, madam, is what I *wish* you to say.'

'But, perhaps, I keep no journal.'

'Perhaps you are not sitting in this room, and I am not sitting by you. These are points in which a doubt is equally possible. Not keep a journal! How are your absent cousins to understand the tenor of your life in Bath without one? How are the civilities and compliments of every day to be related as they ought to be, unless noted down every evening in a journal? How are your various dresses to be remembered, and the particular state of your complexion, and curl of your hair to be described in all their diversities, without having constant recourse to a journal? – My dear madam, I am not so ignorant of young ladies' ways as you wish to believe me; it is this delightful habit of journalizing which largely contributes to form the easy style of writing for which ladies are so generally celebrated. Every body allows that the talent of writing agreeable letters is peculiarly female. Nature may have done something, but I am sure it must be essentially assisted by the practice of keeping a journal.'

'I have sometimes thought,' said Catherine, doubtingly, 'whether ladies do write so much better letters than gentlemen! That is – I should not think the superiority was always on our side.'

'As far as I have had opportunity of judging, it appears to me that the usual style of letter-writing among women is faultless, except in three particulars.'

'And what are they?'

'A general deficiency of subject, a total inattention to stops, and a very frequent ignorance of grammar.'

'Upon my word! I need not have been afraid of disclaiming the compliment. You do not think too highly of us in that way.'

'I should no more lay it down as a general rule that women write better letters than men, than that they sing better duets, or draw better landscapes. In every power, of which taste is the foundation, excellence is pretty fairly divided between the sexes.'

They were interrupted by Mrs. Allen: – 'My dear Catherine,' said she, 'do take this pin out of my sleeve; I am afraid it has torn a hole already; I shall be quite sorry if it has, for this is a favourite gown, though it cost but nine shillings a yard.'

'That is exactly what I should have guessed it, madam,' said Mr. Tilney, looking at the muslin.

'Do you understand muslins, sir?'

'Particularly well; I always buy my own cravats, and am allowed to be an excellent judge; and my sister has often trusted me in the choice of a gown. I bought one for her the other day, and it was pronounced to be a prodigious bargain by every lady who saw it. I gave but five shillings a yard for it, and a true Indian muslin.'

Mrs. Allen was quite struck by his genius. 'Men commonly take so little notice of those things,' said she: 'I can never get Mr. Allen to know one of my gowns from another. You must be a great comfort to your sister, sir.'

'I hope I am, madam.'

'And pray, sir, what do you think of Miss Morland's gown?'

'It is very pretty, madam,' said he, gravely examining it; 'but I do not think it will wash well; I am afraid it will fray.'

'How can you,' said Catherine, laughing, 'be so —' she had almost said, strange.

'I am quite of your opinion, sir,' replied Mrs. Allen; 'and so I told Miss Morland when she bought it.'

'But then you know, madam, muslin always turns to some account or other; Miss Morland will get enough out of it for a handkerchief, or a cap, or a cloak. – Muslin can never be said to be wasted. I have heard my sister say so forty times, when she has been extravagant in buying more than she wanted, or careless in cutting it to pieces.'

'Bath is a charming place, sir; there are so many good shops here. – We are sadly off in the country; not but what we have very good shops in Salisbury, but it is so far to go; – eight miles is a long way; Mr. Allen says it is nine, measured nine; but I am sure it cannot be more than eight; and it is such a fag – I come back tired to death. Now here one can step out of doors and get a thing in five minutes.'

Mr. Tilney was polite enough to seem interested in what she said; and she kept him on the subject of muslins till the dancing recommenced. Catherine feared, as she listened to their discourse, that he indulged himself a little too much with the foibles of others. – 'What are you thinking of so earnestly?' said he, as they walked back to the ball-room; – 'not of your partner, I hope, for, by that shake of the head, your meditations are not satisfactory.'

Catherine coloured, and said, 'I was not thinking of any thing.'

'That is artful and deep, to be sure; but I had rather be told at once that you will not tell me.'

'Well then, I will not.'

'Thank you; for now we shall soon be acquainted, as I am authorized to tease you on this subject whenever we meet, and nothing in the world advances intimacy so much.'

They danced again; and, when the assembly closed, parted, on the lady's side at least, with a strong inclination for continuing the acquaintance. Whether she thought of him so much, while she drank her warm wine and water, and prepared herself for bed, as to dream of him when there, cannot be ascertained; but I hope it was no more than in a slight slumber, or a morning doze at most; for if it be true, as a celebrated writer has maintained, that no young lady can be justified in falling in love before the gentleman's love is declared,* it must be very improper that a young lady should dream of a gentleman before the gentleman is first known to have dreamt of her. How proper Mr. Tilney might be as a dreamer or a lover, had not yet perhaps entered Mr. Allen's head, but that he was not objectionable as a common acquaintance for his young charge he was on inquiry satisfied; for he had early in the evening taken pains to know who her partner was, and had been assured of Mr. Tilney's being a clergyman, and of a very respectable family in Gloucestershire.

* Vide a letter from Mr. Richardson, No. 97, vol ii. Rambler.

CHAPTER IV

WITH MORE than usual eagerness did Catherine hasten to the Pump-room the next day, secure within herself of seeing Mr. Tilney there before the morning were over, and ready to meet him with a smile: — but no smile was demanded — Mr. Tilney did not appear. Every creature in Bath, except himself, was to be seen in the room at different periods of the fashionable hours; crowds of people were every moment passing in and out, up the steps and down; people whom nobody cared about, and nobody wanted to see; and he only was absent. 'What a delightful place Bath is,' said Mrs. Allen, as they sat down near the great clock, after parading the room till they were tired; 'and how pleasant it would be if we had any acquaintance here.'

This sentiment had been uttered so often in vain, that Mrs. Allen had no particular reason to hope it would be followed with more advantage now; but we are told to 'despair of nothing we would attain,' as 'unwearied diligence our point would gain;' and the unwearied diligence with which she had every day wished for the same thing was at length to have its just reward, for hardly had she been seated ten minutes before a lady of about her own age, who was sitting by her, and had been looking at her attentively for several minutes, addressed her with great complaisance in these words: — 'I think, madam, I cannot be mistaken; it is a long time since I had the pleasure of seeing you, but is not your name Allen?' This question answered, as it readily was, the stranger pronounced her's to be Thorpe; and Mrs. Allen immediately recognized the features of a former schoolfellow and intimate, whom she had seen only once since their respective marriages, and that many years ago. Their joy on this meeting was very great, as well it might, since they had been contented to know nothing of each other for the last fifteen years. Compliments on good looks now passed; and, after observing how time had slipped away since they were last together, how little they had thought of meeting in Bath, and what a pleasure it was to see an old friend, they proceeded to make inquiries and give intelligence as to their families, sisters, and cousins, talking both together, far more ready to give than to receive information, and each hearing very little of what the other said. Mrs. Thorpe, however, had one great advantage as a talker, over Mrs. Allen, in a family of children; and when she expatiated on the talents of her sons, and the beauty of her daughters, – when she related their different situations and views, – that John was at Oxford, Edward at Merchant-Taylors', and William at sea, – and all of them more beloved and respected in their different stations than any other three beings ever were, Mrs. Allen had no similar information to give, no similar triumphs to press on the unwilling and unbelieving ear of her friend, and was forced to sit and appear to listen to all these maternal effusions, consoling herself, however, with the discovery, which her keen eye soon made, that the lace on Mrs. Thorpe's pelisse was not half so handsome as that on her own.

'Here come my dear girls,' cried Mrs. Thorpe, pointing at three smart looking females, who, arm in arm, were then moving towards her. 'My dear Mrs. Allen, I long to introduce them; they will be so delighted to see you: the tallest is Isabella, my eldest; is not she a fine young woman? The others are very much admired too, but I believe Isabella is the handsomest.'

The Miss Thorpes were introduced; and Miss Morland, who had been for a short time forgotten, was introduced likewise. The name seemed to strike them all; and, after speaking to her with great civility, the eldest young lady observed aloud to the rest, 'How excessively like her brother Miss Morland is!'

'The very picture of him indeed!' cried the mother – and 'I should have known her any where for his sister!' was repeated by them all, two or three times over. For a moment Catherine was surprised; but Mrs. Thorpe and her daughters had scarcely begun the history of their acquaintance with Mr. James Morland, before she remembered that her eldest brother had lately formed an intimacy with a young man of his own college, of the name of Thorpe; and that he had spent the last week of the Christmas vacation with his family, near London.

The whole being explained, many obliging things were said by the Miss Thorpes of their wish of being better acquainted with her; of being considered as already friends, through the friendship of their brothers, &c. which Catherine heard with pleasure, and answered with all the pretty expressions she could command; and, as the first proof of amity, she was soon invited to accept an arm of the eldest Miss Thorpe, and take a turn with her about the room. Catherine was delighted with this extension of her Bath acquaintance, and almost forgot Mr. Tilney while she talked to Miss Thorpe. Friendship is certainly the finest balm for the pangs of disappointed love.

Their conversation turned upon those subjects, of which the free discussion has generally much to do in perfecting a sudden intimacy between two young ladies; such as dress, balls, flirtations, and quizzes. Miss Thorpe, however, being four years older than Miss Morland, and at least four years better informed, had a very decided advantage in discussing such points; she could compare the balls of Bath with those of Tunbridge; its fashions with the fashions of London; could rectify the opinions of her new friend in many articles of tasteful attire; could discover a flirtation between any gentleman and lady who only smiled on each other; and point out a quiz through the thickness of a crowd. These powers received due admiration from Catherine, to whom they were entirely new; and the respect which they naturally inspired might have been too great for familiarity, had not the easy gaiety of Miss Thorpe's manners, and her frequent expressions of delight on this acquaintance with her, softened down every feeling of awe, and left nothing but tender affection. Their increasing attachment was not to be satisfied with half a dozen turns in the Pump-room, but required, when they all quitted it together, that Miss Thorpe should accompany Miss Morland to the very door of Mr. Allen's house; and that they should there part with a most affectionate and lengthened shake of hands, after learning, to their mutual relief, that they should see each other across the theatre at night, and say their prayers in the same chapel the next morning. Catherine then ran directly up stairs, and watched Miss Thorpe's progress down the street from the drawing-room window; admired the graceful spirit of her walk, the fashionable air of her figure and dress, and felt grateful, as well she might, for the chance which had procured her such a friend.

Mrs. Thorpe was a widow, and not a very rich one; she was a good-humoured, well-meaning woman, and a very indulgent mother. Her eldest daughter had great personal beauty, and the younger ones, by pretending to be as handsome as their sister, imitating her air, and dressing in the same style, did very well.

This brief account of the family is intended to supersede the necessity of a long and minute detail from Mrs. Thorpe herself, of her past adventures and sufferings, which might otherwise be expected to occupy the three or four following chapters; in which the worthlessness of lords and attornies might be set forth, and conversations, which had passed twenty years before, be minutely repeated.

CHAPTER V

CATHERINE WAS not so much engaged at the theatre that evening, in returning the nods and smiles of Miss Thorpe, though they certainly claimed much of her leisure, as to forget to look with an inquiring eye for Mr. Tilney in every box which her eye could reach; but she looked in vain. Mr. Tilney was no fonder of the play than the Pump-room. She hoped to be more fortunate the next day; and when her wishes for fine weather were answered by seeing a beautiful morning, she hardly felt a doubt of it; for a fine Sunday in Bath empties every house of its inhabitants, and all the world appears on such an occasion to walk about and tell their acquaintance what a charming day it is.

As soon as divine service was over, the Thorpes and Allens eagerly joined each other; and after staying long enough in the Pump-room to discover that the crowd was insupportable, and that there was not a genteel face to be seen, which every body discovers every Sunday throughout the season, they hastened away to the Crescent, to breathe the fresh air of better company. Here Catherine and Isabella, arm in arm, again tasted the sweets of friendship in an unreserved conversation; – they talked much, and with much enjoyment; but again was Catherine disappointed in her hope of reseeing her partner. He was no where to be met with; every search for him was equally unsuccessful, in morning lounges or evening assemblies; neither at the upper nor lower rooms, at dressed or undressed balls, was he perceivable; nor among the walkers, the horsemen, or the curricle-drivers of the morning. His name was not in the Pump-room book, and curiosity could do no more. He must be gone from Bath. Yet he had not mentioned that his stay would be so short! This sort of mysteriousness, which is always so becoming in a hero, threw a fresh grace in Catherine's imagination around his person and manners, and increased her anxiety to know more of him. From the Thorpes she could learn nothing, for they had been only two days in Bath before they met with Mrs. Allen. It was a subject, however, in which she often indulged with her fair friend, from whom she received every possible encouragement to continue to think of him; and his impression on her fancy was not suffered therefore to weaken. Isabella was very sure that he must be a charming young man; and was equally sure that he must have been delighted with her dear Catherine, and would therefore shortly return. She liked him the better for being a clergyman, 'for she must confess herself very partial to the profession;' and something like a sigh escaped her as she said it. Perhaps Catherine was wrong in not demanding the cause of that gentle emotion – but she was not experienced enough in the finesse of love, or the duties of friendship, to know when delicate raillery was properly called for, or when a confidence should be forced.

Mrs. Allen was now quite happy – quite satisfied with Bath. She had found some acquaintance, had been so lucky too as to find in them the family of a most worthy old friend; and, as the completion of good fortune, had found these friends by no means so expensively dressed as herself. Her daily expressions were no longer, 'I wish we had some acquaintance in Bath!' They were changed into – 'How glad I am we have met with Mrs. Thorpe!' – and she was as eager in promoting the intercourse of the two families, as her young charge and Isabella themselves could be; never satisfied with the day unless she spent the chief of it by the side of Mrs. Thorpe, in what they called conversation, but in which there was scarcely ever any exchange of opinion, and not often any resemblance of subject, for Mrs. Thorpe talked chiefly of her children, and Mrs. Allen of her gowns.

The progress of the friendship between Catherine and Isabella was quick as its beginning had been warm, and they passed so rapidly through every gradation of increasing tenderness, that there was shortly no fresh proof of it to be given to their friends or themselves. They called each other by their Christian name, were always arm in arm when they walked, pinned up each other's train for the dance, and were not to be divided in the set; and if a rainy morning deprived them of other enjoyments, they were still resolute in meeting in defiance of wet and dirt, and shut themselves up, to read novels together. Yes, novels; – for I will not adopt that ungenerous and impolitic custom so common with novel writers, of degrading by their contemptuous censure the very performances, to the number of which they are themselves adding – joining with their greatest enemies in bestowing the harshest epithets on such works, and scarcely ever permitting them to be read by their own heroine, who, if she accidentally take up a novel, is sure to turn over its insipid pages with disgust. Alas! if the heroine of one novel be not patronized by the heroine of another, from whom can she expect protection and regard? I cannot approve of it. Let us leave it to the Reviewers to abuse such effusions of fancy at their leisure, and over every new novel to talk in threadbare strains of the trash with which the press now groans. Let us not desert one another; we are an injured body. Although our productions have afforded more extensive and unaffected pleasure than those of any other literary corporation in the world, no species of composition has been so much decried. From pride, ignorance, or fashion, our foes are almost as many as our readers. And while the abilities of the nine-hundredth abridger of the History of England, or of the man who collects and publishes in a volume some dozen lines of Milton, Pope, and Prior, with a paper from the Spectator, and a chapter from Sterne, are eulogized by a thousand pens, – there seems almost a general wish of decrying the capacity and undervaluing the labour of the novelist, and of slighting the performances which have only genius, wit, and taste to recommend them. 'I am no novel reader – I seldom look into novels – Do not imagine that *I* often read novels – It is really very well for a novel.' – Such is the common cant. – 'And what are you reading, Miss — ?' 'Oh! it is only a novel!' replies the young lady; while she lays down her book with affected indifference, or momentary shame. – 'It is only Cecilia, or Camilla, or Belinda;' or, in short, only some work in which the greatest powers of the mind are displayed, in which the most thorough knowledge of human nature, the happiest delineation of its varieties, the liveliest effusions of wit and humour are conveyed to the world in the best chosen language. Now, had the same young lady been engaged with a volume of the Spectator, instead of such a work, how proudly would she have produced the book, and told its name; though the chances must be against her being occupied by any part of that voluminous publication, of which either the matter or manner would not disgust a young person of taste: the substance of its papers so often consisting in the statement of improbable circumstances, unnatural characters, and topics of conversation, which no longer concern any one living, and their language, too, frequently so coarse as to give no very favourable idea of the age that could endure it.

CHAPTER VI

THE FOLLOWING conversation, which took place between the two friends in the Pump-room one morning, after an acquaintance of eight or nine days, is given as a specimen of their very warm attachment, and of the delicacy, discretion, originality of thought, and literary taste which marked the reasonableness of that attachment.

They met by appointment; and as Isabella had arrived nearly five minutes before her friend, her first address naturally was – 'My dearest creature, what can have made you so late? I have been waiting for you at least this age!'

'Have you, indeed! – I am very sorry for it; but really I thought I was in very good time. It is but just one. I hope you have not been here long?'

'Oh! these ten ages at least. I am sure I have been here this half hour. But now, let us go and sit down at the other end of the room, and enjoy ourselves. I have an hundred things to say to you. In the first place, I was so afraid it would rain this morning, just as I wanted to set off; it looked very showery, and that would have thrown me into agonies! Do you know, I saw the prettiest hat you can imagine, in a shop window in Milsom-street just now – very like yours, only with coquelicot ribbons instead of green; I quite longed for it. But, my dearest Catherine, what have you been doing with yourself all this morning? – Have you gone on with Udolpho?'

'Yes, I have been reading it ever since I woke; and I am got to the black veil.'

'Are you, indeed? How delightful! Oh! I would not tell you what is behind the black veil for the world! Are not you wild to know?'

'Oh! yes, quite; what can it be? – But do not tell me – I would not be told upon any account. I know it must be a skeleton, I am sure it is Laurentina's skeleton. Oh! I am delighted with the book! I should like to spend my whole life in reading it. I assure you, if it had not been to meet you, I would not have come away from it for all the world.'

'Dear creature! how much I am obliged to you; and when you have finished Udolpho, we will read the Italian together; and I have made out a list of ten or twelve more of the same kind for you.'

'Have you, indeed! How glad I am! – What are they all?'

'I will read you their names directly; here they are, in my pocket-book. Castle of Wolfenbach, Clermont, Mysterious Warnings, Necromancer of the Black Forest, Midnight Bell, Orphan of the Rhine, and Horrid Mysteries. Those will last us some time.'

'Yes, pretty well; but are they all horrid, are you sure they are all horrid?'

'Yes, quite sure; for a particular friend of mine, a Miss Andrews, a sweet girl, one of the sweetest creatures in the world, has read every one of them. I wish you knew Miss Andrews, you would be delighted with her. She is netting herself the sweetest cloak you can conceive. I think her as beautiful as an angel, and I am so vexed with the men for not admiring her! – I scold them all amazingly about it.'

'Scold them! Do you scold them for not admiring her?'

'Yes, that I do. There is nothing I would not do for those who are really my friends. I have no notion of loving people by halves, it is not my nature. My attachments are always excessively strong. I told Capt. Hunt at one of our assemblies this winter, that if he was to tease me all night, I would not dance with him, unless he would allow Miss Andrews to be as beautiful as an angel. The men think us incapable of real friendship you know, and I am determined to shew them the difference. Now, if I were to hear any body speak slightingly of you, I should fire up in a moment: – but that is not at all likely, for *you* are just the kind of girl to be a great favourite with the men.'

'Oh! dear,' cried Catherine, colouring, 'how can you say so?'

'I know you very well; you have so much animation, which is exactly what Miss Andrews wants, for I must confess there is something amazingly insipid about her. Oh! I must tell you, that just after we parted yesterday, I saw a young man looking at you so earnestly – I am sure he is in love with you.' Catherine coloured, and disclaimed again. Isabella laughed. 'It is very true, upon my honour, but I see how it is; you are indifferent to every body's admiration, except that of one gentleman, who shall be nameless. Nay, I cannot blame you – (speaking more seriously) – your feelings are easily understood. Where the heart is really attached, I know very well how little one can be pleased with the attention of any body else. Every thing is so inspid, so uninteresting, that does not relate to the beloved object! I can perfectly comprehend your feelings.'

'But you should not persuade me that I think so very much about Mr. Tilney, for perhaps I may never see him again.'

'Not see him again! My dearest creature, do not talk of it. I am sure you would be miserable if you thought so.'

'No, indeed, I should not. I do not pretend to say that I was not very much pleased with him; but while I have Udolpho to read, I feel as if nobody could make me miserable. Oh! the dreadful black veil! My dear Isabella, I am sure there must be Laurentina's skeleton behind it.'

'It is so odd to me, that you should never have read

Udolpho before; but I suppose Mrs. Morland objects to novels.'

'No, she does not. She very often reads Sir Charles Grandison herself; but new books do not fall in our way.'

'Sir Charles Grandison! That is an amazing horrid book, is it not? – I remember Miss Andrews could not get through the first volume.'

'It is not like Udolpho at all; but yet I think it is very entertaining.'

'Do you indeed! – you surprise me; I thought it had not been readable. But, my dearest Catherine, have you settled what to wear on your head to-night? I am determined at all events to be dressed exactly like you. The men take notice of *that* sometimes you know.'

'But it does not signify if they do;' said Catherine, very innocently.

'Signify! Oh, heavens! I make it a rule never to mind what they say. They are very often amazingly impertinent if you do not treat them with spirit, and make them keep their distance.'

'Are they? – Well, I never observed *that*. They always behave very well to me.'

'Oh! they give themselves such airs. They are the most conceited creatures in the world, and think themselves of so much importance! – By the bye, though I have thought of it a hundred times, I have always forgot to ask you what is your favourite complexion in a man. Do you like them best dark or fair?'

'I hardly know. I never much thought about it. Something between both, I think. Brown – not fair, and not very dark.'

'Very well, Catherine. That is exactly he. I have not forgot your description of Mr. Tilney; – "a brown skin, with dark eyes, and rather dark hair." – Well, my taste is different. I prefer light eyes, and as to complexion – do you know – I like a sallow better than any other.

You must not betray me, if you should ever meet with one of your acquaintance answering that description.'

'Betray you! – What do you mean?'

'Nay, do not distress me. I believe I have said too much. Let us drop the subject.'

Catherine, in some amazement, complied; and after remaining a few moments silent, was on the point of reverting to what interested her at that time rather more than any thing else in the world, Laurentina's skeleton; when her friend prevented her, by saying, – 'For Heaven's sake! let us move away from this end of the room. Do you know, there are two odious young men who have been staring at me this half hour. They really put me quite out of countenance. Let us go and look at the arrivals. They will hardly follow us there.'

Away they walked to the book; and while Isabella examined the names, it was Catherine's employment to watch the proceedings of these alarming young men.

'They are not coming this way, are they? I hope they are not so impertinent as to follow us. Pray let me know if they are coming. I am determined I will not look up.'

In a few moments Catherine, with unaffected pleasure, assured her that she need not be longer uneasy, as the gentlemen had just left the Pump-room.

'And which way are they gone?' said Isabella, turning hastily round. 'One was a very good-looking young man.'

'They went towards the churchyard.'

'Well, I am amazingly glad I have got rid of them! And now, what say you to going to Edgar's Buildings with me, and looking at my new hat? You said you should like to see it.'

Catherine readily agreed. 'Only,' she added, 'perhaps we may overtake the two young men.'

'Oh! never mind that. If we make haste, we shall

pass by them presently, and I am dying to shew you my hat.'

'But if we only wait a few minutes, there will be no danger of our seeing them at all.'

'I shall not pay them any such compliment, I assure you. I have no notion of treating men with such respect. *That* is the way to spoil them.'

Catherine had nothing to oppose against such reasoning; and therefore, to shew the independence of Miss Thorpe, and her resolution of humbling the sex, they set off immediately as fast as they could walk, in pursuit of the two young men.

CHAPTER VII

HALF A minute conducted them through the Pump-yard to the archway, opposite Union-passage; but here they were stopped. Every body acquainted with Bath may remember the difficulties of crossing Cheap-street at this point; it is indeed a street of so impertinent a nature, so unfortunately connected with the great London and Oxford roads, and the principal inn of the city, that a day never passes in which parties of ladies, however important their business, whether in quest of pastry, millinery, or even (as in the present case) of young men, are not detained on one side or other by carriages, horsemen, or carts. This evil had been felt and lamented, at least three times a day, by Isabella since her residence in Bath; and she was now fated to feel and lament it once more, for at the very moment of coming opposite to Union-passage, and within view of the two gentlemen who were proceeding through the crowds, and threading the gutters of that interesting alley, they were prevented crossing by the approach of a gig, driven along on bad pavement by a most knowing-looking coachman with all the vehemence that could most fitly endanger the lives of himself, his companion, and his horse.

'Oh, these odious gigs!' said Isabella, looking up, 'how I detest them.' But this detestation, though so just, was of short duration, for she looked again and exclaimed, 'Delightful! Mr. Morland and my brother!'

'Good heaven! 'tis James!' was uttered at the same moment by Catherine; and, on catching the young men's eyes, the horse was immediately checked with a violence which almost threw him on his haunches, and the servant having now scampered up, the gentlemen jumped out, and the equipage was delivered to his care.

Catherine, by whom this meeting was wholly unexpected, received her brother with the liveliest pleasure; and he, being of a very amiable disposition, and sincerely attached to her, gave every proof on his side of equal satisfaction, which he could have leisure to do, while the bright eyes of Miss Thorpe were incessantly challenging his notice; and to her his devoirs were speedily paid, with a mixture of joy and embarrassment which might have informed Catherine, had she been more expert in the developement of other people's feelings, and less simply engrossed by her own, that her brother thought her friend quite as pretty as she could do herself.

John Thorpe, who in the mean time had been giving orders about the horses, soon joined them, and from him she directly received the amends which were her due; for while he slightly and carelessly touched the hand of Isabella, on her he bestowed a whole scrape and half a short bow. He was a stout young man of middling height, who, with a plain face and ungraceful form, seemed fearful of being too handsome unless he wore the dress of a groom, and too much like a gentleman unless he were easy where he ought to be civil, and impudent where he might be allowed to be easy.

He took out his watch: 'How long do you think we have been running it from Tetbury, Miss Morland?'

'I do not know the distance.' Her brother told her that it was twenty-three miles.

'*Three*-and-twenty!' cried Thorpe; 'five-and-twenty if it is an inch.' Morland remonstrated, pleaded the authority of road-books, innkeepers, and milestones; but his friend disregarded them all; he had a surer test of distance. 'I know it must be five-and-twenty,' said he, 'by the time we have been doing it. It is now half after one; we drove out of the inn-yard at Tetbury as the town-clock struck eleven; and I defy any man in England to make my horse go less than ten miles an hour in harness; that makes it exactly twenty-five.'

'You have lost an hour,' said Morland; 'it was only ten o'clock when we came from Tetbury.'

'Ten o'clock! it was eleven, upon my soul! I counted every stroke. This brother of yours would persuade me out of my senses, Miss Morland; do but look at my horse; did you ever see an animal so made for speed in your life?' (The servant had just mounted the carriage and was driving off.) 'Such true blood! Three hours and a half indeed coming only three-and-twenty miles! look at that creature, and suppose it possible if you can.'

'He *does* look very hot to be sure.'

'Hot! he had not turned a hair till we came to Walcot Church: but look at his forehand; look at his loins; only see how he moves; that horse *cannot* go less than ten miles an hour: tie his legs and he will get on. What do you think of my gig, Miss Morland? a neat one, is not it? Well hung; town built; I have not had it a month. It was built for a Christchurch man, a friend of mine, a very good sort of fellow; he ran it a few weeks, till, I believe, it was convenient to have done with it. I happened just then to be looking out for some light thing of the kind, though I had pretty well determined on a curricle too; but I chanced to meet him on

Magdalen Bridge, as he was driving into Oxford, last term: "Ah! Thorpe," said he, "do you happen to want such a little thing as this? it is a capital one of the kind, but I am cursed tired of it." "Oh! d—," said I, "I am your man; what do you ask?" And how much do you think he did, Miss Morland?'

'I am sure I cannot guess at all.'

'Curricle-hung you see; seat, trunk, sword-case, splashing-board, lamps, silver moulding, all you see complete; the iron-work as good as new, or better. He asked fifty guineas; I closed with him directly, threw down the money, and the carriage was mine.'

'And I am sure,' said Catherine, 'I know so little of such things that I cannot judge whether it was cheap or dear.'

'Neither one nor t'other; I might have got it for less I dare say; but I hate haggling, and poor Freeman wanted cash.'

'That was very good-natured of you,' said Catherine, quite pleased.

'Oh! d— it, when one has the means of doing a kind thing by a friend, I hate to be pitiful.'

An inquiry now took place into the intended movements of the young ladies; and, on finding whither they were going, it was decided that the gentlemen should accompany them to Edgar's Buildings, and pay their respects to Mrs. Thorpe. James and Isabella led the way; and so well satisfied was the latter with her lot, so contentedly was she endeavouring to ensure a pleasant walk to him who brought the double recommendation of being her brother's friend, and her friend's brother, so pure and uncoquettish were her feelings, that, though they overtook and passed the two offending young men in Milsom-street, she was so far from seeking to attract their notice, that she looked back at them only three times.

John Thorpe kept of course with Catherine, and,

after a few minutes' silence, renewed the conversation about his gig – 'You will find, however, Miss Morland, it would be reckoned a cheap thing by some people, for I might have sold it for ten guineas more the next day; Jackson, of Oriel, bid me sixty at once; Morland was with me at the time.'

'Yes,' said Morland, who overheard this; 'but you forget that your horse was included.'

'My horse! oh, d— it! I would not sell my horse for a hundred. Are you fond of an open carriage, Miss Morland?'

'Yes, very; I have hardly ever an opportunity of being in one; but I am particularly fond of it.'

'I am glad of it; I will drive you out in mine every day.'

'Thank you,' said Catherine, in some distress, from a doubt of the propriety of accepting such an offer.

'I will drive you up Lansdown Hill to-morrow.'

'Thank you; but will not your horse want rest?'

'Rest! he has only come three-and-twenty miles to-day; all nonsense; nothing ruins horses so much as rest; nothing knocks them up so soon. No, no; I shall exercise mine at the average of four hours every day while I am here.'

'Shall you indeed!' said Catherine very seriously, 'that will be forty miles a day.'

'Forty! aye fifty, for what I care. Well, I will drive you up Lansdown to-morrow; mind, I am engaged.'

'How delightful that will be!' cried Isabella, turning round; 'my dearest Catherine, I quite envy you; but I am afraid, brother, you will not have room for a third.'

'A third indeed! no, no; I did not come to Bath to drive my sisters about; that would be a good joke, faith! Morland must take care of you.'

This brought on a dialogue of civilities between the other two; but Catherine heard neither the particulars nor the result. Her companion's discourse now sunk from its hitherto animated pitch, to nothing more than a short decisive sentence of praise or condemnation on the face of every woman they met; and Catherine, after listening and agreeing as long as she could, with all the civility and deference of the youthful female mind, fearful of hazarding an opinion of its own in opposition to that of a self-assured man, especially where the beauty of her own sex is concerned, ventured at length to vary the subject by a question which had been long uppermost in her thoughts; it was, 'Have you ever read Udolpho, Mr. Thorpe?'

'Udolpho! Oh, Lord! not I; I never read novels; I have something else to do.'

Catherine, humbled and ashamed, was going to apologize for her question, but he prevented her by saying, 'Novels are all so full of nonsense and stuff; there has not been a tolerably decent one come out since Tom Jones, except the Monk; I read that t'other day; but as for all the others, they are the stupidest things in creation.'

'I think you must like Udolpho, if you were to read it; it is so very interesting.'

'Not I, faith! No, if I read any, it shall be Mrs. Radcliff's; her novels are amusing enough; they are worth reading; some fun and nature in *them*.'

'Udolpho was written by Mrs. Radcliff,' said Catherine, with some hesitation, from the fear of mortifying him.

'No sure; was it? Aye, I remember, so it was; I was thinking of that other stupid book, written by that woman they make such a fuss about, she who married the French emigrant.'

'I suppose you mean Camilla?'

'Yes, that's the book; such unnatural stuff! – An old man playing at see-saw! I took up the first volume once, and looked it over, but I soon found it would not do; indeed I guessed what sort of stuff it must be before I saw it: as soon as I heard she had married an emigrant, I was sure I should never be able to get through it.'

'I have never read it.'

'You had no loss I assure you; it is the horridest nonsense you can imagine; there is nothing in the world in it but an old man's playing at see-saw and learning Latin; upon my soul there is not.'

This critique, the justness of which was unfortunately lost on poor Catherine, brought them to the door of Mrs. Thorpe's lodgings, and the feelings of the discerning and unprejudiced reader of Camilla gave way to the feelings of the dutiful and affectionate son, as they met Mrs. Thorpe, who had descried them from above, in the passage. 'Ah, mother! how do you do?' said he, giving her a hearty shake of the hand: 'where did you get that quiz of a hat, it makes you look like an old witch? Here is Morland and I come to stay a few days with you, so you must look out for a couple of good beds some where near.' And this address seemed to satisfy all the fondest wishes of the mother's heart, for she received him with the most delighted and exulting affection. On his two younger sisters he then bestowed an equal portion of his fraternal tenderness, for he asked each of them how they did, and observed that they both looked very ugly.

These manners did not please Catherine; but he was James's friend and Isabella's brother; and her judgment was further bought off by Isabella's assuring her, when they withdrew to see the new hat, that John thought her the most charming girl in the world, and by John's engaging her before they parted to dance with him that evening. Had she been older or vainer, such attacks might have done little; but, where youth and diffidence are united, it requires uncommon steadiness of reason to resist the attraction of being called the most charming girl in the world, and of being so very early engaged as a partner; and the consequence was, that, when the two Morlands, after sitting an hour with the Thorpes, set off to walk together to Mr. Allen's, and James, as the door was closed on them, said, 'Well, Catherine, how do you like my friend Thorpe?' instead of answering, as she probably would have done, had there been no friendship and no flattery in the case, 'I do not like him at all;' she directly replied, 'I like him very much; he seems very agreeable.'

'He is as good-natured a fellow as ever lived; a little of a rattle; but that will recommend him to your sex I believe: and how do you like the rest of the family?'

'Very, very much indeed: Isabella particularly.'

'I am very glad to hear you say so; she is just the kind of young woman I could wish to see you attached to; she has so much good sense, and is so thoroughly unaffected and amiable; I always wanted you to know her; and she seems very fond of you. She said the highest things in your praise that could possibly be; and the praise of such a girl as Miss Thorpe even you, Catherine,' taking her hand with affection, 'may be proud of.'

'Indeed I am,' she replied; 'I love her exceedingly, and am delighted to find that you like her too. You hardly mentioned any thing of her, when you wrote to me after your visit there.'

'Because I thought I should soon see you myself. I hope you will be a great deal together while you are in Bath. She is a most amiable girl; such a superior understanding! How fond all the family are of her; she is evidently the general favourite; and how much she must be admired in such a place as this – is not she?'

'Yes, very much indeed, I fancy; Mr. Allen thinks her the prettiest girl in Bath.'

'I dare say he does; and I do not know any man who is a better judge of beauty than Mr. Allen. I need not ask you whether you are happy here, my dear

Catherine; with such a companion and friend as Isabella Thorpe, it would be impossible for you to be otherwise; and the Allens I am sure are very kind to you?'

'Yes, very kind; I never was so happy before; and now you are come it will be more delightful than ever; how good it is of you to come so far on purpose to see *me*.'

James accepted this tribute of gratitude, and qualified his conscience for accepting it too, by saying with perfect sincerity, 'Indeed, Catherine, I love you dearly.'

Inquiries and communications concerning brothers and sisters, the situation of some, the growth of the rest, and other family matters, now passed between them, and continued, with only one small digression on James's part, in praise of Miss Thorpe, till they reached Pulteney-street, where he was welcomed with great kindness by Mr. and Mrs. Allen, invited by the former to dine with them, and summoned by the latter to guess the price and weigh the merits of a new muff and tippet. A pre-engagement in Edgar's Buildings prevented his accepting the invitation of one friend, and obliged him to hurry away as soon as he had satisfied the demands of the other. The time of the two parties uniting in the Octagon Room being correctly adjusted, Catherine was then left to the luxury of a raised, restless, and frightened imagination over the pages of Udolpho, lost from all worldly concerns of dressing and dinner, incapable of soothing Mrs. Allen's fears on the delay of an expected dress-maker, and having only one minute in sixty to bestow even on the reflection of her own felicity, in being already engaged for the evening.

CHAPTER VIII

I N SPITE of Udolpho and the dress-maker, however,
the party from Pulteney-street reached the Upper
Rooms in very good time. The Thorpes and James
Morland were there only two minutes before them; and
Isabella having gone through the usual ceremonial of
meeting her friend with the most smiling and affectionate haste, of admiring the set of her gown, and envying
the curl of her hair, they followed their chaperons, arm
in arm, into the ball-room, whispering to each other
whenever a thought occurred, and supplying the place
of many ideas by a squeeze of the hand or a smile of
affection.

The dancing began within a few minutes after they
were seated; and James, who had been engaged quite
as long as his sister, was very importunate with Isabella
to stand up; but John was gone into the card-room to
speak to a friend, and nothing, she declared, should
induce her to join the set before her dear Catherine
could join it too: 'I assure you,' said she, 'I would not
stand up without your dear sister for all the world; for
if I did we should certainly be separated the whole
evening.' Catherine accepted this kindness with gratitude, and they continued as they were for three
minutes longer, when Isabella, who had been talking to
James on the other side of her, turned again to his
sister and whispered, 'My dear creature, I am afraid I
must leave you, your brother is so amazingly impatient
to begin; I know you will not mind my going away, and
I dare say John will be back in a moment, and then you
may easily find me out.' Catherine, though a little disappointed, had too much good-nature to make any
opposition, and the others rising up, Isabella had only
time to press her friend's hand and say, 'Good bye, my

dear love,' before they hurried off. The younger Miss Thorpes being also dancing, Catherine was left to the mercy of Mrs. Thorpe and Mrs. Allen, between whom she now remained. She could not help being vexed at the non-appearance of Mr. Thorpe, for she not only longed to be dancing, but was likewise aware that, as the real dignity of her situation could not be known, she was sharing with the scores of other young ladies still sitting down all the discredit of wanting a partner. To be disgraced in the eye of the world, to wear the appearance of infamy while her heart is all purity, her actions all innocence, and the misconduct of another the true source of her debasement, is one of those circumstances which peculiarly belong to the heroine's life, and her fortitude under it what particularly dignifies her character. Catherine had fortitude too; she suffered, but no murmur passed her lips.

From this state of humiliation, she was roused, at the end of ten minutes, to a pleasanter feeling, by seeing, not Mr. Thorpe, but Mr. Tilney, within three yards of the place where they sat; he seemed to be moving that way, but he did not see her, and therefore the smile and the blush, which his sudden reappearance raised in Catherine, passed away without sullying her heroic importance. He looked as handsome and as lively as ever, and was talking with interest to a fashionable and pleasing-looking young woman, who leant on his arm, and whom Catherine immediately guessed to be his sister; thus unthinkingly throwing away a fair opportunity of considering him lost to her for ever, by being married already. But guided only by what was simple and probable, it had never entered her head that Mr. Tilney could be married; he had not behaved, he had not talked, like the married men to whom she had been used; he had never mentioned a wife, and he had acknowledged a sister. From these circumstances sprang the instant conclusion of his sister's now being by his side; and therefore, instead of turning of a deathlike paleness, and falling in a fit on Mrs. Allen's bosom, Catherine sat erect, in the perfect use of her senses, and with cheeks only a little redder than usual.

Mr. Tilney and his companion, who continued, though slowly, to approach, were immediately preceded by a lady, an acquaintance of Mrs. Thorpe; and this lady stopping to speak to her, they, as belonging to her, stopped likewise, and Catherine, catching Mr. Tilney's eye, instantly received from him the smiling tribute of recognition. She returned it with pleasure, and then advancing still nearer, he spoke both to her and Mrs. Allen, by whom he was very civilly acknowledged. 'I am very happy to see you again, sir, indeed; I was afraid you had left Bath.' He thanked her for her fears, and said that he had quitted it for a week, on the very morning after his having had the pleasure of seeing her.

'Well, sir, and I dare say you are not sorry to be back again, for it is just the place for young people – and indeed for every body else too. I tell Mr. Allen, when he talks of being sick of it, that I am sure he should not complain, for it is so very agreeable a place, that it is much better to be here than at home at this dull time of year. I tell him he is quite in luck to be sent here for his health.'

'And I hope, madam, that Mr. Allen will be obliged to like the place, from finding it of service to him.'

'Thank you, sir. I have no doubt that he will. – A neighbour of ours, Dr. Skinner, was here for his health last winter, and came away quite stout.'

'That circumstance must give great encouragement.'

'Yes, sir – and Dr. Skinner and his family were here three months; so I tell Mr. Allen he must not be in a hurry to get away.'

Here they were interrupted by a request from Mrs. Thorpe to Mrs. Allen, that she would move a little to accommodate Mrs. Hughes and Miss Tilney with seats, as they had agreed to join their party. This was accordingly done, Mr. Tilney still continuing standing before them; and after a few minutes consideration, he asked Catherine to dance with him. This compliment, delightful as it was, produced severe mortification to the lady; and in giving her denial, she expressed her sorrow on the occasion so very much as if she really felt it, that had Thorpe, who joined her just afterwards, been half a minute earlier, he might have thought her sufferings rather too acute. The very easy manner in which he then told her that he had kept her waiting, did not by any means reconcile her more to her lot; nor did the particulars which he entered into while they were standing up, of the horses and dogs of the friend whom he had just left, and of a proposed exchange of terriers between them, interest her so much as to prevent her looking very often towards that part of the room where she had left Mr. Tilney. Of her dear Isabella, to whom she particularly longed to point out that gentleman, she could see nothing. They were in different sets. She was separated from all her party, and away from all her acquaintance; – one mortification succeeded another, and from the whole she deduced this useful lesson, that to go previously engaged to a ball, does not necessarily increase either the dignity or enjoyment of a young lady. From such a moralizing strain as this, she was suddenly roused by a touch on the shoulder, and turning round, perceived Mrs. Hughes directly behind her, attended by Miss Tilney and a gentleman. 'I beg your pardon, Miss Morland,' said she, 'for this liberty, – but I cannot any how get to Miss Thorpe, and Mrs. Thorpe said she was sure you would not have the least objection to letting in this young lady by you.' Mrs. Hughes could not have applied to any creature in the room more happy to oblige her than Catherine. The young ladies were introduced to each other, Miss Tilney expressing a proper sense of such goodness, Miss Morland with the real delicacy of a generous mind making light of the obligation; and Mrs. Hughes, satisfied with having so respectably settled her young charge, returned to her party.

Miss Tilney had a good figure, a pretty face, and a very agreeable countenance; and her air, though it had not all the decided pretension, the resolute stilishness of Miss Thorpe's, had more real elegance. Her manners shewed good sense and good breeding; they were neither shy, nor affectedly open; and she seemed capable of being young, attractive, and at a ball, without wanting to fix the attention of every man near her, and without exaggerated feelings of extatic delight or inconceivable vexation on every little trifling occurrence. Catherine, interested at once by her appearance and her relationship to Mr. Tilney, was desirous of being acquainted with her, and readily talked therefore whenever she could think of any thing to say, and had courage and leisure for saying it. But the hindrance thrown in the way of a very speedy intimacy, by the frequent want of one or more of these requisites, prevented their doing more than going through the first rudiments of an acquaintance, by informing themselves how well the other liked Bath, how much she admired its buildings and surrounding country, whether she drew, or played or sang, and whether she was fond of riding on horseback.

The two dances were scarcely concluded before Catherine found her arm gently seized by her faithful Isabella, who in great spirits exclaimed – 'At last I have got you. My dearest creature, I have been looking for you this hour. What could induce you to come into this set, when you knew I was in the other? I have been quite wretched without you.'

'My dear Isabella, how was it possible for me to get at you? I could not even see where you were.'

'So I told your brother all the time – but he would not believe me. Do go and see for her, Mr. Morland, said I – but all in vain – he would not stir an inch. Was not it so, Mr. Morland? But you men are all so immoderately lazy! I have been scolding him to such a degree, my dear Catherine, you would be quite amazed. – You know I never stand upon ceremony with such people.'

'Look at that young lady with the white beads round her head,' whispered Catherine, detaching her friend from James – 'It is Mr. Tilney's sister.'

'Oh! heavens! You don't say so! Let me look at her this moment. What a delightful girl! I never saw any thing half so beautiful! But where is her all-conquering brother? Is he in the room? Point him out to me this instant, if he is. I die to see him. Mr. Morland, you are not to listen. We are not talking about you.'

'But what is all this whispering about? What is going on?'

'There now, I knew how it would be. You men have such restless curiosity! Talk of the curiosity of women, indeed! – 'tis nothing. But be satisfied, for you are not to know any thing at all of the matter.'

'And is that likely to satisfy me, do you think?'

'Well, I declare I never knew any thing like you. What can it signify to you, what we are talking of? Perhaps we are talking about you, therefore I would advise you not to listen, or you may happen to hear something not very agreeable.'

In this common-place chatter, which lasted some time, the original subject seemed entirely forgotten; and though Catherine was very well pleased to have it dropped for a while, she could not avoid a little suspicion at the total suspension of all Isabella's impatient desire to see Mr. Tilney. When the orchestra struck up a fresh dance, James would have led his fair partner away, but she resisted. 'I tell you, Mr. Morland,' she cried, 'I would not do such a thing for all the world. How can you be so teasing; only conceive, my dear Catherine, what your brother wants me to do. He wants me to dance with him again, though I tell him that it is a most improper thing, and entirely against the rules. It would make us the talk of the place, if we were not to change partners.'

'Upon my honour,' said James, 'in these public assemblies, it is as often done as not.'

'Nonsense, how can you say so? But when you men have a point to carry, you never stick at any thing. My sweet Catherine, do support me, persuade your brother how impossible it is. Tell him, that it would quite shock you to see me do such a thing; now would not it?'

'No, not at all; but if you think it wrong, you had much better change.'

'There,' cried Isabella, 'you hear what your sister says, and yet you will not mind her. Well, remember that it is not my fault, if we set all the old ladies in Bath in a bustle. Come along, my dearest Catherine, for heaven's sake, and stand by me.' And off they went, to regain their former place. John Thorpe, in the meanwhile, had walked away; and Catherine, ever willing to give Mr. Tilney an opportunity of repeating the agreeable request which had already flattered her once, made her way to Mrs. Allen and Mrs. Thorpe as fast as she could, in the hope of finding him still with them – a hope which, when it proved to be fruitless, she felt to have been highly unreasonable. 'Well, my dear,' said Mrs. Thorpe, impatient for praise of her son, 'I hope you have had an agreeable partner.'

'Very agreeable, madam.'

'I am glad of it. John has charming spirits, has not he?'

'Did you meet Mr. Tilney, my dear?' said Mrs. Allen. 'No, where is he?'

'He was with us just now, and said he was so tired

of lounging about, that he was resolved to go and dance; so I thought perhaps he would ask you, if he met with you.'

'Where can he be?' said Catherine, looking round; but she had not looked round long before she saw him leading a young lady to the dance.

'Ah! he has got a partner, I wish he had asked *you*,' said Mrs. Allen; and after a short silence, she added, 'he is a very agreeable young man.'

'Indeed he is, Mrs. Allen,' said Mrs. Thorpe, smiling complacently; 'I must say it, though I *am* his mother, that there is not a more agreeable young man in the world.'

This inapplicable answer might have been too much for the comprehension of many; but it did not puzzle Mrs. Allen, for after only a moment's consideration, she said, in a whisper to Catherine, 'I dare say she thought I was speaking of her son.'

Catherine was disappointed and vexed. She seemed to have missed by so little the very object she had had in view; and this persuasion did not incline her to a very gracious reply, when John Thorpe came up to her soon afterwards, and said, 'Well, Miss Morland, I suppose you and I are to stand up and jig it together again.'

'Oh, no; I am much obliged to you, our two dances are over; and, besides, I am tired, and do not mean to dance any more.'

'Do not you? – then let us walk about and quiz people. Come along with me, and I will shew you the four greatest quizzers in the room; my two younger sisters and their partners. I have been laughing at them this half hour.'

Again Catherine excused herself; and at last he walked off to quiz his sisters by himself. The rest of the evening she found very dull; Mr. Tilney was drawn away from their party at tea, to attend that of his partner; Miss Tilney, though belonging to it, did not sit near her, and James and Isabella were so much engaged in conversing together, that the latter had no leisure to bestow more on her friend than one smile, one squeeze, and one 'dearest Catherine.'

CHAPTER IX

THE PROGRESS of Catherine's unhappiness from the events of the evening, was as follows. It appeared first in a general dissatisfaction with every body about her, while she remained in the rooms, which speedily brought on considerable weariness and a violent desire to go home. This, on arriving in Pulteney-street, took the direction of extraordinary hunger, and when that was appeased, changed into an earnest longing to be in bed; such was the extreme point of her distress; for when there she immediately fell into a sound sleep which lasted nine hours, and from which she awoke perfectly revived, in excellent spirits, with fresh hopes and fresh schemes. The first wish of her heart was to improve her acquaintance with Miss Tilney, and almost her first resolution, to seek her for that purpose, in the Pump-room at noon. In the Pump-room, one so newly arrived in Bath must be met with, and that building she had already found so favourable for the discovery of female excellence, and the completion of female intimacy, so admirably adapted for secret discourses and unlimited confidence, that she was most reasonably encouraged to expect another friend from within its walls. Her plan for the morning thus settled, she sat quietly down to her book after breakfast, resolving to remain in the same place and the same employment till the clock struck one; and from habitude very little incommoded by the remarks and ejaculations of Mrs. Allen, whose vacancy of mind and incapacity for thinking were such, that as she never talked a great deal, so she could never be entirely silent; and, therefore, while she sat at her work, if she lost her needle or broke her thread, if she heard a carriage in the street, or saw a speck upon her gown, she must observe it aloud, whether there were any one at leisure to answer her or not. At about half past twelve, a remarkably loud rap drew her in haste to the window, and scarcely had she time to inform Catherine of there being two open carriages at the door, in the first only a servant, her brother driving Miss Thorpe in the second, before John Thorpe came running up stairs, calling out, 'Well, Miss Morland, here I am. Have you been waiting long? We could not come before; the old devil of a coachmaker was such an eternity finding out a thing fit to be got into, and now it is ten thousand to one, but they break down before we are out of the street. How do you do, Mrs. Allen? a famous ball last night, was not it? Come, Miss Morland, be quick, for the others are in a confounded hurry to be off. They want to get their tumble over.'

'What do you mean?' said Catherine, 'where are you all going to?'

'Going to? why, you have not forgot our engagement! Did not we agree together to take a drive this morning? What a head you have! We are going up Claverton Down.'

'Something was said about it, I remember,' said Catherine, looking at Mrs. Allen for her opinion; 'but really I did not expect you.'

'Not expect me! that's a good one! And what a dust you would have made, if I had not come.'

Catherine's silent appeal to her friend, meanwhile, was entirely thrown away, for Mrs. Allen, not being at all in the habit of conveying any expression herself by a look, was not aware of its being ever intended by any body else; and Catherine, whose desire of seeing Miss Tilney again could at that moment bear a short delay in favour of a drive, and who thought there could be no impropriety in her going with Mr. Thorpe, as Isabella was going at the same time with James, was therefore obliged to speak plainer. 'Well, ma'am, what do you say to it? Can you spare me for an hour or two? shall I go?'

'Do just as you please, my dear,' replied Mrs. Allen, with the most placid indifference. Catherine took the advice, and ran off to get ready. In a very few minutes she re-appeared, having scarcely allowed the two others time enough to get through a few short sentences in her praise, after Thorpe had procured Mrs. Allen's admiration of his gig; and then receiving her friend's parting good wishes, they both hurried down stairs. 'My dearest creature,' cried Isabella, to whom the duty of friendship immediately called her before she could get into the carriage, 'you have been at least three hours getting ready. I was afraid you were ill. What a delightful ball we had last night. I have a thousand things to say to you; but make haste and get in, for I long to be off.'

Catherine followed her orders and turned away, but not too soon to hear her friend exclaim aloud to James, 'What a sweet girl she is! I quite doat on her.'

'You will not be frightened, Miss Morland,' said Thorpe, as he handed her in, 'if my horse should dance about a little at first setting off. He will, most likely, give a plunge or two, and perhaps take the rest for a minute; but he will soon know his master. He is full of spirits, playful as can be, but there is no vice in him.'

Catherine did not think the portrait a very inviting one, but it was too late to retreat, and she was too young to own herself frightened; so, resigning herself to her fate, and trusting to the animal's boasted knowledge of its owner, she sat peaceably down, and saw Thorpe sit down by her. Every thing being then arranged, the servant who stood at the horse's head was bid in an important voice 'to let him go,' and off they went in the quietest manner imaginable, without a plunge or a caper, or any thing like one. Catherine, delighted at so happy an escape, spoke her pleasure aloud with grateful surprise; and her companion immediately made the matter perfectly simple by assuring her that it was entirely owing to the peculiarly judicious manner in which he had then held the reins, and the singular discernment and dexterity with which he had directed his whip. Catherine, though she could not help wondering that with such perfect command of his horse, he should think it necessary to alarm her with a relation of its tricks, congratulated herself sincerely on being under the care of so excellent a coachman; and perceiving that the animal continued to go on in the same quiet manner, without shewing the smallest propensity towards any unpleasant vivacity, and (considering its inevitable pace was ten miles an hour) by no means alarmingly fast, gave herself up to all the enjoyment of air and exercise of the most invigorating kind, in a fine mild day of February, with the consciousness of safety. A silence of several minutes succeeded their first short dialogue; – it was broken by Thorpe's saying very abruptly, 'Old Allen is as rich as a Jew – is not he?' Catherine did not understand him – and he repeated his question, adding in explanation, 'Old Allen, the man you are with.'

'Oh! Mr. Allen, you mean. Yes, I believe, he is very rich.'

'And no children at all?'

'No – not any.'

'A famous thing for his next heirs. He is *your* godfather, is not he?'

'My godfather! – no.'

'But you are always very much with them.'

'Yes, very much.'

'Aye, that is what I meant. He seems a good kind of old fellow enough, and has lived very well in his time, I dare say; he is not gouty for nothing. Does he drink his bottle a-day now?'

'His bottle a-day! – no. Why should you think of such a thing? He is a very temperate man, and you could not fancy him in liquor last night?'

'Lord help you! – You women are always thinking of men's being in liquor. Why you do not suppose a man is overset by a bottle? I am sure of *this* – that if every body was to drink their bottle a-day, there would not be half the disorders in the world there are now. It would be a famous good thing for us all.'

'I cannot believe it.'

'Oh! lord, it would be the saving of thousands. There is not the hundredth part of the wine consumed in this kingdom, that there ought to be. Our foggy climate wants help.'

'And yet I have heard that there is a great deal of wine drank in Oxford.'

'Oxford! There is no drinking at Oxford now, I assure you. Nobody drinks there. You would hardly meet with a man who goes beyond his four pints at the utmost. Now, for instance, it was reckoned a remarkable thing at the last party in my rooms, that upon an average we cleared about five pints a head. It was looked upon as something out of the common way. *Mine* is famous good stuff to be sure. You would not often meet with any thing like it in Oxford – and that may account for it. But this will just give you a notion of the general rate of drinking there.'

'Yes, it does give a notion,' said Catherine, warmly, 'and that is, that you all drink a great deal more wine than I thought you did. However, I am sure James does not drink so much.'

This declaration brought on a loud and overpowering reply, of which no part was very distinct, except the frequent exclamations, amounting almost to oaths, which adorned it, and Catherine was left, when it ended, with rather a strengthened belief of there being a great deal of wine drank in Oxford, and the same happy conviction of her brother's comparative sobriety.

Thorpe's ideas then all reverted to the merits of his own equipage, and she was called on to admire the spirit and freedom with which his horse moved along, and the ease which his paces, as well as the excellence of the springs, gave the motion of the carriage. She followed him in all his admiration as well as she could. To go before, or beyond him was impossible. His knowledge and her ignorance of the subject, his rapidity of expression, and her diffidence of herself put that out of her power; she could strike out nothing new in commendation, but she readily echoed whatever he chose to assert, and it was finally settled between them without any difficulty, that his equipage was altogether the most complete of its kind in England, his carriage the neatest, his horse the best goer, and himself the best coachman. – 'You do not really think, Mr. Thorpe,' said Catherine, venturing after some time to consider the matter as entirely decided, and to offer some little variation on the subject, 'that James's gig will break down?'

'Break down! Oh! lord! Did you ever see such a little tittuppy thing in your life? There is not a sound piece of iron about it. The wheels have been fairly worn out these ten years at least – and as for the body! Upon my soul, you might shake it to pieces yourself with a touch. It is the most devilish little ricketty business I ever beheld! – Thank God! we have got a better. I would not be bound to go two miles in it for fifty thousand pounds.'

'Good heavens!' cried Catherine, quite frightened, 'then pray let us turn back; they will certainly meet with an accident if we go on. Do let us turn back, Mr. Thorpe; stop and speak to my brother, and tell him how very unsafe it is.'

'Unsafe! Oh, lord! what is there in that? they will only get a roll if it does break down; and there is plenty of dirt, it will be excellent falling. Oh, curse it! the carriage is safe enough, if a man knows how to drive it; a thing of that sort in good hands will last above twenty years after it is fairly worn out. Lord bless you! I would undertake for five pounds to drive it to York and back again, without losing a nail.'

Catherine listened with astonishment; she knew not how to reconcile two such very different accounts of the same thing; for she had not been brought up to understand the propensities of a rattle, nor to know to how many idle assertions and impudent falsehoods the excess of vanity will lead. Her own family were plain matter-of-fact people, who seldom aimed at wit of any kind; her father, at the utmost, being contented with a pun, and her mother with a proverb; they were not in the habit therefore of telling lies to increase their importance, or of asserting at one moment what they would contradict the next. She reflected on the affair for some time in much perplexity, and was more than once on the point of requesting from Mr. Thorpe a clearer insight into his real opinion on the subject; but she checked herself, because it appeared to her that he did not excel in giving those clearer insights, in making those things plain which he had before made ambiguous; and, joining to this, the consideration, that he would not really suffer his sister and his friend to be exposed to a danger from which he might easily preserve them, she concluded at last, that he must know the carriage to be in fact perfectly safe, and therefore would alarm herself no longer. By him the whole matter seemed entirely forgotten; and all the rest of his conversation, or rather talk, began and ended with himself and his own concerns. He told her of horses which he had bought for a trifle and sold for incredible sums; of racing matches, in which his judgment had infallibly foretold the winner; of shooting parties, in which he had killed more birds (though without having one good shot) than all his companions together; and described to her some famous day's sport, with the fox-hounds, in which his foresight and skill in directing the dogs had repaired the mistakes of the most experienced huntsman, and in which the boldness of his riding, though it had never endangered his own life for a moment, had been constantly leading others into difficulties, which he calmly concluded had broken the necks of many.

Little as Catherine was in the habit of judging for her self, and unfixed as were her general notions of what men ought to be, she could not entirely repress a doubt, while she bore with the effusions of his endless conceit, of his being altogether completely agreeable. It was a bold surmise, for he was Isabella's brother; and she had been assured by James, that his manners would recommend him to all her sex; but in spite of this, the extreme weariness of his company, which crept over her before they had been out an hour, and which continued unceasingly to increase till they stopped in Pulteney-street again, induced her, in some small degree, to resist such high authority, and to distrust his powers of giving universal pleasure.

When they arrived at Mrs. Allen's door, the astonishment of Isabella was hardly to be expressed, on finding that it was too late in the day for them to attend her friend into the house: — 'Past three o'clock!' it was inconceivable, incredible, impossible! and she would neither believe her own watch, nor her brother's, nor the servant's; she would believe no assurance of it founded on reason or reality, till Morland produced his watch, and ascertained the fact; to have doubted a moment longer *then*, would have been equally inconceivable, incredible, and impossible; and she could only protest, over and over again, that no two hours and a half had ever gone off so swiftly before, as Catherine was called on to confirm; Catherine could not tell a falsehood even to please Isabella; but the latter was spared the misery of her friend's dissenting voice, by not waiting for her answer. Her own feelings entirely engrossed her; her wretchedness was most acute on finding herself obliged to go directly home. – It was ages since she had had a moment's conversation with her dearest Catherine; and, though she had such thousands of things to say to her, it appeared as if they were never to be together again; so, with smiles of most exquisite misery, and the laughing eye of utter despondency, she bade her friend adieu and went on.

Catherine found Mrs. Allen just returned from all the busy idleness of the morning, and was immediately greeted with, 'Well, my dear, here you are;' a truth which she had no greater inclination than power to dispute; 'and I hope you have had a pleasant airing?'

'Yes, ma'am, I thank you; we could not have had a nicer day.'

'So Mrs. Thorpe said; she was vastly pleased at your all going.'

'You have seen Mrs. Thorpe then?'

'Yes, I went to the Pump-room as soon as you were gone, and there I met her, and we had a great deal of talk together. She says there was hardly any veal to be got at market this morning, it is so uncommonly scarce.'

'Did you see any body else of our acquaintance?'

'Yes; we agreed to take a turn in the Crescent, and there we met Mrs. Hughes, and Mr. and Miss Tilney walking with her.'

'Did you indeed? and did they speak to you?'

'Yes, we walked along the Crescent together for half

an hour. They seem very agreeable people. Miss Tilney was in a very pretty spotted muslin, and I fancy, by what I can learn, that she always dresses very handsomely. Mrs. Hughes talked to me a great deal about the family.'

'And what did she tell you of them?'

'Oh! a vast deal indeed; she hardly talked of any thing else.'

'Did she tell you what part of Gloucestershire they come from?'

'Yes, she did; but I cannot recollect now. But they are very good kind of people, and very rich. Mrs. Tilney was a Miss Drummond, and she and Mrs. Hughes were school-fellows; and Miss Drummond had a very large fortune; and, when she married, her father gave her twenty thousand pounds, and five hundred to buy wedding-clothes. Mrs. Hughes saw all the clothes after they came from the warehouse.'

'And are Mr. and Mrs. Tilney in Bath?'

'Yes, I fancy they are, but I am not quite certain. Upon recollection, however, I have a notion they are both dead; at least the mother is; yes, I am sure Mrs. Tilney is dead, because Mrs. Hughes told me there was a very beautiful set of pearls that Mr. Drummond gave his daughter on her wedding-day and that Miss Tilney has got now, for they were put by for her when her mother died.'

'And is Mr. Tilney, my partner, the only son?'

'I cannot be quite positive about that, my dear; I have some idea he is; but, however, he is a very fine young man Mrs. Hughes says, and likely to do very well.'

Catherine inquired no further; she had heard enough to feel that Mrs. Allen had no real intelligence to give, and that she was most particularly unfortunate herself in having missed such a meeting with both brother and sister. Could she have foreseen such a circumstance, nothing should have persuaded her to go out with the others; and, as it was, she could only lament her ill-luck, and think over what she had lost, till it was clear to her, that the drive had by no means been very pleasant and that John Thorpe himself was quite disagreeable.

CHAPTER X

THE ALLENS, Thorpes, and Morlands, all met in the evening at the theatre; and, as Catherine and Isabella sat together, there was then an opportunity for the latter to utter some few of the many thousand things which had been collecting within her for communication, in the immeasurable length of time which had divided them. – 'Oh, heavens! my beloved Catherine, have I got you at last?' was her address on Catherine's entering the box and sitting by her. 'Now, Mr. Morland,' for he was close to her on the other side, 'I shall not speak another word to you all the rest of the evening; so I charge you not to expect it. My sweetest Catherine, how have you been this long age? but I need not ask you, for you look delightfully. You really have done your hair in a more heavenly style than ever: you mischievous creature, do you want to attract every body? I assure you, my brother is quite in love with you already; and as for Mr. Tilney – but *that* is a settled thing – even *your* modesty cannot doubt his attachment now; his coming back to Bath makes it too plain. Oh! what would not I give to see him! I really am quite wild with impatience. My mother says he is the most delightful young man in the world; she saw him this morning you know: you must introduce him to me. Is he in the house now? – Look about for heaven's sake! I assure you, I can hardly exist till I see him.'

'No,' said Catherine, 'he is not here; I cannot see him any where.'

'Oh, horrid! am I never to be acquainted with him? How do you like my gown? I think it does not look amiss; the sleeves were entirely my own thought. Do you know I get so immoderately sick of Bath; your brother and I were agreeing this morning that, though it is vastly well to be here for a few weeks, we would not live here for millions. We soon found out that our tastes were exactly alike in preferring the country to every other place; really, our opinions were so exactly the same, it was quite ridiculous! There was not a single point in which we differed; I would not have had you by for the world; you are such a sly thing, I am sure you would have made some droll remark or other about it.'

'No, indeed I should not.'

'Oh, yes you would indeed; I know you better than you know yourself. You would have told us that we seemed born for each other, or some nonsense of that kind, which would have distressed me beyond conception; my cheeks would have been as red as your roses; I would not have had you by for the world.'

'Indeed you do me injustice; I would not have made so improper a remark upon any account; and besides, I am sure it would never have entered my head.'

Isabella smiled incredulously, and talked the rest of the evening to James.

Catherine's resolution of endeavouring to meet Miss Tilney again continued in full force the next morning; and till the usual moment of going to the Pump-room, she felt some alarm from the dread of a second prevention. But nothing of that kind occurred, no visitors appeared to delay them, and they all three set off in good time for the Pump-room, where the ordinary course of events and conversation took place; Mr. Allen, after drinking his glass of water, joined some

gentlemen to talk over the politics of the day and compare the accounts of their newspapers; and the ladies
walked about together, noticing every new face, and
almost every new bonnet in the room. The female part
of the Thorpe family, attended by James Morland, appeared among the crowd in less than a quarter of an
hour, and Catherine immediately took her usual place
by the side of her friend. James, who was now in constant attendance, maintained a similar position, and
separating themselves from the rest of their party, they
walked in that manner for some time, till Catherine
began to doubt the happiness of a situation which
confining her entirely to her friend and brother, gave
her very little share in the notice of either. They were
always engaged in some sentimental discussion or lively
dispute, but their sentiment was conveyed in such
whispering voices, and their vivacity attended with so
much laughter, that though Catherine's supporting opinion was not unfrequently called for by one or the
other, she was never able to give any, from not having
heard a word of the subject. At length however she was
empowered to disengage herself from her friend, by
the avowed necessity of speaking to Miss Tilney, whom
she most joyfully saw just entering the room with Mrs.
Hughes, and whom she instantly joined, with a firmer
determination to be acquainted, than she might have
had courage to command, had she not been urged by
the disappointment of the day before. Miss Tilney met
her with great civility, returned her advances with equal
good will, and they continued talking together as long
as both parties remained in the room; and though in all
probability not an observation was made, nor an expression used by either which had not been made and
used some thousands of times before, under that roof,
in every Bath season, yet the merit of their being
spoken with simplicity and truth, and without personal
conceit, might be something uncommon. –

'How well your brother dances!' was an artless exclamation of Catherine's towards the close of their conversation, which at once surprised and amused her companion.

'Henry!' she replied with a smile. 'Yes, he does dance very well.'

'He must have thought it very odd to hear me say I was engaged the other evening, when he saw me sitting down. But I really had been engaged the whole day to Mr. Thorpe.' Miss Tilney could only bow. 'You cannot think,' added Catherine after a moment's silence, 'how surprised I was to see him again. I felt so sure of his being quite gone away.'

'When Henry had the pleasure of seeing you before, he was in Bath but for a couple of days. He came only to engage lodgings for us.'

'*That* never occurred to me; and of course, not seeing him any where, I thought he must be gone. Was not the young lady he danced with on Monday a Miss Smith?'

'Yes, an acquaintance of Mrs. Hughes.'

'I dare say she was very glad to dance. Do you think her pretty?'

'Not very.'

'He never comes to the Pump-room, I suppose?'

'Yes, sometimes; but he has rid out this morning with my father.'

Mrs. Hughes now joined them, and asked Miss Tilney if she was ready to go. 'I hope I shall have the pleasure of seeing you again soon,' said Catherine. 'Shall you be at the cotillion ball to-morrow?'

'Perhaps we — yes, I think we certainly shall.'

'I am glad of it, for we shall all be there.' – This civility was duly returned; and they parted – on Miss Tilney's side with some knowledge of her new acquaintance's feelings, and on Catherine's, without the smallest consciousness of having explained them.

She went home very happy. The morning had answered all her hopes, and the evening of the following day was now the object of expectation, the future good. What gown and what head-dress she should wear on the occasion became her chief concern. She cannot be justified in it. Dress is at all times a frivolous distinction, and excessive solicitude about it often destroys its own aim. Catherine knew all this very well; her great aunt had read her a lecture on the subject only the Christmas before; and yet she lay awake ten minutes on Wednesday night debating between her spotted and her tamboured muslin, and nothing but the shortness of the time prevented her buying a new one for the evening. This would have been an error in judgment, great though not uncommon, from which one of the other sex rather than her own, a brother rather than a great aunt might have warned her, for man only can be aware of the insensibility of man towards a new gown. It would be mortifying to the feelings of many ladies, could they be made to understand how little the heart of man is affected by what is costly or new in their attire; how little it is biassed by the texture of their muslin, and how unsusceptible of peculiar tenderness towards the spotted, the sprigged, the mull or the jackonet. Woman is fine for her own satisfaction alone. No man will admire her the more, no woman will like her the better for it. Neatness and fashion are enough for the former, and a something of shabbiness or impropriety will be most endearing to the latter. – But not one of these grave reflections troubled the tranquillity of Catherine.

She entered the rooms on Thursday evening with feelings very different from what had attended her thither the Monday before. She had then been exulting in her engagement to Thorpe, and was now chiefly anxious to avoid his sight, lest he should engage her again; for though she could not, dared not expect that

Mr. Tilney should ask her a third time to dance, her wishes, hopes and plans all centered in nothing less. Every young lady may feel for my heroine in this critical moment, for every young lady has at some time or other known the same agitation. All have been, or at least all have believed themselves to be, in danger from the pursuit of some one whom they wished to avoid; and all have been anxious for the attentions of some one whom they wished to please. As soon as they were joined by the Thorpes, Catherine's agony began; she fidgetted about if John Thorpe came towards her, hid herself as much as possible from his view, and when he spoke to her pretended not to hear him. The cotillions were over, the country-dancing beginning, and she saw nothing of the Tilneys. 'Do not be frightened, my dear Catherine,' whispered Isabella, 'but I am really going to dance with your brother again. I declare positively it is quite shocking. I tell him he ought to be ashamed of himself, but you and John must keep us in countenance. Make haste, my dear creature, and come to us. John is just walked off, but he will be back in a moment.'

Catherine had neither time nor inclination to answer. The others walked away, John Thorpe was still in view, and she gave herself up for lost. That she might not appear, however, to observe or expect him, she kept her eyes intently fixed on her fan; and a self-condemnation for her folly, in supposing that among such a crowd they should even meet with the Tilneys in any reasonable time, had just passed through her mind, when she suddenly found herself addressed and again solicited to dance, by Mr. Tilney himself. With what sparkling eyes and ready motion she granted his request, and with how pleasing a flutter of heart she went with him to the set, may be easily imagined. To escape, and, as she believed, so narrowly escape John Thorpe, and to be asked, so immediately on his joining her, asked by Mr. Tilney, as if he had sought her on purpose! – it did not appear to her that life could supply any greater felicity.

Scarcely had they worked themselves into the quiet possession of a place, however, when her attention was claimed by John Thorpe, who stood behind her. 'Hey-day, Miss Morland!' said he, 'what is the meaning of this? – I thought you and I were to dance together.'

'I wonder you should think so, for you never asked me.' 'That is a good one, by Jove! – I asked you as soon as I came into the room, and I was just going to ask you again, but when I turned round, you were gone! – this is a cursed shabby trick! I only came for the sake of dancing with *you*, and I firmly believe you were engaged to me ever since Monday. Yes; I remember, I asked you while you were waiting in the lobby for your cloak. And here have I been telling all my acquaintance that I was going to dance with the prettiest girl in the room; and when they see you standing up with somebody else, they will quiz me famously.'

'Oh, no; they will never think of *me*, after such a description as that.'

'By heavens, if they do not, I will kick them out of the room for blockheads. What chap have you there?' Catherine satisfied his curiosity. 'Tilney,' he repeated, 'Hum – I do not know him. A good figure of a man; well put together. – Does he want a horse? – Here is a friend of mine, Sam Fletcher, has got one to sell that would suit any body. A famous clever animal for the road – only forty guineas. I had fifty minds to buy it myself, for it is one of my maxims always to buy a good horse when I meet with one; but it would not answer my purpose, it would not do for the field. I would give any money for a real good hunter. I have three now, the best that ever were back'd. I would not take eight hundred guineas for them. Fletcher and I mean to get a house in Leicestershire, against the next season. It is so d— uncomfortable, living at an inn.'

This was the last sentence by which he could weary Catherine's attention, for he was just then borne off by the resistless pressure of a long string of passing ladies. Her partner now drew near, and said, 'That gentleman would have put me out of patience, had he staid with you half a minute longer. He has no business to withdraw the attention of my partner from me. We have entered into a contract of mutual agreeableness for the space of an evening, and all our agreeableness belongs solely to each other for that time. Nobody can fasten themselves on the notice of one, without injuring the rights of the other. I consider a country-dance as an emblem of marriage. Fidelity and complaisance are the principal duties of both; and those men who do not chuse to dance or marry themselves, have no business with the partners or wives of their neighbours.'

'But they are such very different things! –'

' – That you think they cannot be compared together.'

'To be sure not. People that marry can never part, but must go and keep house together. People that dance, only stand opposite each other in a long room for half an hour.'

'And such is your definition of matrimony and dancing. Taken in that light certainly, their resemblance is not striking; but I think I could place them in such a view. – You will allow, that in both, man has the advantage of choice, woman only the power of refusal; that in both, it is an engagement between man and woman, formed for the advantage of each; and that when once entered into, they belong exclusively to each other till the moment of its dissolution; that it is their duty, each to endeavour to give the other no cause for wishing that he or she had bestowed themselves elsewhere, and their best interest to keep their

own imaginations from wandering towards the perfections of their neighbours, or fancying that they should
have been better off with any one else. You will allow
all this?'

'Yes, to be sure, as you state it, all this sounds very
well; but still they are so very different. – I cannot look
upon them at all in the same light, nor think the same
duties belong to them.'

'In one respect, there certainly is a difference. In
marriage, the man is supposed to provide for the support of the woman; the woman to make the home
agreeable to the man; he is to purvey, and she is to
smile. But in dancing, their duties are exactly changed;
the agreeableness, the compliance are expected from
him, while she furnishes the fan and the lavender
water. *That*, I suppose, was the difference of duties
which struck you, as rendering the conditions incapable
of comparison.'

'No, indeed, I never thought of that.'

'Then I am quite at a loss. One thing, however, I
must observe. This disposition on your side is rather
alarming. You totally disallow any similarity in the obli-
gations; and may I not thence infer, that your notions
of the duties of the dancing state are not so strict as
your partner might wish? Have I not reason to fear,
that if the gentleman who spoke to you just now were
to return, or if any other gentleman were to address
you, there would be nothing to restrain you from conversing with him as long as you chose?'

'Mr. Thorpe is such a very particular friend of my
brother's, that if he talks to me, I must talk to him
again; but there are hardly three young men in the
room besides him, that I have any acquaintance with.'

'And is that to be my only security? alas, alas!'

'Nay, I am sure you cannot have a better; for if I do
not know any body, it is impossible for me to talk to
them; and, besides, I do not *want* to talk to any body.'

'Now you have given me a security worth having; and I shall proceed with courage. Do you find Bath as agreeable as when I had the honour of making the inquiry before?'

'Yes, quite – more so, indeed.'

'More so! – Take care, or you will forget to be tired of it at the proper time. – You ought to be tired at the end of six weeks.'

'I do not think I should be tired, if I were to stay here six months.'

'Bath, compared with London, has little variety, and so every body finds out every year. "For six weeks, I allow Bath is pleasant enough; but beyond *that*, it is the most tiresome place in the world." You would be told so by people of all descriptions, who come regularly every winter, lengthen their six weeks into ten or twelve, and go away at last because they can afford to stay no longer.'

'Well, other people must judge for themselves, and those who go to London may think nothing of Bath. But I, who live in a small retired village in the country, can never find greater sameness in such a place as this, than in my own home; for here are a variety of amusements, a variety of things to be seen and done all day long, which I can know nothing of there.'

'You are not fond of the country.'

'Yes, I am. I have always lived there, and always been very happy. But certainly there is much more sameness in a country life than in a Bath life. One day in the country is exactly like another.'

'But then you spend your time so much more rationally in the country.'

'Do I?'

'Do you not?'

'I do not believe there is much difference.'

'Here you are in pursuit only of amusement all day long.'

'And so I am at home – only I do not find so much of it. I walk about here, and so I do there; – but here I see a variety of people in every street, and there I can only go and call on Mrs. Allen.'

Mr. Tilney was very much amused. 'Only go and call on Mrs. Allen!' he repeated. 'What a picture of intellectual poverty! However, when you sink into this abyss again, you will have more to say. You will be able to talk of Bath, and of all that you did here.'

'Oh! yes. I shall never be in want of something to talk of again to Mrs. Allen, or any body else. I really believe I shall always be talking of Bath, when I am at home again – I *do* like it so very much. If I could but have papa and mamma, and the rest of them here, I suppose I should be too happy! James's coming (my eldest brother) is quite delightful – and especially as it turns out, that the very family we are just got so intimate with, are his intimate friends already. Oh! who can ever be tired of Bath?'

'Not those who bring such fresh feelings of every sort to it, as you do. But papas and mammas, and brothers and intimate friends are a good deal gone by, to most of the frequenters of Bath – and the honest relish of balls and plays, and every-day sights, is past with them.'

Here their conversation closed; the demands of the dance becoming now too importunate for a divided attention.

Soon after their reaching the bottom of the set, Catherine perceived herself to be earnestly regarded by a gentleman who stood among the lookers-on, immediately behind her partner. He was a very handsome man, of a commanding aspect, past the bloom, but not past the vigour of life; and with his eye still directed towards her, she saw him presently address Mr. Tilney in a familiar whisper. Confused by his notice, and blushing from the fear of its being excited by something wrong in her appearance, she turned away her head. But while she did so, the gentleman retreated, and her partner coming nearer, said, 'I see that you guess what I have just been asked. That gentleman knows your name, and you have a right to know his. It is General Tilney, my father.'

Catherine's answer was only 'Oh!' – but it was an 'Oh!' expressing every thing needful; attention to his words, and perfect reliance on their truth. With real interest and strong admiration did her eye now follow the General, as he moved through the crowd, and 'How handsome a family they are!' was her secret remark.

In chatting with Miss Tilney before the evening concluded, a new source of felicity arose to her. She had never taken a country walk since her arrival in Bath. Miss Tilney, to whom all the commonly-frequented environs were familiar, spoke of them in terms which made her all eagerness to know them too; and on her openly fearing that she might find nobody to go with her, it was proposed by the brother and sister that they should join in a walk, some morning or other. 'I shall like it,' she cried, 'beyond any thing in the world; and do not let us put it off – let us go to-morrow.' This was readily agreed to, with only a proviso of Miss Tilney's, that it did not rain, which Catherine was sure it would not. At twelve o'clock, they were to call for her in Pulteney-street – and 'remember – twelve o'clock,' was her parting speech to her new friend. Of her other, her older, her more established friend, Isabella, of whose fidelity and worth she had enjoyed a fortnight's experience, she scarcely saw any thing during the evening. Yet, though longing to make her acquainted with her happiness, she cheerfully submitted to the wish of Mr. Allen, which took them rather early away, and her spirits danced within her, as she danced in her chair all the way home.

CHAPTER XI

THE MORROW brought a very sober looking morning; the sun making only a few efforts to appear; and Catherine augured from it, every thing most favourable to her wishes. A bright morning so early in the year, she allowed would generally turn to rain, but a cloudy one foretold improvement as the day advanced. She applied to Mr. Allen for confirmation of her hopes, but Mr. Allen not having his own skies and barometer about him, declined giving any absolute promise of sunshine. She applied to Mrs. Allen, and Mrs. Allen's opinion was more positive. 'She had no doubt in the world of its being a very fine day, if the clouds would only go off, and the sun keep out.'

At about eleven o'clock however, a few specks of small rain upon the windows caught Catherine's watchful eye, and 'Oh! dear, I do believe it will be wet,' broke from her in a most desponding tone.

'I thought how it would be,' said Mrs. Allen.

'No walk for me to-day,' sighed Catherine; — 'but perhaps it may come to nothing, or it may hold up before twelve.'

'Perhaps it may, but then, my dear, it will be so dirty.'

'Oh! that will not signify; I never mind dirt.'

'No,' replied her friend very placidly, 'I know you never mind dirt.'

After a short pause, 'It comes on faster and faster!' said Catherine, as she stood watching at a window.

'So it does indeed. If it keeps raining, the streets will be very wet.'

'There are four umbrellas up already. How I hate the sight of an umbrella!'

'They are disagreeable things to carry. I would much rather take a chair at any time.'

'It was such a nice looking morning! I felt so convinced it would be dry!'

'Any body would have thought so indeed. There will be very few people in the Pump-room, if it rains all the morning. I hope Mr. Allen will put on his great coat when he goes, but I dare say he will not, for he had rather do any thing in the world than walk out in a great coat; I wonder he should dislike it, it must be so comfortable.'

The rain continued – fast, though not heavy. Catherine went every five minutes to the clock, threatening on each return that, if it still kept on raining another five minutes, she would give up the matter as hopeless. The clock struck twelve, and it still rained. – 'You will not be able to go, my dear.'

'I do not quite despair yet. I shall not give it up till a quarter after twelve. This is just the time of day for it to clear up, and I do think it looks a little lighter. There, it is twenty minutes after twelve, and now I *shall* give it up entirely. Oh! that we had such weather here as they had at Udolpho, or at least in Tuscany and the South of France! – the night that poor St. Aubin died! – such beautiful weather!'

At half past twelve, when Catherine's anxious attention to the weather was over, and she could no longer claim any merit from its amendment, the sky began voluntarily to clear. A gleam of sunshine took her quite by surprise; she looked round; the clouds were parting, and she instantly returned to the window to watch over and encourage the happy appearance. Ten minutes more made it certain that a bright afternoon would succeed, and justified the opinion of Mrs. Allen, who had 'always thought it would clear up.' But whether Catherine might still expect her friends, whether there had not been too much rain for Miss Tilney to venture, must yet be a question.

It was too dirty for Mrs. Allen to accompany her

husband to the Pump-room; he accordingly set off by himself, and Catherine had barely watched him down the street, when her notice was claimed by the approach of the same two open carriages, containing the same three people that had surprised her so much a few mornings back.

'Isabella, my brother, and Mr. Thorpe, I declare! They are coming for me perhaps – but I shall not go – I cannot go indeed, for you know Miss Tilney may still call.' Mrs. Allen agreed to it. John Thorpe was soon with them, and his voice was with them yet sooner, for on the stairs he was calling out to Miss Morland to be quick. 'Make haste! make haste!' as he threw open the door – 'put on your hat this moment – there is no time to be lost – we are going to Bristol. – How d'ye do, Mrs. Allen?'

'To Bristol! Is not that a great way off? – But, however, I cannot go with you to-day, because I am engaged; I expect some friends every moment.' This was of course vehemently talked down as no reason at all; Mrs. Allen was called on to second him, and the two others walked in, to give their assistance. 'My sweetest Catherine, is not this delightful? We shall have a most heavenly drive. You are to thank your brother and me for the scheme; it darted into our heads at breakfast-time, I verily believe at the same instant; and we should have been off two hours ago if it had not been for this detestable rain. But it does not signify, the nights are moonlight, and we shall do delightfully. Oh! I am in such extasies at the thoughts of a little country air and quiet! – so much better than going to the Lower Rooms. We shall drive directly to Clifton and dine there; and, as soon as dinner is over, if there is time for it, go on to Kingsweston.'

'I doubt our being able to do so much,' said Morland.

'You croaking fellow!' cried Thorpe, 'we shall be

able to do ten times more. Kingsweston! aye, and
Blaize Castle too, and any thing else we can hear of;
but here is your sister says she will not go.'

'Blaize Castle!' cried Catherine; 'what is that?'

'The finest place in England – worth going fifty
miles at any time to see.'

'What, is it really a castle, an old castle?'

'The oldest in the kingdom.'

'But is it like what one reads of?'

'Exactly – the very same.'

'But now really – are there towers and long gal-
leries?'

'By dozens.'

'Then I should like to see it; but I cannot – I cannot
go.'

'Not go! – my beloved creature, what do you mean?'

'I cannot go, because' – (looking down as she spoke,
fearful of Isabella's smile) 'I expect Miss Tilney and her
brother to call on me to take a country walk. They
promised to come at twelve, only it rained; but now, as
it is so fine, I dare say they will be here soon.'

'Not they indeed,' cried Thorpe; 'for, as we turned
into Broad-street, I saw them – does he not drive a
phaeton with bright chesnuts?'

'I do not know indeed.'

'Yes, I know he does; I saw him. You are talking of
the man you danced with last night, are not you?'

'Yes.'

'Well, I saw him at that moment turn up the Lansdown Road, – driving a smart-looking girl.'

'Did you indeed?'

'Did upon my soul; knew him again directly, and he
seemed to have got some very pretty cattle too.'

'It is very odd! but I suppose they thought it would
be too dirty for a walk.'

'And well they might, for I never saw so much dirt
in my life. Walk! you could no more walk than you

could fly! it has not been so dirty the whole winter; it is ancle-deep every where.'

Isabella corroborated it: – 'My dearest Catherine, you cannot form an idea of the dirt; come, you must go; you cannot refuse going now.'

'I should like to see the castle; but may we go all over it? may we go up every staircase, and into every suite of rooms?'

'Yes, yes, every hole and corner.'

'But then, – if they should only be gone out for an hour till it is drier, and call by and bye?'

'Make yourself easy, there is no danger of that, for I heard Tilney hallooing to a man who was just passing by on horseback, that they were going as far as Wick Rocks.'

'Then I will. Shall I go, Mrs. Allen?'

'Just as you please, my dear.'

'Mrs. Allen, you must persuade her to go,' was the general cry. Mrs. Allen was not inattentive to it: – 'Well, my dear,' said she, 'suppose you go.' – And in two minutes they were off.

Catherine's feelings, as she got into the carriage, were in a very unsettled state; divided between regret for the loss of one great pleasure, and the hope of soon enjoying another, almost its equal in degree, however unlike in kind. She could not think the Tilneys had acted quite well by her, in so readily giving up their engagement, without sending her any message of excuse. It was now but an hour later than the time fixed on for the beginning of their walk; and, in spite of what she had heard of the prodigious accumulation of dirt in the course of that hour, she could not from her own observation help thinking, that they might have gone with very little inconvenience. To feel herself slighted by them was very painful. On the other hand, the delight of exploring an edifice like Udolpho, as her fancy represented Blaize Castle to be, was such a

counterpoise of good, as might console her for almost
any thing.

They passed briskly down Pulteney-street, and
through Laura-place, without the exchange of many
words. Thorpe talked to his horse, and she meditated,
by turns, on broken promises and broken arches,
phaetons and false hangings, Tilneys and trap-doors.
As they entered Argyle-buildings, however, she was
roused by this address from her companion, 'Who is
that girl who looked at you so hard as she went by?'

'Who? – where?'

'On the right-hand pavement – she must be almost
out of sight now.' Catherine looked round and saw
Miss Tilney leaning on her brother's arm, walking slowly down the street. She saw them both looking back at
her. 'Stop, stop, Mr. Thorpe,' she impatiently cried, 'it is
Miss Tilney; it is indeed. – How could you tell me they
were gone? – Stop, stop, I will get out this moment and
go to them.' But to what purpose did she speak? –
Thorpe only lashed his horse into a brisker trot; the
Tilneys, who had soon ceased to look after her, were
in a moment out of sight round the corner of Laura-
place, and in another moment she was herself whisked
into the Market-place. Still, however, and during the
length of another street, she intreated him to stop.
'Pray, pray stop, Mr. Thorpe. – I cannot go on. – I will
not go on. – I must go back to Miss Tilney.' But Mr.
Thorpe only laughed, smacked his whip, encouraged
his horse, made odd noises, and drove on; and Catherine, angry and vexed as she was, having no power of
getting away, was obliged to give up the point and
submit. Her reproaches, however, were not spared.
'How could you deceive me so, Mr. Thorpe? – How
could you say, that you saw them driving up the Lans-
down-road? – I would not have had it happen so for
the world. – They must think it so strange; so rude of
me! to go by them, too, without saying a word! You do

not know how vexed I am. – I shall have no pleasure at Clifton, nor in any thing else. I had rather, ten thousand times rather get out now, and walk back to them. How could you say, you saw them driving out in a phaeton?' Thorpe defended himself very stoutly, declared he had never seen two men so much alike in his life, and would hardly give up the point of its having been Tilney himself.

Their drive, even when this subject was over, was not likely to be very agreeable. Catherine's complaisance was no longer what it had been in their former airing. She listened reluctantly, and her replies were short. Blaize Castle remained her only comfort; towards *that*, she still looked at intervals with pleasure; though rather than be disappointed of the promised walk, and especially rather than be thought ill of by the Tilneys, she would willingly have given up all the happiness which its walls could supply – the happiness of a progress through a long suite of lofty rooms, exhibiting the remains of magnificent furniture, though now for many years deserted – the happiness of being stopped in their way along narrow, winding vaults, by a low, grated door; or even of having their lamp, their only lamp, extinguished by a sudden gust of wind, and of being left in total darkness. In the meanwhile, they proceeded on their journey without any mischance; and were within view of the town of Keynsham, when a halloo from Morland, who was behind them, made his friend pull up, to know what was the matter. The others then came close enough for conversation, and Morland said, 'We had better go back, Thorpe; it is too late to go on to-day; your sister thinks so as well as I. We have been exactly an hour coming from Pulteney-street, very little more than seven miles; and, I suppose, we have at least eight more to go. It will never do. We set out a great deal too late. We had much better put it off till another day, and turn round.'

'It is all one to me,' replied Thorpe rather angrily; and instantly turning his horse, they were on their way back to Bath.

'If your brother had not got such a d— beast to drive,' said he soon afterwards, 'we might have done it very well. My horse would have trotted to Clifton within the hour, if left to himself, and I have almost broke my arm with pulling him in to that cursed broken-winded jade's pace. Morland is a fool for not keeping a horse and gig of his own.'

'No, he is not,' said Catherine warmly, 'for I am sure he could not afford it.'

'And why cannot he afford it?'

'Because he has not money enough.'

'And whose fault is that?'

'Nobody's, that I know of.' Thorpe then said something in the loud, incoherent way to which he had often recourse, about its being a d— thing to be miserly; and that if people who rolled in money could not afford things, he did not know who could; which Catherine did not even endeavour to understand. Disappointed of what was to have been the consolation for her first disappointment, she was less and less disposed either to be agreeable herself, or to find her companion so; and they returned to Pulteney-street without her speaking twenty words.

As she entered the house, the footman told her, that a gentleman and lady had called and inquired for her a few minutes after her setting off; that, when he told them she was gone out with Mr. Thorpe, the lady had asked whether any message had been left for her; and on his saying no, had felt for a card, but said she had none about her, and went away. Pondering over these heart-rending tidings, Catherine walked slowly up stairs. At the head of them she was met by Mr. Allen, who, on hearing the reason of their speedy return, said, 'I am glad your brother had so much sense; I am glad you are come back. It was a strange, wild scheme.'

They all spent the evening together at Thorpe's. Catherine was disturbed and out of spirits; but Isabella seemed to find a pool of commerce, in the fate of which she shared, by private partnership with Morland, a very good equivalent for the quiet and country air of an inn at Clifton. Her satisfaction, too, in not being at the Lower Rooms, was spoken more than once. 'How I pity the poor creatures that are going there! How glad I am that I am not amongst them! I wonder whether it will be a full ball or not! They have not begun dancing yet. I would not be there for all the world. It is so delightful to have an evening now and then to oneself. I dare say it will not be a very good ball. I know the Mitchells will not be there. I am sure I pity every body that is. But I dare say, Mr. Morland, you long to be at it, do not you? I am sure you do. Well, pray do not let any body here be a restraint on you. I dare say we could do very well without you; but you men think yourselves of such consequence.'

Catherine could almost have accused Isabella of being wanting in tenderness towards herself and her sorrows; so very little did they appear to dwell on her mind, and so very inadequate was the comfort she offered. 'Do not be so dull, my dearest creature,' she whispered. 'You will quite break my heart. It was amazingly shocking to be sure; but the Tilneys were entirely to blame. Why were not they more punctual? It was dirty, indeed, but what did that signify? I am sure John and I should not have minded it. I never mind going through any thing, where a friend is concerned; that is my disposition, and John is just the same; he has amazing strong feelings. Good heavens! what a delightful hand you have got! Kings, I vow! I never was so happy in my life! I would fifty times rather you should have them than myself.'

And now I may dismiss my heroine to the sleepless couch, which is the true heroine's portion; to a pillow strewed with thorns and wet with tears. And lucky may she think herself, if she get another good night's rest in the course of the next three months.

CHAPTER XII

'MRS. ALLEN,' said Catherine the next morning, 'will there be any harm in my calling on Miss Tilney to-day? I shall not be easy till I have explained every thing.'

'Go by all means, my dear; only put on a white gown; Miss Tilney always wears white.'

Catherine cheerfully complied; and being properly equipped, was more impatient than ever to be at the Pump-room, that she might inform herself of General Tilney's lodgings, for though she believed they were in Milsom-street, she was not certain of the house, and Mrs. Allen's wavering convictions only made it more doubtful. To Milsom-street she was directed; and having made herself perfect in the number, hastened away with eager steps and a beating heart to pay her visit, explain her conduct, and be forgiven; tripping lightly through the church-yard, and resolutely turning away her eyes, that she might not be obliged to see her beloved Isabella and her dear family, who, she had reason to believe, were in a shop hard by. She reached the house without any impediment, looked at the number, knocked at the door, and inquired for Miss Tilney. The man believed Miss Tilney to be at home, but was not quite certain. Would she be pleased to send up her name? She gave her card. In a few minutes the servant returned, and with a look which did not quite confirm his words, said he had been mistaken, for that Miss Tilney was walked out. Catherine, with a blush of mortification, left the house. She felt almost persuaded that Miss Tilney *was* at home, and too much offended to admit her; and as she retired down the street, could not withhold one glance at the drawing-room windows, in expectation of seeing her there, but no one appeared at them. At the bottom of the street, however, she looked back again, and then, not at a window, but issuing from the door, she saw Miss Tilney herself. She was followed by a gentleman, whom Catherine believed to be her father, and they turned up towards Edgar's-buildings. Catherine, in deep mortification, proceeded on her way. She could almost be angry herself at such angry incivility; but she checked the resentful sensation; she remembered her own ignorance. She knew not how such an offence as her's might be classed by the laws of worldly politeness, to what a degree of unforgivingness it might with propriety lead, nor to what rigours of rudeness in return it might justly make her amenable.

Dejected and humbled, she had even some thoughts of not going with the others to the theatre that night; but it must be confessed that they were not of long continuance: for she soon recollected, in the first place, that she was without any excuse for staying at home; and, in the second, that it was a play she wanted very much to see. To the theatre accordingly they all went; no Tilneys appeared to plague or please her; she feared that, amongst the many perfections of the family, a fondness for plays was not to be ranked; but perhaps it was because they were habituated to the finer performances of the London stage, which she knew, on Isabella's authority, rendered every thing else of the kind 'quite horrid.' She was not deceived in her own expectation of pleasure; the comedy so well suspended her care, that no one, observing her during the first four acts, would have supposed she had any wretchedness about her. On the beginning of the fifth, however, the

sudden view of Mr. Henry Tilney and his father, joining a party in the opposite box, recalled her to anxiety
and distress. The stage could no longer excite genuine
merriment – no longer keep her whole attention. Every
other look upon an average was directed towards the
opposite box; and, for the space of two entire scenes,
did she thus watch Henry Tilney, without being once
able to catch his eye. No longer could he be suspected
of indifference for a play; his notice was never withdrawn from the stage during two whole scenes. At
length, however, he did look towards her, and he
bowed – but such a bow! no smile, no continued observ-
ance attended it; his eyes were immediately returned
to their former direction. Catherine was restlessly
miserable; she could almost have run round to the box
in which he sat, and forced him to hear her explanation. Feelings rather natural than heroic possessed her;
instead of considering her own dignity injured by this
ready condemnation – instead of proudly resolving, in
conscious innocence, to shew her resentment towards
him who could harbour a doubt of it, to leave to him
all the trouble of seeking an explanation, and to en-
lighten him on the past only by avoiding his sight, or
flirting with somebody else, she took to herself all the
shame of misconduct, or at least of its appearance, and
was only eager for an opportunity of explaining its
cause.

The play concluded – the curtain fell – Henry Tilney
was no longer to be seen where he had hitherto sat,
but his father remained, and perhaps he might be now
coming round to their box. She was right; in a few
minutes he appeared, and, making his way through the
then thinning rows, spoke with like calm politeness to
Mrs. Allen and her friend. – Not with such calmness
was he answered by the latter: 'Oh! Mr. Tilney, I have
been quite wild to speak to you, and make my apologies. You must have thought me so rude; but indeed

it was not my own fault, – was it, Mrs. Allen? Did not they tell me that Mr. Tilney and his sister were gone out in a phaeton together? and then what could I do? But I had ten thousand times rather have been with you; now had not I, Mrs. Allen?'

'My dear, you tumble my gown,' was Mrs. Allen's reply.

Her assurance, however, standing sole as it did, was not thrown away; it brought a more cordial, more natural smile into his countenance, and he replied in a tone which retained only a little affected reserve: – 'We were much obliged to you at any rate for wishing us a pleasant walk after our passing you in Argyle-street: you were so kind as to look back on purpose.'

'But indeed I did not wish you a pleasant walk; I never thought of such a thing; but I begged Mr. Thorpe so earnestly to stop; I called out to him as soon as ever I saw you; now, Mrs. Allen, did not — Oh! you were not there; but indeed I did; and, if Mr. Thorpe would only have stopped, I would have jumped out and run after you.'

Is there a Henry in the world who could be insensible to such a declaration? Henry Tilney at least was not. With a yet sweeter smile, he said every thing that need be said of his sister's concern, regret, and dependence on Catherine's honour. – 'Oh! do not say Miss Tilney was not angry,' cried Catherine, 'because I know she was; for she would not see me this morning when I called; I saw her walk out of the house the next minute after my leaving it; I was hurt, but I was not affronted. Perhaps you did not know I had been there.'

'I was not within at the time; but I heard of it from Eleanor, and she has been wishing ever since to see you, to explain the reason of such incivility; but perhaps I can do it as well. It was nothing more than that my father – they were just preparing to walk out, and he being hurried for time, and not caring to have it put off, made a point of her being denied. That was all, I do assure you. She was very much vexed, and meant to make her apology as soon as possible.'

Catherine's mind was greatly eased by this information, yet a something of solicitude remained, from which sprang the following question, thoroughly artless in itself, though rather distressing to the gentleman: — 'But, Mr. Tilney, why were *you* less generous than your sister? If she felt such confidence in my good intentions, and could suppose it to be only a mistake, why should *you* be so ready to take offence?'

'Me! — I take offence!'

'Nay, I am sure by your look, when you came into the box, you were angry.'

'I angry! I could have no right.'

'Well, nobody would have thought you had no right who saw your face.' He replied by asking her to make room for him, and talking of the play.

He remained with them some time, and was only too agreeable for Catherine to be contented when he went away. Before they parted, however, it was agreed that the projected walk should be taken as soon as possible; and, setting aside the misery of his quitting their box, she was, upon the whole, left one of the happiest creatures in the world.

While talking to each other, she had observed with some surprise, that John Thorpe, who was never in the same part of the house for ten minutes together, was engaged in conversation with General Tilney; and she felt something more than surprise, when she thought she could perceive herself the object of their attention and discourse. What could they have to say of her? She feared General Tilney did not like her appearance: she found it was implied in his preventing her admittance to his daughter, rather than postpone his own walk a few minutes. 'How came Mr. Thorpe to know your father?' was her anxious inquiry, as she pointed them out to her companion. He knew nothing about it; but his father, like every military man, had a very large acquaintance.

When the entertainment was over, Thorpe came to assist them in getting out. Catherine was the immediate object of his gallantry; and, while they waited in the lobby for a chair, he prevented the inquiry which had travelled from her heart almost to the tip of her tongue, by asking, in a consequential manner, whether she had seen him talking with General Tilney: – 'He is a fine old fellow, upon my soul! – stout, active, – looks as young as his son. I have a great regard for him, I assure you: a gentleman-like, good sort of fellow as ever lived.'

'But how came you to know him?'

'Know him! – There are few people much about town that I do not know. I have met him for ever at the Bedford; and I knew his face again to-day the moment he came into the billiard-room. One of the best players we have, by the bye; and we had a little touch together, though I was almost afraid of him at first: the odds were five to four against me; and, if I had not made one of the cleanest strokes that perhaps ever was made in this world – I took his ball exactly – but I could not make you understand it without a table; – however I *did* beat him. A very fine fellow; as rich as a Jew. I should like to dine with him; I dare say he gives famous dinners. But what do you think we have been talking of? – You. Yes, by heavens! – and the General thinks you the finest girl in Bath.'

'Oh! nonsense! how can you say so?'

'And what do you think I said?' (lowering his voice) 'Well done, General, said I, I am quite of your mind.'

Here, Catherine, who was much less gratified by his admiration than by General Tilney's, was not sorry to be called away by Mr. Allen. Thorpe, however, would see her to her chair, and, till she entered it, continued the same kind of delicate flattery, in spite of her entreating him to have done.

That General Tilney, instead of disliking, should admire her, was very delightful; and she joyfully thought, that there was not one of the family whom she need now fear to meet. – The evening had done more, much more, for her, than could have been expected.

CHAPTER XIII

Monday, Tuesday, Wednesday, Thursday, Friday and Saturday have now passed in review before the reader; the events of each day, its hopes and fears, mortifications and pleasures have been separately stated, and the pangs of Sunday only now remain to be described, and close the week. The Clifton scheme had been deferred, not relinquished, and on the afternoon's Crescent of this day, it was brought forward again. In a private consultation between Isabella and James, the former of whom had particularly set her heart upon going, and the latter no less anxiously placed his upon pleasing her, it was agreed that, provided the weather were fair, the party should take place on the following morning; and they were to set off very early, in order to be at home in good time. The affair thus determined, and Thorpe's approbation secured, Catherine only remained to be apprized of it. She had left them for a few minutes to speak to Miss Tilney. In that interval the plan was completed, and as soon as she came again, her agreement was demanded; but instead of the gay acquiescence expected by Isabella, Catherine looked grave, was very sorry, but could not go. The engagement which ought to have kept her from joining in the former attempt, would make it impossible for her to accompany them now. She had that moment

settled with Miss Tilney to take their promised walk
to-morrow; it was quite determined, and she would
not, upon any account, retract. But that she *must* and
should retract, was instantly the eager cry of both the
Thorpes; they must go to Clifton to-morrow, they
would not go without her, it would be nothing to put
off a mere walk for one day longer, and they would not
hear of a refusal. Catherine was distressed, but not
subdued. 'Do not urge me, Isabella. I am engaged to
Miss Tilney. I cannot go.' This availed nothing. The
same arguments assailed her again; she must go, she
should go, and they would not hear of a refusal. 'It
would be so easy to tell Miss Tilney that you had just
been reminded of a prior engagement, and must only
beg to put off the walk till Tuesday.'

'No, it would not be easy. I could not do it. There
has been no prior engagement.' But Isabella became
only more and more urgent; calling on her in the most
affectionate manner; addressing her by the most endearing names. She was sure her dearest, sweetest
Catherine would not seriously refuse such a trifling request to a friend who loved her so dearly. She knew
her beloved Catherine to have so feeling a heart, so
sweet a temper, to be so easily persuaded by those she
loved. But all in vain; Catherine felt herself to be in the
right, and though pained by such tender, such flattering
supplication, could not allow it to influence her. Isabella then tried another method. She reproached her
with having more affection for Miss Tilney, though she
had known her so little a while, than for her best and
oldest friends; with being grown cold and indifferent,
in short, towards herself. 'I cannot help being jealous,
Catherine, when I see myself slighted for strangers, I,
who love you so excessively! When once my affections
are placed, it is not in the power of any thing to change
them. But I believe my feelings are stronger than any
body's; I am sure they are too strong for my own

peace; and to see myself supplanted in your friendship by strangers, does cut me to the quick, I own. These Tilneys seem to swallow up every thing else.'

Catherine thought this reproach equally strange and unkind. Was it the part of a friend thus to expose her feelings to the notice of others? Isabella appeared to her ungenerous and selfish, regardless of every thing but her own gratification. These painful ideas crossed her mind, though she said nothing. Isabella, in the meanwhile, had applied her handkerchief to her eyes; and Morland, miserable at such a sight, could not help saying, 'Nay, Catherine. I think you cannot stand out any longer now. The sacrifice is not much; and to oblige such a friend – I shall think you quite unkind, if you still refuse.'

This was the first time of her brother's openly siding against her, and anxious to avoid his displeasure, she proposed a compromise. If they would only put off their scheme till Tuesday, which they might easily do, as it depended only on themselves, she could go with them, and every body might then be satisfied. But 'No, no, no!' was the immediate answer; 'that could not be, for Thorpe did not know that he might not go to town on Tuesday.' Catherine was sorry, but could do no more; and a short silence ensued, which was broken by Isabella; who in a voice of cold resentment said, 'Very well, then there is an end of the party. If Catherine does not go, I cannot. I cannot be the only woman. I would not, upon any account in the world, do so improper a thing.'

'Catherine, you must go,' said James.

'But why cannot Mr. Thorpe drive one of his other sisters? I dare say either of them would like to go.'

'Thank ye,' cried Thorpe, 'but I did not come to Bath to drive my sisters about, and look like a fool. No, if you do not go, d— me if I do. I only go for the sake of driving you.'

'That is a compliment which gives me no pleasure.' But her words were lost on Thorpe, who had turned abruptly away.

The three others still continued together, walking in a most uncomfortable manner to poor Catherine; some times not a word was said, sometimes she was again attacked with supplications or reproaches, and her arm was still linked within Isabella's, though their hearts were at war. At one moment she was softened, at an-other irritated; always distressed, but always steady.

'I did not think you had been so obstinate, Cath-erine,' said James; 'you were not used to be so hard to persuade; you once were the kindest, best-tempered of my sisters.'

'I hope I am not less so now,' she replied, very feelingly; 'but indeed I cannot go. If I am wrong, I am doing what I believe to be right.'

'I suspect,' said Isabella, in a low voice, 'there is no great struggle.'

Catherine's heart swelled; she drew away her arm, and Isabella made no opposition. Thus passed a long ten minutes, till they were again joined by Thorpe, who coming to them with a gayer look, said, 'Well, I have settled the matter, and now we may all go to-morrow with a safe conscience. I have been to Miss Tilney, and made your excuses.'

'You have not!' cried Catherine.

'I have, upon my soul. Left her this moment. Told her you had sent me to say, that having just recol-lected a prior engagement of going to Clifton with us to-morrow, you could not have the pleasure of walking with her till Tuesday. She said very well, Tues-day was just as convenient to her; so there is an end of all our difficulties. – A pretty good thought of mine – hey?'

Isabella's countenance was once more all smiles and good-humour, and James too looked happy again.

'A most heavenly thought indeed! Now, my sweet Catherine, all our distresses are over; you are honourably acquitted, and we shall have a most delightful party.'

'This will not do,' said Catherine; 'I cannot submit to this. I must run after Miss Tilney directly and set her right.'

Isabella, however, caught hold of one hand; Thorpe of the other; and remonstrances poured in from all three. Even James was quite angry. When every thing was settled, when Miss Tilney herself said that Tuesday would suit her as well, it was quite ridiculous, quite absurd to make any further objection.

'I do not care. Mr. Thorpe had no business to invent any such message. If I had thought it right to put it off, I could have spoken to Miss Tilney myself. This is only doing it in a ruder way; and how do I know that Mr. Thorpe has – he may be mistaken again perhaps; he led me into one act of rudeness by his mistake on Friday. Let me go, Mr. Thorpe; Isabella, do not hold me.'

Thorpe told her it would be in vain to go after the Tilneys; they were turning the corner into Brock-street, when he had overtaken them, and were at home by this time.

'Then I will go after them,' said Catherine; 'wherever they are I will go after them. It does not signify talking. If I could not be persuaded into doing what I thought wrong, I never will be tricked into it.' And with these words she broke away and hurried off. Thorpe would have darted after her, but Morland withheld him. 'Let her go, let her go, if she will go.'

'She is as obstinate as –'

Thorpe never finished the simile, for it could hardly have been a proper one.

Away walked Catherine in great agitation, as fast as the crowd would permit her, fearful of being pursued,

yet determined to persevere. As she walked, she reflected on what had passed. It was painful to her to
disappoint and displease them, particularly to displease
her brother; but she could not repent her resistance.
Setting her own inclination apart, to have failed a second time in her engagement to Miss Tilney, to have
retracted a promise voluntarily made only five minutes
before, and on a false pretence too, must have been
wrong. She had not been withstanding them on selfish
principles alone, she had not consulted merely her own
gratification; *that* might have been ensured in some degree by the excursion itself, by seeing Blaize Castle; no,
she had attended to what was due to others, and to her
own character in their opinion. Her conviction of
being right however was not enough to restore her
composure, till she had spoken to Miss Tilney she
could not be at ease; and quickening her pace when she
got clear of the Crescent, she almost ran over the remaining ground till she gained the top of Milsom-
street. So rapid had been her movements, that in spite
of the Tilneys' advantage in the outset, they were but
just turning into their lodgings as she came within view
of them; and the servant still remaining at the open
door, she used only the ceremony of saying that she
must speak with Miss Tilney that moment, and hurrying by him proceeded up stairs. Then, opening the first
door before her, which happened to be the right, she
immediately found herself in the drawing-room with
General Tilney, his son and daughter. Her explanation,
defective only in being – from her irritation of nerves
and shortness of breath – no explanation at all, was
instantly given. 'I am come in a great hurry – It was all
a mistake – I never promised to go – I told them from
the first I could not go. – I ran away in a great hurry
to explain it. – I did not care what you thought of me.
– I would not stay for the servant.'

The business however, though not perfectly eluci-

dated by this speech, soon ceased to be a puzzle. Catherine found that John Thorpe *had* given the message;
and Miss Tilney had no scruple in owning herself
greatly surprised by it. But whether her brother had
still exceeded her in resentment, Catherine, though she
instinctively addressed herself as much to one as to the
other in her vindication, had no means of knowing.
Whatever might have been felt before her arrival, her
eager declarations immediately made every look and
sentence as friendly as she could desire.

The affair thus happily settled, she was introduced
by Miss Tilney to her father, and received by him with
such ready, such solicitous politeness as recalled
Thorpe's information to her mind, and made her think
with pleasure that he might be sometimes depended
on. To such anxious attention was the General's civility
carried, that not aware of her extraordinary swiftness
in entering the house, he was quite angry with the servant whose neglect had reduced her to open the door
of the apartment herself. 'What did William mean by
it? He should make a point of inquiring into the
matter.' And if Catherine had not most warmly asserted
his innocence, it seemed likely that William would lose
the favour of his master for ever, if not his place, by
her rapidity.

After sitting with them a quarter of an hour, she
rose to take leave, and was then most agreeably surprised by General Tilney's asking her if she would do
his daughter the honour of dining and spending the
rest of the day with her. Miss Tilney added her own
wishes. Catherine was greatly obliged; but it was quite
out of her power. Mr. and Mrs. Allen would expect her
back every moment. The General declared he could say
no more; the claims of Mr. and Mrs. Allen were not to
be superseded; but on some other day he trusted, when
longer notice could be given, they would not refuse to
spare her to her friend. 'Oh, no; Catherine was sure

they would not have the least objection, and she should have great pleasure in coming.' The General attended her himself to the street-door, saying every thing gallant as they went down stairs, admiring the elasticity of her walk, which corresponded exactly with the spirit of her dancing, and making her one of the most graceful bows she had ever beheld, when they parted.

Catherine, delighted by all that had passed, proceeded gaily to Pulteney-street; walking, as she concluded, with great elasticity, though she had never thought of it before. She reached home without seeing any thing more of the offended party; and now that she had been triumphant throughout, had carried her point and was secure of her walk, she began (as the flutter of her spirits subsided) to doubt whether she had been perfectly right. A sacrifice was always noble; and if she had given way to their entreaties, she should have been spared the distressing idea of a friend displeased, a brother angry, and a scheme of great happiness to both destroyed, perhaps through her means. To ease her mind, and ascertain by the opinion of an unprejudiced person what her own conduct had really been, she took occasion to mention before Mr. Allen the half-settled scheme of her brother and the Thorpes for the following day. Mr. Allen caught at it directly. 'Well,' said he, 'and do you think of going too?'

'No; I had just engaged myself to walk with Miss Tilney before they told me of it; and therefore you know I could not go with them, could I?'

'No, certainly not; and I am glad you do not think of it. These schemes are not at all the thing. Young men and women driving about the country in open carriages! Now and then it is very well; but going to inns and public places together! It is not right; and I wonder Mrs. Thorpe should allow it. I am glad you do not think of going; I am sure Mrs. Morland would not be pleased. Mrs. Allen, are not you of my way of thinking? Do not you think these kind of projects objectionable?'

'Yes, very much so indeed. Open carriages are nasty things. A clean gown is not five minutes wear in them. You are splashed getting in and getting out; and the wind takes your hair and your bonnet in every direction. I hate an open carriage myself.'

'I know you do; but that is not the question. Do not you think it has an odd appearance, if young ladies are frequently driven about in them by young men, to whom they are not even related?'

'Yes, my dear, a very odd appearance indeed. I cannot bear to see it.'

'Dear madam,' cried Catherine, 'then why did not you tell me so before? I am sure if I had known it to be improper, I would not have gone with Mr. Thorpe at all; but I always hoped you would tell me, if you thought I was doing wrong.'

'And so I should, my dear, you may depend on it; for as I told Mrs. Morland at parting, I would always do the best for you in my power. But one must not be over particular. Young people *will* be young people, as your good mother says herself. You know I wanted you, when we first came, not to buy that sprigged muslin, but you would. Young people do not like to be always thwarted.'

'But this was something of real consequence; and I do not think you would have found me hard to persuade.'

'As far as it has gone hitherto, there is no harm done,' said Mr. Allen; 'and I would only advise you, my dear, not to go out with Mr. Thorpe any more.'

'That is just what I was going to say,' added his wife.

Catherine, relieved for herself, felt uneasy for Isabella; and after a moment's thought, asked Mr. Allen whether it would not be both proper and kind in her to write to Miss Thorpe, and explain the indecorum of which she must be as insensible as herself; for she considered that Isabella might otherwise perhaps be going to Clifton the next day, in spite of what had passed. Mr. Allen however discouraged her from doing any such thing. 'You had better leave her alone, my dear, she is old enough to know what she is about; and if not, has a mother to advise her. Mrs. Thorpe is too indulgent beyond a doubt; but however you had better not interfere. She and your brother chuse to go, and you will be only getting ill-will.'

Catherine submitted; and though sorry to think that Isabella should be doing wrong, felt greatly relieved by Mr. Allen's approbation of her own conduct, and truly rejoiced to be preserved by his advice from the danger of falling into such an error herself. Her escape from being one of the party to Clifton was now an escape indeed; for what would the Tilneys have thought of her, if she had broken her promise to them in order to do what was wrong in itself? if she had been guilty of one breach of propriety, only to enable her to be guilty of another?

CHAPTER XIV

THE NEXT morning was fair, and Catherine almost expected another attack from the assembled party. With Mr. Allen to support her, she felt no dread of the event: but she would gladly be spared a contest, where victory itself was painful; and was heartily rejoiced therefore at neither seeing nor hearing any thing of them. The Tilneys called for her at the appointed time; and no new difficulty arising, no sudden recollection, no unexpected summons, no impertinent intrusion to disconcert their measures, my heroine was most un-naturally able to fulfil her engagement, though it was made with the hero himself. They determined on walking round Beechen Cliff, that noble hill, whose beautiful verdure and hanging coppice render it so striking an object from almost every opening in Bath.

'I never look at it,' said Catherine, as they walked along the side of the river, 'without thinking of the south of France.'

'You have been abroad then?' said Henry, a little surprised.

'Oh! no, I only mean what I have read about. It always puts me in mind of the country that Emily and her father travelled through, in the "Mysteries of Udolpho." But you never read novels, I dare say?'

'Why not?'

'Because they are not clever enough for you – gentlemen read better books.'

'The person, be it gentleman or lady, who has not pleasure in a good novel, must be intolerably stupid. I have read all Mrs. Radcliffe's works, and most of them with great pleasure. "The Mysteries of Udolpho", when I had once begun it, I could not lay down again; – I remember finishing it in two days – my hair standing on end the whole time.'

'Yes,' added Miss Tilney, 'and I remember that you undertook to read it aloud to me, and that when I was called away for only five minutes to answer a note, instead of waiting for me, you took the volume into the Hermitage-walk, and I was obliged to stay till you had finished it.'

'Thank you, Eleanor; – a most honourable testimony. You see, Miss Morland, the injustice of your suspicions. Here was I, in my eagerness to get on, refusing to wait only five minutes for my sister; breaking the promise I had made of reading it aloud, and keeping her in suspense at a most interesting part, by running away with the volume, which, you are to observe, was her own, particularly her own. I am proud when I reflect on it, and I think it must establish me in your good opinion.'

'I am very glad to hear it indeed, and now I shall never be ashamed of liking Udolpho myself. But I really thought before, young men despised novels amazingly.'

'It is *amazingly*; it may well suggest *amazement* if they do – for they read nearly as many as women. I myself have read hundreds and hundreds. Do not imagine that you can cope with me in a knowledge of Julias and Louisas. If we proceed to particulars, and engage in the never-ceasing inquiry of "Have you read this?" and "Have you read that?" I shall soon leave you as far behind me as – what shall I say? – I want an appropriate simile; – as far as your friend Emily herself left poor Valancourt when she went with her aunt into Italy. Consider how many years I have had the start of you. I had entered on my studies at Oxford, while you were a good little girl working your sampler at home!'

'Not very good I am afraid. But now really, do not you think Udolpho the nicest book in the world?'

'The nicest; – by which I suppose you mean the neatest. That must depend upon the binding.'

'Henry,' said Miss Tilney, 'you are very impertinent. Miss Morland, he is treating you exactly as he does his sister. He is for ever finding fault with me, for some incorrectness of language, and now he is taking the same liberty with you. The word "nicest," as you used it, did not suit him; and you had better change it as soon as you can, or we shall be overpowered with Johnson and Blair all the rest of the way.'

'I am sure,' cried Catherine, 'I did not mean to say any thing wrong; but it *is* a nice book, and why should not I call it so?'

'Very true,' said Henry, 'and this is a very nice day, and we are taking a very nice walk, and you are two very nice young ladies. Oh! it is a very nice word indeed! – it does for every thing. Originally perhaps it was applied only to express neatness, propriety, delicacy, or refinement; – people were nice in their dress, in their sentiments, or their choice. But now every commendation on every subject is comprised in that one word.'

'While, in fact,' cried his sister, 'it ought only to be applied to you, without any commendation at all. You are more nice than wise. Come, Miss Morland, let us leave him to meditate over our faults in the utmost propriety of diction, while we praise Udolpho in whatever terms we like best. It is a most interesting work. You are fond of that kind of reading?'

'To say the truth, I do not much like any other.'

'Indeed!'

'That is, I can read poetry and plays, and things of that sort, and do not dislike travels. But history, real solemn history, I cannot be interested in. Can you?'

'Yes, I am fond of history.'

'I wish I were too. I read it a little as a duty, but it tells me nothing that does not either vex or weary me. The quarrels of popes and kings, with wars or pestilences, in every page; the men all so good for nothing, and hardly any women at all – it is very tiresome: and yet I often think it odd that it should be so dull, for a great deal of it must be invention. The speeches that are put into the heroes' mouths, their thoughts and designs – the chief of all this must be invention, and invention is what delights me in other books.'

'Historians, you think,' said Miss Tilney, 'are not happy in their flights of fancy. They display imagination without raising interest. I am fond of history – and am very well contented to take the false with the true. In the principal facts they have sources of intelligence in former histories and records, which may be as much depended on, I conclude, as any thing that does not actually pass under one's own observation; and as for the little embellishments you speak of, they are embellishments, and I like them as such. If a speech be well drawn up, I read it with pleasure, by whomsoever it may be made – and probably with much greater, if the production of Mr. Hume or Mr. Robertson, than if the genuine words of Caractacus, Agricola, or Alfred the Great.'

'You are fond of history! – and so are Mr. Allen and my father; and I have two brothers who do not dislike it. So many instances within my small circle of friends is remarkable! At this rate, I shall not pity the writers of history any longer. If people like to read their books, it is all very well, but to be at so much trouble in filling great volumes, which, as I used to think, nobody would willingly ever look into, to be labouring only for the torment of little boys and girls, always struck me as a hard fate; and though I know it is all very right and necessary, I have often wondered at the person's courage that could sit down on purpose to do it.'

'That little boys and girls should be tormented,' said Henry, 'is what no one at all acquainted with human nature in a civilized state can deny; but in behalf of our most distinguished historians, I must observe, that they might well be offended at being supposed to have no higher aim; and that by their method and style, they are perfectly well qualified to torment readers of the most advanced reason and mature time of life. I use the verb "to torment," as I observed to be your own method, instead of "to instruct," supposing them to be now admitted as synonimous.'

'You think me foolish to call instruction a torment, but if you had been as much used as myself to hear poor little children first learning their letters and then learning to spell, if you had ever seen how stupid they can be for a whole morning together, and how tired my poor mother is at the end of it, as I am in the habit of seeing almost every day of my life at home, you would allow that to *torment* and to *instruct* might sometimes be used as synonimous words.'

'Very probably. But historians are not accountable for the difficulty of learning to read; and even you yourself, who do not altogether seem particularly friendly to very severe, very intense application, may perhaps be brought to acknowledge that it is very well worth while to be tormented for two or three years of one's life, for the sake of being able to read all the rest of it. Consider – if reading had not been taught, Mrs. Radcliffe would have written in vain – or perhaps might not have written at all.'

Catherine assented – and a very warm panegyric from her on that lady's merits, closed the subject. – The Tilneys were soon engaged in another on which she had nothing to say. They were viewing the country with the eyes of persons accustomed to drawing, and decided on its capability of being formed into pictures, with all the eagerness of real taste. Here Catherine was quite lost. She knew nothing of drawing – nothing of taste: – and she listened to them with an attention which brought her little profit, for they talked in phrases which conveyed scarcely any idea to her. The little which she could understand however appeared to contradict the very few notions she had entertained on the matter before. It seemed as if a good view were no longer to be taken from the top of an high hill, and that a clear blue sky was no longer a proof of a fine day. She was heartily ashamed of her ignorance. A misplaced shame. Where people wish to attach, they should always be ignorant. To come with a well-informed mind, is to come with an inability of administering to the vanity of others, which a sensible person would always wish to avoid. A woman especially, if she have the misfortune of knowing any thing, should conceal it as well as she can.

The advantages of natural folly in a beautiful girl have been already set forth by the capital pen of a sister author; – and to her treatment of the subject I will only add in justice to men, that though to the larger and more trifling part of the sex, imbecility in females is a great enhancement of their personal charms, there is a portion of them too reasonable and too well informed themselves to desire any thing more in woman than ignorance. But Catherine did not know her own advantages – did not know that a good-looking girl, with an affectionate heart and a very ignorant mind, cannot fail of attracting a clever young man, unless circumstances are particularly untoward. In the present instance, she confessed and lamented her want of knowledge; declared that she would give any thing in the world to be able to draw; and a lecture on the picturesque immediately followed, in which his instructions were so clear that she soon began to see beauty in every thing admired by him, and her attention was so earnest, that he became perfectly satisfied of her having a great deal of natural taste. He talked of foregrounds, distances, and second distances – side-screens and perspectives – lights and shades; – and Catherine was so hopeful a scholar, that when they gained the top of Beechen Cliff, she voluntarily rejected the whole city of Bath, as unworthy to make part of a landscape. Delighted with her progress, and fearful of wearying her with too much wisdom at once, Henry suffered the subject to decline, and by an easy transition from a piece of rocky fragment and the withered oak which he had placed near its summit, to oaks in general, to forests, the inclosure of them, waste lands, crown lands and government, he shortly found himself arrived at politics; and from politics, it was an easy step to silence. The general pause which succeeded his short disquisition on the state of the nation, was put an end to by Catherine, who, in rather a solemn tone of voice, uttered these words, 'I have heard that something very shocking indeed, will soon come out in London.'

Miss Tilney, to whom this was chiefly addressed,

was startled, and hastily replied, 'Indeed! – and of what nature?'

'That I do not know, nor who is the author. I have only heard that it is to be more horrible than any thing we have met with yet.'

'Good heaven! – Where could you hear of such a thing?'

'A particular friend of mine had an account of it in a letter from London yesterday. It is to be uncommonly dreadful. I shall expect murder and every thing of the kind.'

'You speak with astonishing composure! But I hope your friend's accounts have been exaggerated; – and if such a design is known beforehand, proper measures will undoubtedly be taken by government to prevent its coming to effect.'

'Government,' said Henry, endeavouring not to smile, 'neither desires nor dares to interfere in such matters. There must be murder; and government cares not how much.'

The ladies stared. He laughed, and added, 'Come, shall I make you understand each other, or leave you to puzzle out an explanation as you can? No – I will be noble. I will prove myself a man, no less by the generosity of my soul than the clearness of my head. I have no patience with such of my sex as disdain to let themselves sometimes down to the comprehension of yours. Perhaps the abilities of women are neither sound nor acute – neither vigorous nor keen. Perhaps they may want observation, discernment, judgment, fire, genius, and wit.'

'Miss Morland, do not mind what he says; – but have the goodness to satisfy me as to this dreadful riot.'

'Riot! – what riot?'

'My dear Eleanor, the riot is only in your own brain. The confusion there is scandalous. Miss Morland has been talking of nothing more dreadful than a new pub-lication which is shortly to come out, in three duo-decimo volumes, two hundred and seventy-six pages in each, with a frontispiece to the first, of two tombstones and a lantern – do you understand? – And you, Miss Morland – my stupid sister has mistaken all your clearest expressions. You talked of expected horrors in London – and instead of instantly conceiving, as any rational creature would have done, that such words could relate only to a circulating library, she immedi-ately pictured to herself a mob of three thousand men assembling in St. George's Fields; the Bank attacked, the Tower threatened, the streets of London flowing with blood, a detachment of the 12th Light Dragoons, (the hopes of the nation,) called up from Northampton to quell the insurgents, and the gallant Capt. Frederick Tilney, in the moment of charging at the head of his troop, knocked off his horse by a brickbat from an upper window. Forgive her stupidity. The fears of the sister have added to the weakness of the woman; but she is by no means a simpleton in general.'

Catherine looked grave. 'And now, Henry,' said Miss Tilney, 'that you have made us understand each other, you may as well make Miss Morland understand your-self – unless you mean to have her think you intoler-ably rude to your sister, and a great brute in your opinion of women in general. Miss Morland is not used to your odd ways.'

'I shall be most happy to make her better acquainted with them.'

'No doubt; – but that is no explanation of the pres-ent.'

'What am I to do?'

'You know what you ought to do. Clear your char-acter handsomely before her. Tell her that you think very highly of the understanding of women.'

'Miss Morland, I think very highly of the understanding of all the women in the world – especially of those – whoever they may be – with whom I happen to be in company.'

'That is not enough. Be more serious.'

'Miss Morland, no one can think more highly of the understanding of women than I do. In my opinion, nature has given them so much, that they never find it necessary to use more than half.'

'We shall get nothing more serious from him now, Miss Morland. He is not in a sober mood. But I do assure you that he must be entirely misunderstood, if he can ever appear to say an unjust thing of any woman at all, or an unkind one of me.'

It was no effort to Catherine to believe that Henry Tilney could never be wrong. His manner might sometimes surprise, but his meaning must always be just: – and what she did not understand, she was almost as ready to admire, as what she did. The whole walk was delightful, and though it ended too soon, its conclusion was delightful too; – her friends attended her into the house, and Miss Tilney, before they parted, addressing herself with respectful form, as much to Mrs. Allen as to Catherine, petitioned for the pleasure of her company to dinner on the day after the next. No difficulty was made on Mrs. Allen's side – and the only difficulty on Catherine's was in concealing the excess of her pleasure.

The morning had passed away so charmingly as to banish all her friendship and natural affection; for no thought of Isabella or James had crossed her during their walk. When the Tilneys were gone, she became amiable again, but she was amiable for some time to little effect; Mrs. Allen had no intelligence to give that could relieve her anxiety, she had heard nothing of any of them. Towards the end of the morning however, Catherine having occasion for some indispensable yard of ribbon which must be bought without a moment's delay, walked out into the town, and in Bond-street overtook the second Miss Thorpe, as she was loitering towards Edgar's Buildings between two of the sweetest girls in the world, who had been her dear friends all the morning. From her, she soon learned that the party to Clifton had taken place. 'They set off at eight this morning,' said Miss Anne, 'and I am sure I do not envy them their drive. I think you and I are very well off to be out of the scrape. – It must be the dullest thing in the world, for there is not a soul at Clifton at this time of year. Belle went with your brother, and John drove Maria.'

Catherine spoke the pleasure she really felt on hearing this part of the arrangement.

'Oh! yes,' rejoined the other, 'Maria is gone. She was quite wild to go. She thought it would be something very fine. I cannot say I admire her taste; and for my part I was determined from the first not to go, if they pressed me ever so much.'

Catherine, a little doubtful of this, could not help answering, 'I wish you could have gone too. It is a pity you could not all go.'

'Thank you; but it is quite a matter of indifference to me. Indeed, I would not have gone on any account. I was saying so to Emily and Sophia when you overtook us.'

Catherine was still unconvinced; but glad that Anne should have the friendship of an Emily and a Sophia to console her, she bade her adieu without much uneasiness, and returned home, pleased that the party had not been prevented by her refusing to join it, and very heartily wishing that it might be too pleasant to allow either James or Isabella to resent her resistance any longer.

CHAPTER XV

EARLY THE next day, a note from Isabella, speaking peace and tenderness in every line, and entreating the immediate presence of her friend on a matter of the utmost importance, hastened Catherine, in the happiest state of confidence and curiosity, to Edgar's Buildings. – The two youngest Miss Thorpes were by themselves in the parlour; and, on Anne's quitting it to call her sister, Catherine took the opportunity of asking the other for some particulars of their yesterday's party. Maria desired no greater pleasure than to speak of it; and Catherine immediately learnt that it had been altogether the most delightful scheme in the world; that nobody could imagine how charming it had been, and that it had been more delightful than any body could conceive. Such was the information of the first five minutes; the second unfolded thus much in detail, – that they had driven directly to the York Hotel, ate some soup, and bespoke an early dinner, walked down to the Pump-room, tasted the water, and laid out some shillings in purses and spars; thence adjourned to eat ice at a pastry-cook's, and hurrying back to the Hotel, swallowed their dinner in haste, to prevent being in the dark; and then had a delightful drive back, only the moon was not up, and it rained a little, and Mr. Morland's horse was so tired he could hardly get it along.

Catherine listened with heartfelt satisfaction. It appeared that Blaize Castle had never been thought of; and, as for all the rest, there was nothing to regret for half an instant. – Maria's intelligence concluded with a tender effusion of pity for her sister Anne, whom she represented as insupportably cross, from being excluded the party.

'She will never forgive me, I am sure; but, you know, how could I help it? John would have me go, for he vowed he would not drive her, because she had such thick ancles. I dare say she will not be in good humour again this month; but I am determined I will not be cross; it is not a little matter that puts me out of temper.'

Isabella now entered the room with so eager a step, and a look of such happy importance, as engaged all her friend's notice. Maria was without ceremony sent away, and Isabella, embracing Catherine, thus began: – 'Yes, my dear Catherine, it is so indeed; your penetration has not deceived you. – Oh! that arch eye of yours! – It sees through every thing.'

Catherine replied only by a look of wondering ignorance.

'Nay, my beloved, sweetest friend,' continued the other, 'compose yourself. – I am amazingly agitated, as you perceive. Let us sit down and talk in comfort. Well, and so you guessed it the moment you had my note? – Sly creature! – Oh! my dear Catherine, you alone who know my heart can judge of my present happiness. Your brother is the most charming of men. I only wish I were more worthy of him. – But what will your excellent father and mother say? – Oh! heavens! when I think of them I am so agitated!'

Catherine's understanding began to awake: an idea of the truth suddenly darted into her mind; and, with the natural blush of so new an emotion, she cried out, 'Good heaven! – my dear Isabella, what do you mean? Can you – can you really be in love with James?'

This bold surmise, however, she soon learnt comprehended but half the fact. The anxious affection, which she was accused of having continually watched in Isabella's every look and action, had, in the course of their yesterday's party, received the delightful confession of an equal love. Her heart and faith were alike engaged to James. – Never had Catherine listened to any thing so full of interest, wonder, and joy. Her brother and her friend engaged! – New to such circumstances, the importance of it appeared unspeakably great, and she contemplated it as one of those grand events, of which the ordinary course of life can hardly afford a return. The strength of her feelings she could not express; the nature of them, however, contented her friend. The happiness of having such a sister was their first effusion, and the fair ladies mingled in embraces and tears of joy.

Delighting, however, as Catherine sincerely did in the prospect of the connexion, it must be acknowledged that Isabella far surpassed her in tender anticipations. – 'You will be so infinitely dearer to me, my Catherine, than either Anne or Maria: I feel that I shall be so much more attached to my dear Morland's family than to my own.'

This was a pitch of friendship beyond Catherine.

'You are so like your dear brother,' continued Isabella, 'that I quite doated on you the first moment I saw you. But so it always is with me; the first moment settles every thing. The very first day that Morland came to us last Christmas – the very first moment I beheld him – my heart was irrecoverably gone. I remember I wore my yellow gown, with my hair done up in braids; and when I came into the drawing-room, and John introduced him, I thought I never saw any body so handsome before.'

Here Catherine secretly acknowledged the power of love; for, though exceedingly fond of her brother, and partial to all his endowments, she had never in her life thought him handsome.

'I remember too, Miss Andrews drank tea with us that evening, and wore her puce-coloured sarsenet; and she looked so heavenly, that I thought your brother must certainly fall in love with her; I could not sleep a wink all night for thinking of it. Oh! Catherine, the many sleepless nights I have had on your brother's account! – I would not have you suffer half what I have done! I am grown wretchedly thin I know; but I will not pain you by describing my anxiety; you have seen enough of it. I feel that I have betrayed myself perpetually; – so unguarded in speaking of my partiality for the church! – But my secret I was always sure would be safe with *you*.'

Catherine felt that nothing could have been safer; but ashamed of an ignorance little expected, she dared no longer contest the point, nor refuse to have been as full of arch penetration and affectionate sympathy as Isabella chose to consider her. Her brother she found was preparing to set off with all speed to Fullerton, to make known his situation and ask consent; and here was a source of some real agitation to the mind of Isabella. Catherine endeavoured to persuade her, as she was herself persuaded, that her father and mother would never oppose their son's wishes. – 'It is impossible,' said she, 'for parents to be more kind, or more desirous of their children's happiness; I have no doubt of their consenting immediately.'

'Morland says exactly the same,' replied Isabella; 'and yet I dare not expect it; my fortune will be so small; they never can consent to it. Your brother, who might marry any body!'

Here Catherine again discerned the force of love.

'Indeed, Isabella, you are too humble. – The difference of fortune can be nothing to signify.'

'Oh! my sweet Catherine, in *your* generous heart I know it would signify nothing; but we must not expect such disinterestedness in many. As for myself, I am sure I only wish our situations were reversed. Had I the command of millions, were I mistress of the whole world, your brother would be my only choice.'

This charming sentiment, recommended as much by

sense as novelty, gave Catherine a most pleasing remembrance of all the heroines of her acquaintance; and
she thought her friend never looked more lovely than
in uttering the grand idea. – 'I am sure they will consent,' was her frequent declaration; 'I am sure they will
be delighted with you.'

'For my own part,' said Isabella, 'my wishes are so
moderate, that the smallest income in nature would be
enough for me. Where people are really attached, poverty itself is wealth: grandeur I detest: I would not
settle in London for the universe. A cottage in some
retired village would be extasy. There are some charming little villas about Richmond.'

'Richmond!' cried Catherine. – 'You must settle near
Fullerton. You must be near us.'

'I am sure I shall be miserable if we do not. If I can
but be near *you*, I shall be satisfied. But this is idle
talking! I will not allow myself to think of such things,
till we have your father's answer. Morland says that by
sending it to-night to Salisbury, we may have it to-
morrow. -- To-morrow? -- I know I shall never have
courage to open the letter. I know it will be the death
of me.'

A reverie succeeded this conviction – and when Isabella spoke again, it was to resolve on the quality of
her wedding-gown.

Their conference was put an end to by the anxious
young lover himself, who came to breathe his parting
sigh before he set off for Wiltshire. Catherine wished
to congratulate him, but knew not what to say, and her
eloquence was only in her eyes. From them however
the eight parts of speech shone out most expressively,
and James could combine them with ease. Impatient
for the realization of all that he hoped at home, his
adieus were not long; and they would have been yet
shorter, had he not been frequently detained by the
urgent entreaties of his fair one that he would go.

Twice was he called almost from the door by her eagerness to have him gone. 'Indeed, Morland, I must drive you away. Consider how far you have to ride. I cannot bear to see you linger so. For Heaven's sake, waste no more time. There, go, go – I insist on it.'

The two friends, with hearts now more united than ever, were inseparable for the day; and in schemes of sisterly happiness the hours flew along. Mrs. Thorpe and her son, who were acquainted with every thing, and who seemed only to want Mr. Morland's consent, to consider Isabella's engagement as the most fortunate circumstance imaginable for their family, were allowed to join their counsels, and add their quota of significant looks and mysterious expressions to fill up the measure of curiosity to be raised in the unprivileged younger sisters. To Catherine's simple feelings, this odd sort of reserve seemed neither kindly meant, nor consistently supported; and its unkindness she would hardly have forborn pointing out, had its inconsistency been less their friend; – but Anne and Maria soon set her heart at ease by the sagacity of their 'I know what;' and the evening was spent in a sort of war of wit, a display of family ingenuity; on one side in the mystery of an affected secret, on the other of undefined discovery, all equally acute.

Catherine was with her friend again the next day, endeavouring to support her spirits, and while away the many tedious hours before the delivery of the letters; a needful exertion, for as the time of reasonable expectation drew near, Isabella became more and more desponding, and before the letter arrived, had worked herself into a state of real distress. But when it did come, where could distress be found? 'I have had no difficulty in gaining the consent of my kind parents, and am promised that every thing in their power shall be done to forward my happiness,' were the first three lines, and in one moment all was joyful security. The

brightest glow was instantly spread over Isabella's features, all care and anxiety seemed removed, her spirits
became almost too high for controul, and she called
herself without scruple the happiest of mortals.

Mrs. Thorpe, with tears of joy, embraced her
daughter, her son, her visitor, and could have embraced half the inhabitants of Bath with satisfaction.
Her heart was overflowing with tenderness. It was
'dear John,' and 'dear Catherine' at every word; – 'dear
Anne and dear Maria' must immediately be made
sharers in their felicity; and two 'dears' at once before
the name of Isabella were not more than that beloved
child had now well earned. John himself was no skulker
in joy. He not only bestowed on Mr. Morland the high
commendation of being one of the finest fellows in the
world, but swore off many sentences in his praise.

The letter, whence sprang all this felicity, was short,
containing little more than this assurance of success;
and every particular was deferred till James could write
again. But for particulars Isabella could well afford to
wait. The needful was comprised in Mr. Morland's
promise; his honour was pledged to make every thing
easy; and by what means their income was to be
formed, whether landed property were to be resigned,
or funded money made over, was a matter in which her
disinterested spirit took no concern. She knew enough
to feel secure of an honourable and speedy establishment, and her imagination took a rapid flight over
its attendant felicities. She saw herself at the end of
a few weeks, the gaze and admiration of every new
acquaintance at Fullerton, the envy of every valued old
friend in Putney, with a carriage at her command, a
new name on her tickets, and a brilliant exhibition of
hoop rings on her finger.

When the contents of the letter were ascertained,
John Thorpe, who had only waited its arrival to begin
his journey to London, prepared to set off. 'Well, Miss

Morland,' said he, on finding her alone in the parlour, 'I am come to bid you good bye.' Catherine wished him a good journey. Without appearing to hear her, he walked to the window, fidgetted about, hummed a tune, and seemed wholly self-occupied.

'Shall not you be late at Devizes?' said Catherine. He made no answer; but after a minute's silence burst out with, 'A famous good thing this marrying scheme, upon my soul! A clever fancy of Morland's and Belle's. What do you think of it, Miss Morland? *I* say it is no bad notion.'

'I am sure I think it a very good one.'

'Do you? – that's honest, by heavens! I am glad you are no enemy to matrimony however. Did you ever hear the old song, "Going to one wedding brings on another?" I say, you will come to Belle's wedding, I hope.'

'Yes; I have promised your sister to be with her, if possible.'

'And then you know' – twisting himself about and forcing a foolish laugh – 'I say, then you know, we may try the truth of this same old song.'

'May we? – but I never sing. Well, I wish you a good journey. I dine with Miss Tilney to-day, and must now be going home.'

'Nay, but there is no such confounded hurry. – Who knows when we may be together again? – Not but that I shall be down again by the end of a fortnight, and a devilish long fortnight it will appear to me.'

'Then why do you stay away so long?' replied Catherine – finding that he waited for an answer.

'That is kind of you, however – kind and good-natured. – I shall not forget it in a hurry. – But you have more good-nature and all that, than any body living I believe. A monstrous deal of good-nature, and it is not only good-nature, but you have so much, so much of every thing; and then you have such – upon my soul I do not know any body like you.'

'Oh! dear, there are a great many people like me, I dare say, only a great deal better. Good morning to you.'

'But I say, Miss Morland, I shall come and pay my respects at Fullerton before it is long, if not disagreeable.'

'Pray do. – My father and mother will be very glad to see you.'

'And I hope – I hope, Miss Morland, *you* will not be sorry to see me.'

'Oh! dear, not at all. There are very few people I am sorry to see. Company is always cheerful.'

'That is just my way of thinking. Give me but a little cheerful company, let me only have the company of the people I love, let me only be where I like and with whom I like, and the devil take the rest, say I. – And I am heartily glad to hear you say the same. But I have a notion, Miss Morland, you and I think pretty much alike upon most matters.'

'Perhaps we may; but it is more than I ever thought of. And as to *most matters*, to say the truth, there are not many that I know my own mind about.'

'By Jove, no more do I. It is not my way to bother my brains with what does not concern me. My notion of things is simple enough. Let me only have the girl I like, say I, with a comfortable house over my head, and what care I for all the rest? Fortune is nothing. I am sure of a good income of my own; and if she had not a penny, why so much the better.'

'Very true. I think like you there. If there is a good fortune on one side, there can be no occasion for any on the other. No matter which has it, so that there is enough. I hate the idea of one great fortune looking out for another. And to marry for money I think the wickedest thing in existence. – Good day. – We shall be very glad to see you at Fullerton, whenever it is convenient.' And away she went. It was not in the power of all his gallantry to detain her longer. With such news to communicate, and such a visit to prepare for, her departure was not to be delayed by any thing in his nature to urge; and she hurried away, leaving him to the undivided consciousness of his own happy address, and her explicit encouragement.

The agitation which she had herself experienced on first learning her brother's engagement, made her expect to raise no inconsiderable emotion in Mr. and Mrs. Allen, by the communication of the wonderful event. How great was her disappointment! The important affair, which many words of preparation ushered in, had been foreseen by them both ever since her brother's arrival; and all that they felt on the occasion was comprehended in a wish for the young people's happiness, with a remark, on the gentleman's side, in favour of Isabella's beauty, and on the lady's, of her great good luck. It was to Catherine the most surprising insensibility. The disclosure however of the great secret of James's going to Fullerton the day before, did raise some emotion in Mrs. Allen. She could not listen to that with perfect calmness; but repeatedly regretted the necessity of its concealment, wished she could have known his intention, wished she could have seen him before he went, as she should certainly have troubled him with her best regards to his father and mother, and her kind compliments to all the Skinners.

END OF VOL. I.

VOLUME II

NORTHANGER ABBEY

CHAPTER I

CATHERINE'S EXPECTATIONS of pleasure from her visit in Milsom-street were so very high, that disappointment was inevitable; and accordingly, though she was most politely received by General Tilney, and kindly welcomed by his daughter, though Henry was at home, and no one else of the party, she found, on her return, without spending many hours in the examination of her feelings, that she had gone to her appointment preparing for happiness which it had not afforded. Instead of finding herself improved in acquaintance with Miss Tilney, from the intercourse of the day, she seemed hardly so intimate with her as before; instead of seeing Henry Tilney to greater advantage than ever, in the ease of a family party, he had never said so little, nor been so little agreeable; and, in spite of their father's great civilities to her – in spite of his thanks, invitations, and compliments – it had been a release to get away from him. It puzzled her to account for all this. It could not be General Tilney's fault. That he was perfectly agreeable and good-natured, and altogether a very charming man, did not admit of a doubt, for he was tall and handsome, and Henry's father. *He* could not be accountable for his children's want of spirits, or for her want of enjoyment in his company. The former she hoped at last might have been accidental, and the latter she could only attribute to her own stupidity. Isabella, on hearing the particulars of the visit, gave a different explanation: 'It was all pride, pride, insufferable haughtiness and pride! She had long suspected the family to be very high, and this made it certain. Such insolence of behaviour as Miss Tilney's she had never heard of in her life! Not to do the honours of her house with common good-breeding! – To behave to her guest with such superciliousness! – Hardly even to speak to her!'

'But it was not so bad as that, Isabella; there was no superciliousness; she was very civil.'

'Oh! don't defend her! And then the brother, he, who had appeared so attached to you! Good heavens! well, some people's feelings are incomprehensible. And so he hardly looked once at you the whole day?'

'I do not say so; but he did not seem in good spirits.'

'How contemptible! Of all things in the world inconstancy is my aversion. Let me entreat you never to think of him again, my dear Catherine; indeed he is unworthy of you.'

'Unworthy! I do not suppose he ever thinks of me.'

'That is exactly what I say; he never thinks of you. – Such fickleness! Oh! how different to your brother and to mine! I really believe John has the most constant heart.'

'But as for General Tilney, I assure you it would be impossible for any body to behave to me with greater civility and attention; it seemed to be his only care to entertain and make me happy.'

'Oh! I know no harm of him; I do not suspect him of pride. I believe he is a very gentleman-like man. John thinks very well of him, and John's judgment — '

'Well, I shall see how they behave to me this evening; we shall meet them at the rooms.'

'And must I go?'

'Do not you intend it? I thought it was all settled.'

'Nay, since you make such a point of it, I can refuse you nothing. But do not insist upon my being very agreeable, for my heart, you know, will be some forty

miles off. And as for dancing, do not mention it I beg;
that is quite out of the question. Charles Hodges will
plague me to death I dare say; but I shall cut him very
short. Ten to one but he guesses the reason, and that
is exactly what I want to avoid, so I shall insist on his
keeping his conjecture to himself.'

Isabella's opinion of the Tilneys did not influence
her friend; she was sure there had been no insolence in
the manners either of brother or sister; and she did not
credit there being any pride in their hearts. The evening
rewarded her confidence; she was met by one with the
same kindness, and by the other with the same attention as heretofore: Miss Tilney took pains to be near
her, and Henry asked her to dance.

Having heard the day before in Milsom-street, that
their elder brother, Captain Tilney, was expected almost every hour, she was at no loss for the name of a
very fashionable-looking, handsome young man, whom
she had never seen before, and who now evidently be-
longed to their party. She looked at him with great
admiration, and even supposed it possible, that some
people might think him handsomer than his brother,
though, in her eyes, his air was more assuming, and his
countenance less prepossessing. His taste and manners
were beyond a doubt decidedly inferior; for, within her
hearing, he not only protested against every thought of
dancing himself, but even laughed openly at Henry for
finding it possible. From the latter circumstance it may
be presumed, that, whatever might be our heroine's
opinion of him, his admiration of her was not of a very
dangerous kind; not likely to produce animosities between the brothers, nor persecutions to the lady. *He*
cannot be the instigator of the three villains in horsemen's great coats, by whom she will hereafter be
forced into a travelling-chaise and four, which will
drive off with incredible speed. Catherine, meanwhile,
undisturbed by presentiments of such an evil, or of any

evil at all, except that of having but a short set to dance down, enjoyed her usual happiness with Henry Tilney, listening with sparkling eyes to every thing he said; and, in finding him irresistible, becoming so herself.

At the end of the first dance, Captain Tilney came towards them again, and, much to Catherine's dissatisfaction, pulled his brother away. They retired whispering together; and, though her delicate sensibility did not take immediate alarm, and lay it down as fact, that Captain Tilney must have heard some malevolent misrepresentation of her, which he now hastened to communicate to his brother, in the hope of separating them for ever, she could not have her partner conveyed from her sight without very uneasy sensations. Her suspense was of full five minutes' duration; and she was beginning to think it a very long quarter of an hour, when they both returned, and an explanation was given, by Henry's requesting to know, if she thought her friend, Miss Thorpe, would have any objection to dancing, as his brother would be most happy to be introduced to her. Catherine, without hesitation, replied, that she was very sure Miss Thorpe did not mean to dance at all. The cruel reply was passed on to the other, and he immediately walked away.

'Your brother will not mind it I know,' said she, 'because I heard him say before, that he hated dancing; but it was very good-natured in him to think of it. I suppose he saw Isabella sitting down, and fancied she might wish for a partner; but he is quite mistaken, for she would not dance upon any account in the world.'

Henry smiled, and said, 'How very little trouble it can give you to understand the motive of other people's actions.'

'Why? – What do you mean?'

'With you, it is not, How is such a one likely to be influenced? What is the inducement most likely to act upon such a person's feelings, age, situation, and probable habits of life considered? – but, how should *I* be influenced, what would be *my* inducement in acting so and so?'

'I do not understand you.'

'Then we are on very unequal terms, for I understand you perfectly well.'

'Me? – yes; I cannot speak well enough to be unintelligible.'

'Bravo! – an excellent satire on modern language.'

'But pray tell me what you mean.'

'Shall I indeed? – Do you really desire it? – But you are not aware of the consequences; it will involve you in a very cruel embarrassment, and certainly bring on a disagreement between us.'

'No, no; it shall not do either; I am not afraid.'

'Well then, I only meant that your attributing my brother's wish of dancing with Miss Thorpe to good-nature alone, convinced me of your being superior in good-nature yourself to all the rest of the world.'

Catherine blushed and disclaimed, and the gentleman's predictions were verified. There was a something, however, in his words which repaid her for the pain of confusion; and that something occupied her mind so much, that she drew back for some time, forgetting to speak or to listen, and almost forgetting where she was; till, roused by the voice of Isabella, she looked up and saw her with Captain Tilney preparing to give them hands across.

Isabella shrugged her shoulders and smiled, the only explanation of this extraordinary change which could at that time be given; but as it was not quite enough for Catherine's comprehension, she spoke her astonishment in very plain terms to her partner.

'I cannot think how it could happen! Isabella was so determined not to dance.'

'And did Isabella never change her mind before?'

'Oh! but, because — and your brother! – After what you told him from me, how could he think of going to ask her?'

'I cannot take surprise to myself on that head. You bid me be surprised on your friend's account, and therefore I am; but as for my brother, his conduct in the business, I must own, has been no more than I believed him perfectly equal to. The fairness of your friend was an open attraction; her firmness, you know, could only be understood by yourself.'

'You are laughing; but, I assure you, Isabella is very firm in general.'

'It is as much as should be said of any one. To be always firm must be to be often obstinate. When properly to relax is the trial of judgment; and, without reference to my brother, I really think Miss Thorpe has by no means chosen ill in fixing on the present hour.'

The friends were not able to get together for any confidential discourse till all the dancing was over; but then, as they walked about the room arm in arm, Isabella thus explained herself: – 'I do not wonder at your surprise; and I am really fatigued to death. He is such a rattle! – Amusing enough, if my mind had been disengaged; but I would have given the world to sit still.'

'Then why did not you?'

'Oh! my dear! it would have looked so particular; and you know how I abhor doing that. I refused him as long as I possibly could, but he would take no denial. You have no idea how he pressed me. I begged him to excuse me, and get some other partner – but no, not he; after aspiring to my hand, there was nobody else in the room he could bear to think of; and it was not that he wanted merely to dance, he wanted to be with *me*. Oh! such nonsense! – I told him he had taken a very unlikely way to prevail upon me; for, of all things in the world, I hated fine speeches and compliments; – and so — and so then I found there would be no peace if I did not stand up. Besides, I thought Mrs. Hughes, who introduced him, might take it ill if I did not: and your dear brother, I am sure he would have been miserable if I had sat down the whole evening. I am so glad it is over! My spirits are quite jaded with listening to his nonsense: and then, – being such a smart young fellow, I saw every eye was upon us.'

'He is very handsome indeed.'

'Handsome! – Yes, I suppose he may. I dare say people would admire him in general; but he is not at all in my style of beauty. I hate a florid complexion and dark eyes in a man. However, he is very well. Amazingly conceited, I am sure. I took him down several times you know in my way.'

When the young ladies next met, they had a far more interesting subject to discuss. James Morland's second letter was then received, and the kind intentions of his father fully explained. A living, of which Mr. Morland was himself patron and incumbent, of about four hundred pounds yearly value, was to be resigned to his son as soon as he should be old enough to take it; no trifling deduction from the family income, no niggardly assignment to one of ten children. An estate of at least equal value, moreover, was assured as his future inheritance.

James expressed himself on the occasion with becoming gratitude; and the necessity of waiting between two and three years before they could marry, being, however unwelcome, no more than he had expected, was borne by him without discontent. Catherine, whose expectations had been as unfixed as her ideas of her father's income, and whose judgment was now entirely led by her brother, felt equally well satisfied, and heartily congratulated Isabella on having every thing so pleasantly settled.

'It is very charming indeed,' said Isabella, with a grave face. 'Mr. Morland has behaved vastly handsome indeed,' said the gentle Mrs. Thorpe, looking anxiously at her daughter. 'I only wish I could do as much. One could not expect more from him you know. If he finds he *can* do more by and bye, I dare say he will, for I am sure he must be an excellent good hearted man. Four hundred is but a small income to begin on indeed, but your wishes, my dear Isabella, are so moderate, you do not consider how little you ever want, my dear.'

'It is not on my own account I wish for more; but I cannot bear to be the means of injuring my dear Morland, making him sit down upon an income hardly enough to find one in the common necessaries of life. For myself, it is nothing; I never think of myself.'

'I know you never do, my dear; and you will always find your reward in the affection it makes every body feel for you. There never was a young woman so beloved as you are by every body that knows you; and I dare say when Mr. Morland sees you, my dear child – but do not let us distress our dear Catherine by talking of such things. Mr. Morland has behaved so very handsome you know. I always heard he was a most excellent man; and you know, my dear, we are not to suppose but what, if you had had a suitable fortune, he would have come down with something more, for I am sure he must be a most liberal-minded man.'

'Nobody can think better of Mr. Morland than I do, I am sure. But every body has their failing you know, and every body has a right to do what they like with their own money.' Catherine was hurt by these insinuations. 'I am very sure,' said she, 'that my father has promised to do as much as he can afford.'

Isabella recollected herself. 'As to that, my sweet Catherine, there cannot be a doubt, and you know me well enough to be sure that a much smaller income would satisfy me. It is not the want of more money that makes me just at present a little out of spirits; I hate money; and if our union could take place now upon only fifty pounds a year, I should not have a wish unsatisfied. Ah! my Catherine, you have found me out. There's the sting. The long, long, endless two years and half that are to pass before your brother can hold the living.'

'Yes, yes, my darling Isabella,' said Mrs. Thorpe, 'we perfectly see into your heart. You have no disguise. We perfectly understand the present vexation; and every body must love you the better for such a noble honest affection.'

Catherine's uncomfortable feelings began to lessen. She endeavoured to believe that the delay of the marriage was the only source of Isabella's regret; and when she saw her at their next interview as cheerful and amiable as ever, endeavoured to forget that she had for a minute thought otherwise. James soon followed his letter, and was received with the most gratifying kindness.

CHAPTER II

THE ALLENS had now entered on the sixth week of their stay in Bath; and whether it should be the last, was for some time a question, to which Catherine listened with a beating heart. To have her acquaintance with the Tilneys end so soon, was an evil which nothing could counterbalance. Her whole happiness seemed at stake, while the affair was in suspense, and every thing secured when it was determined that the lodgings should be taken for another fortnight. What this additional fortnight was to produce to her beyond the pleasure of sometimes seeing Henry Tilney, made but a small part of Catherine's speculation. Once or twice indeed, since James's engagement had taught her what *could* be done, she had got so far as to indulge in a secret 'perhaps,' but in general the felicity of being with him for the present bounded her views: the present was now comprised in another three weeks, and her happiness being certain for that period, the rest of her life was at such a distance as to excite but little interest. In the course of the morning which saw this business arranged, she visited Miss Tilney, and poured forth her joyful feelings. It was doomed to be a day of trial. No sooner had she expressed her delight in Mr. Allen's lengthened stay, than Miss Tilney told her of her father's having just determined upon quitting Bath by the end of another week. Here was a blow! The past suspense of the morning had been ease and quiet to the present disappointment. Catherine's countenance fell, and in a voice of most sincere concern she echoed Miss Tilney's concluding words, 'By the end of another week!'

'Yes, my father can seldom be prevailed on to give the waters what I think a fair trial. He has been disappointed of some friends' arrival whom he expected to meet here, and as he is now pretty well, is in a hurry to get home.'

'I am very sorry for it,' said Catherine dejectedly, 'if I had known this before —'

'Perhaps,' said Miss Tilney in an embarrassed manner, 'you would be so good — it would make me very happy if —'

The entrance of her father put a stop to the civility, which Catherine was beginning to hope might introduce a desire of their corresponding. After addressing her with his usual politeness, he turned to his daughter and said, 'Well, Eleanor, may I congratulate you on being successful in your application to your fair friend?'

'I was just beginning to make the request, sir, as you came in.'

'Well, proceed by all means. I know how much your heart is in it. My daughter, Miss Morland,' he continued, without leaving his daughter time to speak, 'has been forming a very bold wish. We leave Bath, as she has perhaps told you, on Saturday se'nnight. A letter from my steward tells me that my presence is wanted at home; and being disappointed in my hope of seeing the Marquis of Longtown and General Courteney here, some of my very old friends, there is nothing to detain me longer in Bath. And could we carry our selfish point with you, we should leave it without a single regret. Can you, in short, be prevailed on to quit this scene of public triumph and oblige your friend Eleanor with your company in Gloucestershire? I am almost ashamed to make the request, though its presumption would certainly appear greater to every creature in Bath than yourself. Modesty such as your's – but not for the world would I pain it by open praise. If you can be induced to honour us with a visit, you will make us happy beyond expression. 'Tis true, we can offer you nothing like the gaieties of this lively place; we can tempt you neither by amusement nor splendour, for our mode of living, as you see, is plain and unpretending; yet no endeavours shall be wanting on our side to make Northanger Abbey not wholly disagreeable.'

Northanger Abbey! – These were thrilling words, and wound up Catherine's feelings to the highest point of extasy. Her grateful and gratified heart could hardly restrain its expressions within the language of tolerable calmness. To receive so flattering an invitation! To have her company so warmly solicited! Every thing honourable and soothing, every present enjoyment, and every future hope was contained in it; and her acceptance, with only the saving clause of papa and mamma's approbation, was eagerly given. – 'I will write home directly,' said she, 'and if they do not object, as I dare say they will not' –

General Tilney was not less sanguine, having already waited on her excellent friends in Pulteney-street, and obtained their sanction of his wishes. 'Since they can consent to part with you,' said he, 'we may expect philosophy from all the world.'

Miss Tilney was earnest, though gentle, in her secondary civilities, and the affair became in a few minutes as nearly settled, as this necessary reference to Fullerton would allow.

The circumstances of the morning had led Catherine's feelings through the varieties of suspense, security, and disappointment; but they were now safely lodged in perfect bliss; and with spirits elated to rapture, with Henry at her heart, and Northanger Abbey on her lips, she hurried home to write her letter. Mr. and Mrs. Morland, relying on the discretion of the friends to whom they had already entrusted their daughter, felt no doubt of the propriety of an acquaintance which had been formed under their eye, and sent therefore by return of post their ready consent to her visit in Gloucestershire. This indulgence, though not more than Catherine had hoped for, completed her conviction of being favoured beyond every other human creature, in friends and fortune, circumstance and chance. Every thing seemed to co-operate for her advantage. By the kindness of her first friends the Allens, she had been introduced into scenes, where pleasures of every kind had met her. Her feelings, her preferences had each known the happiness of a return. Wherever she felt attachment, she had been able to create it. The affection of Isabella was to be secured to her in a sister. The Tilneys, they, by whom above all, she desired to be favourably thought of, outstripped even her wishes in the flattering measures by which their intimacy was to be continued. She was to be their chosen visitor, she was to be for weeks under the same roof with the person whose society she mostly prized – and, in addition to all the rest, this roof was to be the roof of an abbey! – Her passion for ancient edifices

was next in degree to her passion for Henry Tilney –
and castles and abbies made usually the charm of those
reveries which his image did not fill. To see and explore either the ramparts and keep of the one, or the
cloisters of the other, had been for many weeks a darling wish, though to be more than the visitor of an
hour, had seemed too nearly impossible for desire. And
yet, this was to happen. With all the chances against
her of house, hall, place, park, court, and cottage,
Northanger turned up an abbey, and she was to be its
inhabitant. Its long, damp passages, its narrow cells and
ruined chapel, were to be within her daily reach, and
she could not entirely subdue the hope of some tradi-
tional legends, some awful memorials of an injured and
ill-fated nun.

It was wonderful that her friends should seem so
little elated by the possession of such a home; that the
consciousness of it should be so meekly borne. The
power of early habit only could account for it. A distinction to which they had been born gave no pride.
Their superiority of abode was no more to them than
their superiority of person.

Many were the inquiries she was eager to make of
Miss Tilney; but so active were her thoughts, that when
these inquiries were answered, she was hardly more
assured than before, of Northanger Abbey having been
a richly-endowed convent at the time of the Reforma-
tion, of its having fallen into the hands of an ancestor
of the Tilneys on its dissolution, of a large portion of
the ancient building still making a part of the present
dwelling although the rest was decayed, or of its standing low in a valley, sheltered from the north and east
by rising woods of oak.

CHAPTER III

WITH A mind thus full of happiness, Catherine was hardly aware that two or three days had passed away, without her seeing Isabella for more than a few minutes together. She began first to be sensible of this, and to sigh for her conversation, as she walked along the Pump-room one morning, by Mrs. Allen's side, without any thing to say or to hear; and scarcely had she felt a five minutes' longing of friendship, before the object of it appeared, and inviting her to a secret conference, led the way to a seat. 'This is my favourite place,' said she, as they sat down on a bench between the doors, which commanded a tolerable view of every body entering at either, 'it is so out of the way.'

Catherine, observing that Isabella's eyes were continually bent towards one door or the other, as in eager expectation, and remembering how often she had been falsely accused of being arch, thought the present a fine opportunity for being really so; and therefore gaily said, 'Do not be uneasy, Isabella. James will soon be here.'

'Psha! my dear creature,' she replied, 'do not think me such a simpleton as to be always wanting to confine him to my elbow. It would be hideous to be always together; we should be the jest of the place. And so you are going to Northanger! – I am amazingly glad of it. It is one of the finest old places in England, I understand. I shall depend upon a most particular description of it.'

'You shall certainly have the best in my power to give. But who are you looking for? Are your sisters coming?'

'I am not looking for any body. One's eyes must be somewhere, and you know what a foolish trick I have of fixing mine, when my thoughts are an hundred miles off. I am amazingly absent; I believe I am the most absent creature in the world. Tilney says it is always the case with minds of a certain stamp.'

'But I thought, Isabella, you had something in particular to tell me?'

'Oh! yes, and so I have. But here is a proof of what I was saying. My poor head! I had quite forgot it. Well, the thing is this, I have just had a letter from John; – you can guess the contents.'

'No, indeed, I cannot.'

'My sweet love, do not be so abominably affected. What can he write about, but yourself? You know he is over head and ears in love with you.'

'With *me*, dear Isabella!'

'Nay, my sweetest Catherine, this is being quite absurd! Modesty, and all that, is very well in its way, but really a little common honesty is sometimes quite as becoming. I have no idea of being so overstrained! It is fishing for compliments. His attentions were such as a child must have noticed. And it was but half an hour before he left Bath, that you gave him the most positive encouragement. He says so in this letter, says that he as good as made you an offer, and that you received his advances in the kindest way; and now he wants me to urge his suit, and say all manner of pretty things to you. So it is in vain to affect ignorance.'

Catherine, with all the earnestness of truth, expressed her astonishment at such a charge, protesting her innocence of every thought of Mr. Thorpe's being in love with her, and the consequent impossibility of her having ever intended to encourage him. 'As to any attentions on his side, I do declare, upon my honour, I never was sensible of them for a moment – except just his asking me to dance the first day of his coming. And as to making me an offer, or any thing like it, there must be some unaccountable mistake. I could not have misunderstood a thing of that kind, you know! – and, as I ever wish to be believed, I solemnly protest that no syllable of such a nature ever passed between us. The last half hour before he went away! – It must be all and completely a mistake – for I did not see him once that whole morning.'

'But *that* you certainly did, for you spent the whole morning in Edgar's Buildings – it was the day your father's consent came – and I am pretty sure that you and John were alone in the parlour, some time before you left the house.'

'Are you? – Well, if you say it, it was so, I dare say – but for the life of me, I cannot recollect it. – I *do* remember now being with you, and seeing him as well as the rest – but that we were ever alone for five minutes – However, it is not worth arguing about, for whatever might pass on his side, you must be convinced, by my having no recollection of it, that I never thought, nor expected, nor wished for any thing of the kind from him. I am excessively concerned that he should have any regard for me – but indeed it has been quite unintentional on my side, I never had the smallest idea of it. Pray undeceive him as soon as you can, and tell him I beg his pardon – that is – I do not know what I ought to say – but make him understand what I mean, in the properest way. I would not speak disrespectfully of a brother of your's, Isabella, I am sure; but you know very well that if I could think of one man more than another – *he* is not the person.' Isabella was silent. 'My dear friend, you must not be angry with me. I cannot suppose your brother cares so very much about me. And, you know, we shall still be sisters.'

'Yes, yes,' (with a blush) 'there are more ways than one of our being sisters. – But where am I wandering to? – Well, my dear Catherine, the case seems to be, that you are determined against poor John – is not it so?'

'I certainly cannot return his affection, and as certainly never meant to encourage it.'

'Since that is the case, I am sure I shall not tease you any further. John desired me to speak to you on the subject, and therefore I have. But I confess, as soon as I read his letter, I thought it a very foolish, imprudent business, and not likely to promote the good of either; for what were you to live upon, supposing you came together? You have both of you something to be sure, but it is not a trifle that will support a family now-a-days; and after all that romancers may say, there is no doing without money. I only wonder John could think of it; he could not have received my last.'

'You *do* acquit me then of any thing wrong? – You are convinced that I never meant to deceive your brother, never suspected him of liking me till this moment?'

'Oh! as to that,' answered Isabella laughingly, 'I do not pretend to determine what your thoughts and designs in time past may have been. All that is best known to yourself. A little harmless flirtation or so will occur, and one is often drawn on to give more encouragement than one wishes to stand by. But you may be assured that I am the last person in the world to judge you severely. All those things should be allowed for in youth and high spirits. What one means one day, you know, one may not mean the next. Circumstances change, opinions alter.'

'But my opinion of your brother never did alter; it was always the same. You are describing what never happened.'

'My dearest Catherine,' continued the other without at all listening to her, 'I would not for all the world be the means of hurrying you into an engagement before you knew what you were about. I do not think any thing would justify me in wishing you to sacrifice all your happiness merely to oblige my brother, because he is my brother, and who perhaps after all, you know, might be just as happy without you, for people seldom know what they would be at, young men especially, they are so amazingly changeable and inconstant. What I say is, why should a brother's happiness be dearer to me than a friend's? You know I carry my notions of friendship pretty high. But, above all things, my dear Catherine, do not be in a hurry. Take my word for it, that if you are in too great a hurry, you will certainly live to repent it. Tilney says, there is nothing people are so often deceived in, as the state of their own affections, and I believe he is very right. Ah! here he comes; never mind, he will not see us, I am sure.'

Catherine, looking up, perceived Captain Tilney; and Isabella, earnestly fixing her eye on him as she spoke, soon caught his notice. He approached immediately, and took the seat to which her movements invited him. His first address made Catherine start. Though spoken low, she could distinguish, 'What! always to be watched, in person or by proxy!'

'Psha, nonsense!' was Isabella's answer in the same half whisper. 'Why do you put such things into my head? If I could believe it – my spirit, you know, is pretty independent.'

'I wish your heart were independent. That would be enough for me.'

'My heart, indeed! What can you have to do with hearts? You men have none of you any hearts.'

'If we have not hearts, we have eyes; and they give us torment enough.'

'Do they? I am sorry for it; I am sorry they find any thing so disagreeable in me. I will look another way. I hope this pleases you, (turning her back on him,) I hope your eyes are not tormented now.'

'Never more so; for the edge of a blooming cheek is still in view – at once too much and too little.'

Catherine heard all this, and quite out of counten-

ance could listen no longer. Amazed that Isabella could
endure it, and jealous for her brother, she rose up, and
saying she should join Mrs. Allen, proposed their walking. But for this Isabella shewed no inclination. She
was so amazingly tired, and it was so odious to parade
about the Pump-room; and if she moved from her seat
she should miss her sisters, she was expecting her
sisters every moment; so that her dearest Catherine
must excuse her, and must sit quietly down again. But
Catherine could be stubborn too; and Mrs. Allen just
then coming up to propose their returning home, she
joined her and walked out of the Pump-room, leaving
Isabella still sitting with Captain Tilney. With much
uneasiness did she thus leave them. It seemed to her
that Captain Tilney was falling in love with Isabella,
and Isabella unconsciously encouraging him; unconsciously it must be, for Isabella's attachment to James
was as certain and well acknowledged as her engagement. To doubt her truth or good intentions was
impossible; and yet, during the whole of their conversation her manner had been odd. She wished Isabella
had talked more like her usual self, and not so much
about money; and had not looked so well pleased at
the sight of Captain Tilney. How strange that she
should not perceive his admiration! Catherine longed
to give her a hint of it, to put her on her guard, and
prevent all the pain which her too lively behaviour
might otherwise create both for him and her brother.

The compliment of John Thorpe's affection did not
make amends for this thoughtlessness in his sister. She
was almost as far from believing as from wishing it to
be sincere; for she had not forgotten that he could
mistake, and his assertion of the offer and of her encouragement convinced her that his mistakes could
sometimes be very egregious. In vanity therefore she
gained but little, her chief profit was in wonder. That
he should think it worth his while to fancy himself in

love with her, was a matter of lively astonishment. Isabella talked of his attentions; *she* had never been sensible of any; but Isabella had said many things which she hoped had been spoken in haste, and would never be said again; and upon this she was glad to rest altogether for present ease and comfort.

CHAPTER IV

A FEW days passed away, and Catherine, though not allowing herself to suspect her friend, could not help watching her closely. The result of her observations was not agreeable. Isabella seemed an altered creature. When she saw her indeed surrounded only by their immediate friends in Edgar's Buildings or Pulteney-street, her change of manners was so trifling that, had it gone no farther, it might have passed unnoticed. A something of languid indifference, or of that boasted absence of mind which Catherine had never heard of before, would occasionally come across her; but had nothing worse appeared, *that* might only have spread a new grace and inspired a warmer interest. But when Catherine saw her in public, admitting Captain Tilney's attentions as readily as they were offered, and allowing him almost an equal share with James in her notice and smiles, the alteration became too positive to be past over. What could be meant by such unsteady conduct, what her friend could be at, was beyond her comprehension. Isabella could not be aware of the pain she was inflicting; but it was a degree of wilful thoughtlessness which Catherine could not but resent. James was the sufferer. She saw him grave and uneasy; and however careless of his present comfort the woman might be who had given him her heart, to *her* it was always an object. For poor Captain Tilney too she was greatly concerned. Though his looks did not please her, his name was a passport to her good will, and she thought with sincere compassion of his approaching disappointment; for, in spite of what she had believed herself to overhear in the Pump-room, his behaviour was so incompatible with a knowledge of Isabella's engagement, that she could not, upon reflection, imagine him aware of it. He might be jealous of her brother as a rival, but if more had seemed implied, the fault must have been in her misapprehension. She wished, by a gentle remonstrance, to remind Isabella of her situation, and make her aware of this double unkindness; but for remonstrance, either opportunity or comprehension was always against her. If able to suggest a hint, Isabella could never understand it. In this distress, the intended departure of the Tilney family became her chief consolation; their journey into Gloucestershire was to take place within a few days, and Captain Tilney's removal would at least restore peace to every heart but his own. But Captain Tilney had at present no intention of removing; he was not to be of the party to Northanger, he was to continue at Bath. When Catherine knew this, her resolution was directly made. She spoke to Henry Tilney on the subject, regretting his brother's evident partiality for Miss Thorpe, and entreating him to make known her prior engagement.

'My brother does know it,' was Henry's answer.

'Does he? – then why does he stay here?'

He made no reply, and was beginning to talk of something else; but she eagerly continued, 'Why do not you persuade him to go away? The longer he stays, the worse it will be for him at last. Pray advise him for his own sake, and for every body's sake, to leave Bath directly. Absence will in time make him comfortable again; but he can have no hope here, and it is only staying to be miserable.' Henry smiled and said, 'I am sure my brother would not wish to do that.'

'Then you will persuade him to go away?'

'Persuasion is not at command; but pardon me, if I cannot even endeavour to persuade him. I have myself told him that Miss Thorpe is engaged. He knows what he is about, and must be his own master.'

'No, he does not know what he is about,' cried Catherine; 'he does not know the pain he is giving my brother. Not that James has ever told me so, but I am sure he is very uncomfortable.'

'And are you sure it is my brother's doing?'

'Yes, very sure.'

'Is it my brother's attentions to Miss Thorpe, or Miss Thorpe's admission of them, that gives the pain?'

'Is not it the same thing?'

'I think Mr. Morland would acknowledge a difference. No man is offended by another man's admiration of the woman he loves; it is the woman only who can make it a torment.'

Catherine blushed for her friend, and said, 'Isabella is wrong. But I am sure she cannot mean to torment, for she is very much attached to my brother. She has been in love with him ever since they first met, and while my father's consent was uncertain, she fretted herself almost into a fever. You know she must be attached to him.'

'I understand: she is in love with James, and flirts with Frederick.'

'Oh! no, not flirts. A woman in love with one man cannot flirt with another.'

'It is probable that she will neither love so well, nor flirt so well, as she might do either singly. The gentlemen must each give up a little.'

After a short pause, Catherine resumed with 'Then you do not believe Isabella so very much attached to my brother?'

'I can have no opinion on that subject.'

'But what can your brother mean? If he knows her engagement, what can he mean by his behaviour?'

'You are a very close questioner.'

'Am I? – I only ask what I want to be told.'

'But do you only ask what I can be expected to tell?'

'Yes, I think so; for you must know your brother's heart.'

'My brother's heart, as you term it, on the present occasion, I assure you I can only guess at.'

'Well?'

'Well! – Nay, if it is to be guess-work, let us all guess for ourselves. To be guided by second-hand conjecture is pitiful. The premises are before you. My brother is a lively, and perhaps sometimes a thoughtless young man; he has had about a week's acquaintance with your friend, and he has known her engagement almost as long as he has known her.'

'Well,' said Catherine, after some moments' consideration, '*you* may be able to guess at your brother's intentions from all this; but I am sure I cannot. But is not your father uncomfortable about it? – Does not he want Captain Tilney to go away? – Sure, if your father were to speak to him, he would go.'

'My dear Miss Morland,' said Henry, 'in this amiable solicitude for your brother's comfort, may you not be a little mistaken? Are you not carried a little too far? Would he thank you, either on his own account or Miss Thorpe's, for supposing that her affection, or at least her good-behaviour, is only to be secured by her seeing nothing of Captain Tilney? Is he safe only in solitude? – or, is her heart constant to him only when unsolicited by any one else? – He cannot think this – and you may be sure that he would not have you think it. I will not say, "Do not be uneasy," because I know that you are so, at this moment; but be as little uneasy as you can. You have no doubt of the mutual attachment of your brother and your friend; depend upon it therefore, that real jealousy never can exist between them; depend upon it that no disagreement between them can be of any duration. Their hearts are open to each other, as neither heart can be to you; they know exactly what is required and what can be borne; and you may be certain, that one will never tease the other beyond what is known to be pleasant.'

Perceiving her still to look doubtful and grave, he added, 'Though Frederick does not leave Bath with us, he will probably remain but a very short time, perhaps only a few days behind us. His leave of absence will soon expire, and he must return to his regiment. – And what will then be their acquaintance? – The mess-room will drink Isabella Thorpe for a fortnight, and she will laugh with your brother over poor Tilney's passion for a month.'

Catherine would contend no longer against comfort. She had resisted its approaches during the whole length of a speech, but it now carried her captive. Henry Tilney must know best. She blamed herself for the extent of her fears, and resolved never to think so seriously on the subject again.

Her resolution was supported by Isabella's behaviour in their parting interview. The Thorpes spent the last evening of Catherine's stay in Pulteney-street, and nothing passed between the lovers to excite her uneasiness, or make her quit them in apprehension. James was in excellent spirits, and Isabella most engagingly placid. Her tenderness for her friend seemed rather the first feeling of her heart; but that at such a moment was allowable; and once she gave her lover a flat contradiction, and once she drew back her hand; but Catherine remembered Henry's instructions, and placed it all to judicious affection. The embraces, tears, and promises of the parting fair ones may be fancied.

CHAPTER V

MR. AND Mrs. Allen were sorry to lose their young friend, whose good-humour and cheerfulness had made her a valuable companion, and in the promotion of whose enjoyment their own had been gently increased. Her happiness in going with Miss Tilney, however, prevented their wishing it otherwise; and, as they were to remain only one more week in Bath themselves, her quitting them now would not long be felt. Mr. Allen attended her to Milsom-street, where she was to breakfast, and saw her seated with the kindest welcome among her new friends; but so great was her agitation in finding herself as one of the family, and so fearful was she of not doing exactly what was right, and of not being able to preserve their good opinion, that, in the embarrassment of the first five minutes, she could almost have wished to return with him to Pulteney-street.

Miss Tilney's manners and Henry's smile soon did away some of her unpleasant feelings; but still she was far from being at ease; nor could the incessant attentions of the General himself entirely reassure her. Nay, perverse as it seemed, she doubted whether she might not have felt less, had she been less attended to. His anxiety for her comfort – his continual solicitations that she would eat, and his often-expressed fears of her seeing nothing to her taste – though never in her life before had she beheld half such variety on a breakfast-table – made it impossible for her to forget for a moment that she was a visitor. She felt utterly unworthy of such respect, and knew not how to reply to it. Her tranquillity was not improved by the General's impatience for the appearance of his eldest son, nor by the displeasure he expressed at his laziness when Captain

Tilney at last came down. She was quite pained by the severity of his father's reproof, which seemed disproportionate to the offence; and much was her concern increased, when she found herself the principal cause of the lecture; and that his tardiness was chiefly resented from being disrespectful to her. This was placing her in a very uncomfortable situation, and she felt great compassion for Captain Tilney, without being able to hope for his good-will.

He listened to his father in silence, and attempted not any defence, which confirmed her in fearing, that the inquietude of his mind, on Isabella's account, might, by keeping him long sleepless, have been the real cause of his rising late. – It was the first time of her being decidedly in his company, and she had hoped to be now able to form her opinion of him; but she scarcely heard his voice while his father remained in the room; and even afterwards, so much were his spirits affected, she could distinguish nothing but these words, in a whisper to Eleanor, 'How glad I shall be when you are all off.'

The bustle of going was not pleasant. – The clock struck ten while the trunks were carrying down, and the General had fixed to be out of Milsom-street by that hour. His great coat, instead of being brought for him to put on directly, was spread out in the curricle in which he was to accompany his son. The middle seat of the chaise was not drawn out, though there were three people to go in it, and his daughter's maid had so crowded it with parcels, that Miss Morland would not have room to sit; and, so much was he influenced by this apprehension when he handed her in, that she had some difficulty in saving her own new writing-desk from being thrown out into the street. – At last, however, the door was closed upon the three females, and they set off at the sober pace in which the handsome, highly-fed four horses of a gentleman usually perform a journey of thirty miles: such was the distance of Northanger from Bath, to be now divided into two equal stages. Catherine's spirits revived as they drove from the door; for with Miss Tilney she felt no restraint; and, with the interest of a road entirely new to her, of an abbey before, and a curricle behind, she caught the last view of Bath without any regret, and met with every mile-stone before she expected it. The tediousness of a two hours' bait at Petty-France, in which there was nothing to be done but to eat without being hungry, and loiter about without any thing to see, next followed – and her admiration of the style in which they travelled, of the fashionable chaise-and-four – postilions handsomely liveried, rising so regularly in their stirrups, and numerous out-riders properly mounted, sunk a little under this consequent inconvenience. Had their party been perfectly agreeable, the delay would have been nothing; but General Tilney, though so charming a man, seemed always a check upon his children's spirits, and scarcely any thing was said but by himself; the observation of which, with his discontent at whatever the inn afforded, and his angry impatience at the waiters, made Catherine grow every moment more in awe of him, and appeared to lengthen the two hours into four. – At last, however, the order of release was given; and much was Catherine then surprised by the General's proposal of her taking his place in his son's curricle for the rest of the journey: – 'the day was fine, and he was anxious for her seeing as much of the country as possible.'

The remembrance of Mr. Allen's opinion, respecting young men's open carriages, made her blush at the mention of such a plan, and her first thought was to decline it; but her second was of greater deference for General Tilney's judgment; he could not propose any thing improper for her; and, in the course of a few minutes, she found herself with Henry in the curricle, as happy a being as ever existed. A very short trial convinced her that a curricle was the prettiest equipage in the world; the chaise-and-four wheeled off with some grandeur, to be sure, but it was a heavy and troublesome business, and she could not easily forget its having stopped two hours at Petty-France. Half the time would have been enough for the curricle, and so nimbly were the light horses disposed to move, that, had not the General chosen to have his own carriage lead the way, they could have passed it with ease in half a minute. But the merit of the curricle did not all belong to the horses; – Henry drove so well, – so quietly – without making any disturbance, without parading to her, or swearing at them; so different from the only gentleman-coachman whom it was in her power to compare him with! – And then his hat sat so well, and the innumerable capes of his great coat looked so becomingly important! – To be driven by him, next to being dancing with him, was certainly the greatest happiness in the world. In addition to every other delight, she had now that of listening to her own praise; of being thanked at least, on his sister's account, for her kindness in thus becoming her visitor; of hearing it ranked as real friendship, and described as creating real gratitude. His sister, he said, was uncomfortably circumstanced – she had no female companion – and, in the frequent absence of her father, was sometimes without any companion at all.

'But how can that be?' said Catherine, 'are not you with her?'

'Northanger is not more than half my home; I have an establishment at my own house in Woodston, which is nearly twenty miles from my father's, and some of my time is necessarily spent there.'

'How sorry you must be for that!'

'I am always sorry to leave Eleanor.'

'Yes; but besides your affection for her, you must be

so fond of the abbey! – After being used to such a home as the abbey, an ordinary parsonage-house must be very disagreeable.'

He smiled, and said, 'You have formed a very favourable idea of the abbey.'

'To be sure I have. Is not it a fine old place, just like what one reads about?'

'And are you prepared to encounter all the horrors that a building such as "what one reads about" may produce? – Have you a stout heart? – Nerves fit for sliding pannels and tapestry?'

'Oh! yes – I do not think I should be easily frightened, because there would be so many people in the house – and besides, it has never been uninhabited and left deserted for years, and then the family come back to it unawares, without giving any notice, as generally happens.'

'No, certainly. – We shall not have to explore our way into a hall dimly lighted by the expiring embers of a wood fire – nor be obliged to spread our beds on the floor of a room without windows, doors, or furniture. But you must be aware that when a young lady is (by whatever means) introduced into a dwelling of this kind, she is always lodged apart from the rest of the family. While they snugly repair to their own end of the house, she is formally conducted by Dorothy the ancient housekeeper up a different staircase, and along many gloomy passages, into an apartment never used since some cousin or kin died in it about twenty years before. Can you stand such a ceremony as this? Will not your mind misgive you, when you find yourself in this gloomy chamber – too lofty and extensive for you, with only the feeble rays of a single lamp to take in its size – its walls hung with tapestry exhibiting figures as large as life, and the bed, of dark green stuff or purple velvet, presenting even a funereal appearance. Will not your heart sink within you?'

'Oh! but this will not happen to me, I am sure.'

'How fearfully will you examine the furniture of your apartment! – And what will you discern? – Not tables, toilettes, wardrobes, or drawers, but on one side perhaps the remains of a broken lute, on the other a ponderous chest which no efforts can open, and over the fire-place the portrait of some handsome warrior, whose features will so incomprehensibly strike you, that you will not be able to withdraw your eyes from it. Dorothy meanwhile, no less struck by your appearance, gazes on you in great agitation, and drops a few unintelligible hints. To raise your spirits, moreover, she gives you reason to suppose that the part of the abbey you inhabit is undoubtedly haunted, and informs you that you will not have a single domestic within call. With this parting cordial she curtseys off – you listen to the sound of her receding footsteps as long as the last echo can reach you – and when, with fainting spirits, you attempt to fasten your door, you discover, with increased alarm, that it has no lock.'

'Oh! Mr. Tilney, how frightful! – This is just like a book! – But it cannot really happen to me. I am sure your housekeeper is not really Dorothy. – Well, what then?'

'Nothing further to alarm perhaps may occur the first night. After surmounting your *unconquerable* horror of the bed, you will retire to rest, and get a few hours' unquiet slumber. But on the second, or at farthest the *third* night after your arrival, you will probably have a violent storm. Peals of thunder so loud as to seem to shake the edifice to its foundation will roll round the neighbouring mountains – and during the frightful gusts of wind which accompany it, you will probably think you discern (for your lamp is not extinguished) one part of the hanging more violently agitated than the rest. Unable of course to repress your curiosity in so favourable a moment for indulging it, you will instantly arise, and throwing your dressing-gown around you, proceed to examine this mystery. After a very short search, you will discover a division in the tapestry so artfully constructed as to defy the minutest inspection, and on opening it, a door will immediately appear – which door being only secured by massy bars and a padlock, you will, after a few efforts, succeed in opening, – and, with your lamp in your hand, will pass through it into a small vaulted room.'

'No, indeed; I should be too much frightened to do any such thing.'

'What! not when Dorothy has given you to understand that there is a secret subterraneous communication between your apartment and the chapel of St. Anthony, scarcely two miles off – Could you shrink from so simple an adventure? No, no, you will proceed into this small vaulted room, and through this into several others, without perceiving any thing very remarkable in either. In one perhaps there may be a dagger, in another a few drops of blood, and in a third the remains of some instrument of torture; but there being nothing in all this out of the common way, and your lamp being nearly exhausted, you will return towards your own apartment. In repassing through the small vaulted room, however, your eyes will be attracted towards a large, old-fashioned cabinet of ebony and gold, which, though narrowly examining the furniture before, you had passed unnoticed. Impelled by an irresistible presentiment, you will eagerly advance to it, unlock its folding doors, and search into every drawer; – but for some time without discovering any thing of importance – perhaps nothing but a considerable hoard of diamonds. At last, however, by touching a secret spring, an inner compartment will open – a roll of paper appears: – you seize it – it contains many sheets of manuscript – you hasten with the precious treasure into your own chamber, but scarcely have you been able to decipher "Oh! thou – whomsoever thou mayst be, into whose hands these memoirs of the wretched Matilda may fall" – when your lamp suddenly expires in the socket, and leaves you in total darkness.'

'Oh! no, no – do not say so. Well, go on.'

But Henry was too much amused by the interest he had raised, to be able to carry it farther; he could no longer command solemnity either of subject or voice, and was obliged to entreat her to use her own fancy in the perusal of Matilda's woes. Catherine, recollecting herself, grew ashamed of her eagerness, and began earnestly to assure him that her attention had been fixed without the smallest apprehension of really meeting with what he related. 'Miss Tilney, she was sure, would never put her into such a chamber as he had described! – She was not at all afraid.'

As they drew near the end of their journey, her impatience for a sight of the Abbey – for some time suspended by his conversation on subjects very different – returned in full force, and every bend in the road was expected with solemn awe to afford a glimpse of its massy walls of grey stone, rising amidst a grove of ancient oaks, with the last beams of the sun playing in beautiful splendour on its high Gothic windows. But so low did the building stand, that she found herself passing through the great gates of the lodge into the very grounds of Northanger, without having discerned even an antique chimney.

She knew not that she had any right to be surprised, but there was a something in this mode of approach which she certainly had not expected. To pass between lodges of a modern appearance, to find herself with such ease in the very precincts of the Abbey, and driven so rapidly along a smooth, level road of fine gravel, without obstacle, alarm or solemnity of any kind, struck her as odd and inconsistent. She was not long at leisure however for such considerations. A sud-

den scud of rain driving full in her face, made it impossible for her to observe any thing further, and fixed
all her thoughts on the welfare of her new straw bonnet: – and she was actually under the Abbey walls, was
springing, with Henry's assistance, from the carriage,
was beneath the shelter of the old porch, and had even
passed on to the hall, where her friend and the General
were waiting to welcome her, without feeling one awe-
ful foreboding of future misery to herself, or one moment's suspicion of any past scenes of horror being
acted within the solemn edifice. The breeze had not
seemed to waft the sighs of the murdered to her; it had
wafted nothing worse than a thick mizzling rain; and
having given a good shake to her habit, she was ready
to be shewn into the common drawing-room, and
capable of considering where she was.

An abbey! – yes, it was delightful to be really in an
abbey! – but she doubted, as she looked round the
room, whether any thing within her observation, would
have given her the consciousness. The furniture was in
all the profusion and elegance of modern taste. The
fire-place, where she had expected the ample width and
ponderous carving of former times, was contracted to
a Rumford, with slabs of plain though handsome
marble, and ornaments over it of the prettiest English
china. The windows, to which she looked with peculiar
dependence, from having heard the General talk of his
preserving them in their Gothic form with reverential
care, were yet less what her fancy had portrayed. To be
sure, the pointed arch was preserved – the form of
them was Gothic – they might be even casements – but
every pane was so large, so clear, so light! To an imagination which had hoped for the smallest divisions,
and the heaviest stone-work, for painted glass, dirt and
cobwebs, the difference was very distressing.

The General, perceiving how her eye was employed,
began to talk of the smallness of the room and

simplicity of the furniture, where every thing being for daily use, pretended only to comfort, &c.; flattering himself however that there were some apartments in the Abbey not unworthy her notice – and was proceeding to mention the costly gilding of one in particular, when taking out his watch, he stopped short to pronounce it with surprise within twenty minutes of five! This seemed the word of separation, and Catherine found herself hurried away by Miss Tilney in such a manner as convinced her that the strictest punctuality to the family hours would be expected at Northanger.

Returning through the large and lofty hall, they ascended a broad staircase of shining oak, which, after many flights and many landing-places, brought them upon a long wide gallery. On one side it had a range of doors, and it was lighted on the other by windows which Catherine had only time to discover looked into a quadrangle, before Miss Tilney led the way into a chamber, and scarcely staying to hope she would find it comfortable, left her with an anxious entreaty that she would make as little alteration as possible in her dress.

CHAPTER VI

A MOMENT'S glance was enough to satisfy Catherine that her apartment was very unlike the one which Henry had endeavoured to alarm her by the description of. – It was by no means unreasonably large, and contained neither tapestry nor velvet. – The walls were papered, the floor was carpeted; the windows were neither less perfect, nor more dim than those of the drawing-room below; the furniture, though not of the latest fashion, was handsome and comfortable, and the air of the room altogether far from uncheerful. Her heart instantaneously at ease on this point, she resolved to lose no time in particular examination of any thing, as she greatly dreaded disobliging the General by any delay. Her habit therefore was thrown off with all possible haste, and she was preparing to unpin the linen package, which the chaise-seat had conveyed for her immediate accommodation, when her eye suddenly fell on a large high chest, standing back in a deep recess on one side of the fire-place. The sight of it made her start; and, forgetting every thing else, she stood gazing on it in motionless wonder, while these thoughts crossed her: –

'This is strange indeed! I did not expect such a sight as this! – An immense heavy chest! – What can it hold? – Why should it be placed here? – Pushed back too, as if meant to be out of sight! – I will look into it – cost me what it may, I will look into it – and directly too – by day-light. – If I stay till evening my candle may go out.' She advanced and examined it closely: it was of cedar, curiously inlaid with some darker wood, and raised, about a foot from the ground, on a carved stand of the same. The lock was silver, though tarnished from age; at each end were the imperfect remains of handles also of silver, broken perhaps prematurely by some strange violence; and, on the centre of the lid, was a mysterious cypher, in the same metal. Catherine bent over it intently, but without being able to distinguish any thing with certainty. She could not, in whatever direction she took it, believe the last letter to be a *T*; and yet that it should be any thing else in that house was a circumstance to raise no common degree of astonishment. If not originally their's, by what strange events could it have fallen into the Tilney family?

Her fearful curiosity was every moment growing greater; and seizing, with trembling hands, the hasp of the lock, she resolved at all hazards to satisfy herself at least as to its contents. With difficulty, for something seemed to resist her efforts, she raised the lid a few inches; but at that moment a sudden knocking at the door of the room made her, starting, quit her hold, and the lid closed with alarming violence. This ill-timed intruder was Miss Tilney's maid, sent by her mistress to be of use to Miss Morland; and though Catherine immediately dismissed her, it recalled her to the sense of what she ought to be doing, and forced her, in spite of her anxious desire to penetrate this mystery, to proceed in her dressing without further delay. Her progress was not quick, for her thoughts and her eyes were still bent on the object so well calculated to interest and alarm; and though she dared not waste a moment upon a second attempt, she could not remain many paces from the chest. At length, however, having slipped one arm into her gown, her toilette seemed so nearly finished, that the impatience of her curiosity might safely be indulged. One moment surely might be spared; and, so desperate should be the exertion of her strength, that, unless secured by supernatural means, the lid in one moment should be thrown back. With this spirit she sprang forward, and her confidence did not deceive her. Her resolute effort threw back the lid, and gave to her astonished eyes the view of a white cotton counterpane, properly folded, reposing at one end of the chest in undisputed possession!

She was gazing on it with the first blush of surprise, when Miss Tilney, anxious for her friend's being ready, entered the room, and to the rising shame of having harboured for some minutes an absurd expectation, was then added the shame of being caught in so idle a search. 'That is a curious old chest, is not it?' said Miss Tilney, as Catherine hastily closed it and turned away to the glass. 'It is impossible to say how many generations it has been here. How it came to be first put in this room I know not, but I have not had it moved, because I thought it might sometimes be of use in holding hats and bonnets. The worst of it is that its weight makes it difficult to open. In that corner, however, it is at least out of the way.'

Catherine had no leisure for speech, being at once blushing, tying her gown, and forming wise resolutions with the most violent dispatch. Miss Tilney gently hinted her fear of being late; and in half a minute they ran down stairs together, in an alarm not wholly unfounded, for General Tilney was pacing the drawing-room, his watch in his hand, and having, on the very instant of their entering, pulled the bell with violence, ordered 'Dinner to be on table *directly*!'

Catherine trembled at the emphasis with which he spoke, and sat pale and breathless, in a most humble mood, concerned for his children, and detesting old chests; and the General recovering his politeness as he looked at her, spent the rest of his time in scolding his daughter, for so foolishly hurrying her fair friend, who was absolutely out of breath from haste, when there was not the least occasion for hurry in the world: but Catherine could not at all get over the double distress of having involved her friend in a lecture and been a great simpleton herself, till they were happily seated at the dinner-table, when the General's complacent smiles, and a good appetite of her own, restored her to peace. The dining-parlour was a noble room, suitable in its dimensions to a much larger drawing-room than the one in common use, and fitted up in a style of luxury and expense which was almost lost on the unpractised eye of Catherine, who saw little more than its spaciousness and the number of their attendants. Of the former, she spoke aloud her admiration; and the General, with a very gracious countenance, acknowledged that it was by no means an ill-sized room; and further confessed, that, though as careless on such subjects as most people, he did look upon a tolerably large eating-room as one of the necessaries of life; he supposed, however, 'that she must have been used to much better sized apartments at Mr. Allen's?'

'No, indeed,' was Catherine's honest assurance; 'Mr. Allen's dining-parlour was not more than half as large:' and she had never seen so large a room as this in her life. The General's good-humour increased. – Why, as he *had* such rooms, he thought it would be simple not to make use of them; but, upon his honour, he believed there might be more comfort in rooms of only half their size. Mr. Allen's house, he was sure, must be exactly of the true size for rational happiness.

The evening passed without any further disturbance, and, in the occasional absence of General Tilney, with much positive cheerfulness. It was only in his presence that Catherine felt the smallest fatigue from her journey; and even then, even in moments of languor or restraint, a sense of general happiness preponderated, and she could think of her friends in Bath without one wish of being with them.

The night was stormy; the wind had been rising at intervals the whole afternoon; and by the time the party broke up, it blew and rained violently. Catherine, as she crossed the hall, listened to the tempest with sensations of awe; and, when she heard it rage round a corner of the ancient building and close with sudden fury a distant door, felt for the first time that she was really in an abbey. – Yes, these were characteristic sounds; – they brought to her recollection a countless variety of dreadful situations and horrid scenes, which such buildings had witnessed, and such storms ushered in; and most heartily did she rejoice in the happier circumstances attending her entrance within walls so solemn! – *She* had nothing to dread from midnight assassins or drunken gallants. Henry had certainly been only in jest in what he had told her that morning. In a house so furnished, and so guarded, she could have nothing to explore or to suffer; and might go to her bedroom as securely as if it had been her own chamber at Fullerton. Thus wisely fortifying her mind, as she proceeded up stairs, she was enabled, especially on perceiving that Miss Tilney slept only two doors from her, to enter her room with a tolerably stout heart; and her spirits were immediately assisted by the cheerful blaze of a wood fire. 'How much better is this,' said she, as she walked to the fender – 'how much better to find a fire ready lit, than to have to wait shivering in the cold till all the family are in bed, as so many poor girls have been obliged to do, and then to have a faithful old servant frightening one by coming in with a faggot! How glad I am that Northanger is what it is! If it had been like some other places, I do not know that, in such a night as this, I could have answered for my courage: – but now, to be sure, there is nothing to alarm one.'

She looked round the room. The window curtains seemed in motion. It could be nothing but the violence of the wind penetrating through the divisions of the shutters; and she stept boldly forward, carelessly humming a tune, to assure herself of its being so, peeped courageously behind each curtain, saw nothing on either low window seat to scare her, and on placing a hand against the shutter, felt the strongest conviction of the wind's force. A glance at the old chest, as she turned away from this examination, was not without its use; she scorned the causeless fears of an idle fancy, and began with a most happy indifference to prepare herself for bed. 'She should take her time; she should not hurry herself; she did not care if she were the last person up in the house. But she would not make up her fire; *that* would seem cowardly, as if she wished for the protection of light after she were in bed.' The fire therefore died away, and Catherine, having spent the best part of an hour in her arrangements, was beginning to think of stepping into bed, when, on giving a parting glance round the room, she was struck by the appearance of a high, old-fashioned black cabinet, which, though in a situation conspicuous enough, had never caught her notice before. Henry's words, his description of the ebony cabinet which was to escape her observation at first, immediately rushed across her; and though there could be nothing really in it, there was something whimsical, it was certainly a very remarkable coincidence! She took her candle and looked closely at the cabinet. It was not absolutely ebony and gold; but it was Japan, black and yellow Japan of the handsomest kind; and as she held her candle, the yellow had very much the effect of gold. The key was in the door, and she had a strange fancy to look into it; not however with the smallest expectation of finding any thing, but it was so very odd, after what Henry had said. In short, she could not sleep till she had examined it. So, placing the candle with great caution on a chair, she seized the key with a very tremulous hand and tried to turn it; but it resisted her utmost strength. Alarmed, but not discouraged, she tried it another way; a bolt flew, and she believed herself successful; but how strangely mysterious! – the door was still immoveable. She paused a moment in breathless wonder. The wind roared down the chimney, the rain beat in torrents against the windows, and every thing seemed to speak the awfulness of her situation. To retire to bed, however, unsatisfied on such a point, would be vain, since sleep must be impossible with the consciousness of a cabinet so mysteriously closed in her immediate vicinity. Again therefore she applied herself to the key, and after moving it in every possible way for some instants with the determined celerity of hope's last effort, the door suddenly yielded to her hand: her heart leaped with exultation at such a victory, and having thrown open each folding door, the second being secured only by bolts of less wonderful construction than the lock, though in that her eye could not discern any thing unusual, a double range of small drawers appeared in view, with some larger drawers above and below them; and in the centre, a small door, closed also with a lock and key, secured in all probability a cavity of importance.

Catherine's heart beat quick, but her courage did not fail her. With a cheek flushed by hope, and an eye straining with curiosity, her fingers grasped the handle of a drawer and drew it forth. It was entirely empty. With less alarm and greater eagerness she seized a second, a third, a fourth; each was equally empty. Not one was left unsearched, and in not one was any thing found. Well read in the art of concealing a treasure, the possibility of false linings to the drawers did not escape her, and she felt round each with anxious acuteness in vain. The place in the middle alone remained now unexplored; and though she had 'never from the first had the smallest idea of finding any thing in any part of the cabinet, and was not in the least disappointed at her ill success thus far, it would be foolish not to examine it thoroughly while she was about it.' It was some time however before she could unfasten the door, the same difficulty occurring in the management of this inner lock as of the outer; but at length it did open; and not vain, as hitherto, was her search; her quick eyes directly fell on a roll of paper pushed back into the further part of the cavity, apparently for concealment, and her feelings at that moment were indescribable. Her heart fluttered, her knees trembled, and her cheeks grew pale. She seized, with an unsteady hand, the precious manuscript, for half a glance sufficed to ascertain written characters; and while she acknowledged with awful sensations this striking exemplification of what Henry had foretold, resolved instantly to peruse every line before she attempted to rest.

The dimness of the light her candle emitted made her turn to it with alarm; but there was no danger of its sudden extinction, it had yet some hours to burn; and that she might not have any greater difficulty in distinguishing the writing than what its ancient date might occasion, she hastily snuffed it. Alas! it was snuffed and extinguished in one. A lamp could not have expired with more awful effect. Catherine, for a few moments, was motionless with horror. It was done completely; not a remnant of light in the wick could give hope to the rekindling breath. Darkness impenetrable and immoveable filled the room. A violent gust of wind, rising with sudden fury, added fresh horror to the moment. Catherine trembled from head to foot. In the pause which succeeded, a sound like receding footsteps and the closing of a distant door struck on her affrighted ear. Human nature could support no more. A cold sweat stood on her forehead, the manuscript fell from her hand, and groping her way to the bed, she jumped hastily in, and sought some suspension of agony by creeping far underneath the clothes. To close her eyes in sleep that night, she felt must be entirely out of the question. With a curiosity so justly awakened, and feelings in every way so agitated, repose must be absolutely impossible. The storm too abroad so dreadful! – She had not been used to feel alarm from wind, but now every blast seemed fraught with awful intelligence. The manuscript so wonderfully found, so wonderfully accomplishing the morning's prediction, how was it to be accounted for? – What could it contain? – to whom could it relate? – by what means could it have been so long concealed? – and how singularly strange that it should fall to her lot to discover it! Till she had made herself mistress of its contents, however, she could have neither repose nor comfort; and with the sun's first rays she was determined to peruse it. But many were the tedious hours which must yet intervene. She shuddered, tossed about in her bed, and envied every quiet sleeper. The storm still raged, and various were the noises, more terrific even than the wind, which struck at intervals on her startled ear. The very curtains of her bed seemed at one moment in motion, and at another the lock of her door was agitated, as if by the attempt of somebody to enter. Hollow murmurs seemed to creep along the gallery, and more than once her blood was chilled by the sound of distant moans. Hour after hour passed away, and the wearied Catherine had heard three proclaimed by all the clocks in the house, before the tempest subsided, or she unknowingly fell fast asleep.

CHAPTER VII

T HE HOUSEMAID'S folding back her window-shutters at eight o'clock the next day, was the sound which first roused Catherine; and she opened her eyes, wondering that they could ever have been closed, on objects of cheerfulness; her fire was already burning, and a bright morning had succeeded the tempest of the night. Instantaneously with the consciousness of existence, returned her recollection of the manuscript; and springing from the bed in the very moment of the maid's going away, she eagerly collected every scattered sheet which had burst from the roll on its falling to the ground, and flew back to enjoy the luxury of their perusal on her pillow. She now plainly saw that she must not expect a manuscript of equal length with the generality of what she had shuddered over in books, for the roll, seeming to consist entirely of small disjointed sheets, was altogether but of trifling size, and much less than she had supposed it to be at first.

Her greedy eye glanced rapidly over a page. She started at its import. Could it be possible, or did not her senses play her false? – An inventory of linen, in coarse and modern characters, seemed all that was before her! If the evidence of sight might be trusted, she held a washing-bill in her hand. She seized another sheet, and saw the same articles with little variation; a third, a fourth, and a fifth presented nothing new. Shirts, stockings, cravats and waistcoats faced her in each. Two others, penned by the same hand, marked an expenditure scarcely more interesting, in letters, hair-powder, shoe-string and breeches-ball. And the larger sheet, which had inclosed the rest, seemed by its first cramp line, 'To poultice chesnut mare,' – a farrier's bill! Such was the collection of papers, (left perhaps, as she could then suppose, by the negligence of a servant in the place whence she had taken them,) which had filled her with expectation and alarm, and robbed her of half her night's rest! She felt humbled to the dust. Could not the adventure of the chest have taught her wisdom? A corner of it catching her eye as she lay, seemed to rise up in judgment against her. Nothing could now be clearer than the absurdity of her recent fancies. To suppose that a manuscript of many generations back could have remained undiscovered in a room such as that, so modern, so habitable! – or that she should be the first to possess the skill of unlocking a cabinet, the key of which was open to all!

How could she have so imposed on herself? – Heaven forbid that Henry Tilney should ever know her folly! And it was in a great measure his own doing, for had not the cabinet appeared so exactly to agree with his description of her adventures, she should never have felt the smallest curiosity about it. This was the only comfort that occurred. Impatient to get rid of those hateful evidences of her folly, those detestable papers then scattered over the bed, she rose directly, and folding them up as nearly as possible in the same shape as before, returned them to the same spot within the cabinet, with a very hearty wish that no untoward accident might ever bring them forward again, to disgrace her even with herself.

Why the locks should have been so difficult to open however, was still something remarkable, for she could now manage them with perfect ease. In this there was surely something mysterious, and she indulged in the flattering suggestion for half a minute, till the possibility of the door's having been at first unlocked, and of being herself its fastener, darted into her head, and cost her another blush.

She got away as soon as she could from a room in which her conduct produced such unpleasant reflections, and found her way with all speed to the breakfast-parlour, as it had been pointed out to her by Miss Tilney the evening before. Henry was alone in it; and his immediate hope of her having been undisturbed by the tempest, with an arch reference to the character of the building they inhabited, was rather distressing. For the world would she not have her weakness suspected; and yet, unequal to an absolute falsehood, was constrained to acknowledge that the wind had kept her awake a little. 'But we have a charming morning after it,' she added, desiring to get rid of the subject; 'and storms and sleeplessness are nothing when they are over. What beautiful hyacinths! – I have just learnt to love a hyacinth.'

'And how might you learn? – By accident or argument?'

'Your sister taught me; I cannot tell how. Mrs. Allen used to take pains, year after year, to make me like them; but I never could, till I saw them the other day in Milsom-street; I am naturally indifferent about flowers.'

'But now you love a hyacinth. So much the better. You have gained a new source of enjoyment, and it is well to have as many holds upon happiness as possible. Besides, a taste for flowers is always desirable in your sex, as a means of getting you out of doors, and tempting you to more frequent exercise than you would otherwise take. And though the love of a hyacinth may be rather domestic, who can tell, the sentiment once raised, but you may in time come to love a rose?'

'But I do not want any such pursuit to get me out of doors. The pleasure of walking and breathing fresh air is enough for me, and in fine weather I am out more than half my time. – Mamma says, I am never within.'

'At any rate, however, I am pleased that you have learnt to love a hyacinth. The mere habit of learning to love is the thing; and a teachableness of disposition in a young lady is a great blessing. – Has my sister a pleasant mode of instruction?'

Catherine was saved the embarrassment of attempting an answer, by the entrance of the General, whose smiling compliments announced a happy state of mind, but whose gentle hint of sympathetic early rising did not advance her composure.

The elegance of the breakfast set forced itself on Catherine's notice when they were seated at table; and, luckily, it had been the General's choice. He was enchanted by her approbation of his taste, confessed it to be neat and simple, thought it right to encourage the manufacture of his country; and for his part, to his uncritical palate, the tea was as well flavoured from the clay of Staffordshire, as from that of Dresden or Sève. But this was quite an old set, purchased two years ago. The manufacture was much improved since that time; he had seen some beautiful specimens when last in town, and had he not been perfectly without vanity of that kind, might have been tempted to order a new set. He trusted, however, that an opportunity might ere long occur of selecting one – though not for himself. Catherine was probably the only one of the party who did not understand him.

Shortly after breakfast Henry left them for Wood-ston, where business required and would keep him two or three days. They all attended in the hall to see him mount his horse, and immediately on re-entering the breakfast-room, Catherine walked to a window in the hope of catching another glimpse of his figure. 'This is a somewhat heavy call upon your brother's fortitude,' observed the General to Eleanor. 'Woodston will make but a sombre appearance to-day.'

'Is it a pretty place?' asked Catherine.

'What say you, Eleanor? – speak your opinion, for ladies can best tell the taste of ladies in regard to places as well as men. I think it would be acknowledged by the most impartial eye to have many recommendations. The house stands among fine meadows facing the south-east, with an excellent kitchen-garden in the same as-pect; the walls surrounding which I built and stocked myself about ten years ago, for the benefit of my son. It is a family living, Miss Morland; and the property in the place being chiefly my own, you may believe I take care that it shall not be a bad one. Did Henry's income depend solely on this living, he would not be ill pro-vided for. Perhaps it may seem odd, that with only two younger children, I should think any profession neces-sary for him; and certainly there are moments when we could all wish him disengaged from every tie of busi-ness. But though I may not exactly make converts of you young ladies, I am sure your father, Miss Morland, would agree with me in thinking it expedient to give every young man some employment. The money is nothing, it is not an object, but employment is the thing. Even Frederick, my eldest son, you see, who will perhaps inherit as considerable a landed property as any private man in the county, has his profession.'

The imposing effect of this last argument was equal to his wishes. The silence of the lady proved it to be unanswerable.

Something had been said the evening before of her being shewn over the house, and he now offered himself as her conductor; and though Catherine had hoped to explore it accompanied only by his daughter, it was a proposal of too much happiness in itself, under any circumstances, not to be gladly accepted; for she had been already eighteen hours in the Abbey, and had seen only a few of its rooms. The netting-box, just leisurely drawn forth, was closed with joyful haste, and she was ready to attend him in a moment. 'And when they had gone over the house, he promised himself moreover the pleasure of accompanying her into the shrubberies and garden.' She curtsied her acquiescence. 'But perhaps it might be more agreeable to her to make those her first object. The weather was at present favourable, and at this time of year the uncertainty was very great of its continuing so. – Which would she prefer? He was equally at her service. – Which did his daughter think would most accord with her fair friend's wishes? – But he thought he could discern. – Yes, he certainly read in Miss Morland's eyes a judicious desire of making use of the present smiling weather. – But when did she judge amiss? – The Abbey would be always safe and dry. – He yielded implicitly, and would fetch his hat and attend them in a moment.' He left the room, and Catherine, with a disappointed, anxious face, began to speak of her unwillingness that he should be taking them out of doors against his own inclination, under a mistaken idea of pleasing her; but she was stopt by Miss Tilney's saying, with a little confusion, 'I believe it will be wisest to take the morning while it is so fine; and do not be uneasy on my father's account, he always walks out at this time of day.'

Catherine did not exactly know how this was to be understood. Why was Miss Tilney embarrassed? Could there be any unwillingness on the General's side to shew her over the Abbey? The proposal was his own.

And was not it odd that he should *always* take his walk so early? Neither her father nor Mr. Allen did so. It was certainly very provoking. She was all impatience to see the house, and had scarcely any curiosity about the grounds. If Henry had been with them indeed! – but now she should not know what was picturesque when she saw it. Such were her thoughts, but she kept them to herself, and put on her bonnet in patient discontent.

She was struck however, beyond her expectation, by the grandeur of the Abbey, as she saw it for the first time from the lawn. The whole building enclosed a large court; and two sides of the quadrangle, rich in Gothic ornaments, stood forward for admiration. The remainder was shut off by knolls of old trees, or lux-uriant plantations, and the steep woody hills rising be-hind to give it shelter, were beautiful even in the leafless month of March. Catherine had seen nothing to compare with it; and her feelings of delight were so strong, that without waiting for any better authority, she boldly burst forth in wonder and praise. The General listened with assenting gratitude; and it seemed as if his own estimation of Northanger had waited unfixed till that hour.

The kitchen-garden was to be next admired, and he led the way to it across a small portion of the park.

The number of acres contained in this garden was such as Catherine could not listen to without dismay, being more than double the extent of all Mr. Allen's, as well as her father's, including church-yard and or-chard. The walls seemed countless in number, endless in length; a village of hot-houses seemed to arise among them, and a whole parish to be at work within the inclosure. The General was flattered by her looks of surprise, which told him almost as plainly, as he soon forced her to tell him in words, that she had never seen any gardens at all equal to them before; – and he then modestly owned that, 'without any ambition of that sort himself – without any solicitude about it, – he did believe them to be unrivalled in the kingdom. If he had a hobby-horse, it was *that*. He loved a garden. Though careless enough in most matters of eating, he loved good fruit – or if he did not, his friends and children did. There were great vexations however attending such a garden as his. The utmost care could not always secure the most valuable fruits. The pinery had yielded only one hundred in the last year. Mr. Allen, he supposed, must feel these inconveniences as well as himself.'

'No, not at all. Mr. Allen did not care about the garden, and never went into it.'

With a triumphant smile of self-satisfaction, the General wished he could do the same, for he never entered his, without being vexed in some way or other, by its falling short of his plan.

'How were Mr. Allen's succession-houses worked?' describing the nature of his own as they entered them.

'Mr. Allen had only one small hot-house, which Mrs. Allen had the use of for her plants in winter, and there was a fire in it now and then.'

'He is a happy man!' said the General, with a look of very happy contempt.

Having taken her into every division, and led her under every wall, till she was heartily weary of seeing and wondering, he suffered the girls at last to seize the advantage of an outer door, and then expressing his wish to examine the effect of some recent alterations about the tea-house, proposed it as no unpleasant extension of their walk, if Miss Morland were not tired. 'But where are you going, Eleanor? – Why do you chuse that cold, damp path to it? Miss Morland will get wet. Our best way is across the park.'

'This is so favourite a walk of mine,' said Miss Tilney, 'that I always think it the best and nearest way. But perhaps it may be damp.'

It was a narrow winding path through a thick grove of old Scotch firs; and Catherine, struck by its gloomy aspect, and eager to enter it, could not, even by the General's disapprobation, be kept from stepping forward. He perceived her inclination, and having again urged the plea of health in vain, was too polite to make further opposition. He excused himself however from attending them: – 'The rays of the sun were not too cheerful for him, and he would meet them by another course.' He turned away; and Catherine was shocked to find how much her spirits were relieved by the separation. The shock however being less real than the relief, offered it no injury; and she began to talk with easy gaiety of the delightful melancholy which such a grove inspired.

'I am particularly fond of this spot,' said her companion, with a sigh. 'It was my mother's favourite walk.'

Catherine had never heard Mrs. Tilney mentioned in the family before, and the interest excited by this tender remembrance, shewed itself directly in her altered countenance, and in the attentive pause with which she waited for something more.

'I used to walk here so often with her!' added Eleanor; 'though I never loved it then, as I have loved it since. At that time indeed I used to wonder at her choice. But her memory endears it now.'

'And ought it not,' reflected Catherine, 'to endear it to her husband? Yet the General would not enter it.' Miss Tilney continuing silent, she ventured to say, 'Her death must have been a great affliction!'

'A great and increasing one,' replied the other, in a low voice. 'I was only thirteen when it happened; and though I felt my loss perhaps as strongly as one so young could feel it, I did not, I could not then know what a loss it was.' She stopped for a moment, and then added, with great firmness, 'I have no sister, you

know – and though Henry – though my brothers are
very affectionate, and Henry is a great deal here, which
I am most thankful for, it is impossible for me not to
be often solitary.'

'To be sure you must miss him very much.'

'A mother would have been always present. A
mother would have been a constant friend; her influence would have been beyond all other.'

'Was she a very charming woman? Was she handsome? Was there any picture of her in the Abbey? And
why had she been so partial to that grove? Was it from
dejection of spirits?' – were questions now eagerly
poured forth; – the first three received a ready affirma-
tive, the two others were passed by; and Catherine's
interest in the deceased Mrs. Tilney augmented with
every question, whether answered or not. Of her unhappiness in marriage, she felt persuaded. The General
certainly had been an unkind husband. He did not love
her walk: – could he therefore have loved her? And
besides, handsome as he was, there was a something in
the turn of his features which spoke his not having
behaved well to her.

'Her picture, I suppose,' blushing at the consum-
mate art of her own question, 'hangs in your father's
room?'

'No; – it was intended for the drawing-room; but my
father was dissatisfied with the painting, and for some
time it had no place. Soon after her death I obtained it
for my own, and hung it in my bed-chamber – where
I shall be happy to shew it you; – it is very like.' – Here
was another proof. A portrait – very like – of a de-
parted wife, not valued by the husband! – He must
have been dreadfully cruel to her!

Catherine attempted no longer to hide from herself
the nature of the feelings which, in spite of all his
attentions, he had previously excited; and what had
been terror and dislike before, was now absolute

aversion. Yes, aversion! His cruelty to such a charming woman made him odious to her. She had often read of such characters; characters, which Mr. Allen had been used to call unnatural and overdrawn; but here was proof positive of the contrary.

She had just settled this point, when the end of the path brought them directly upon the General; and in spite of all her virtuous indignation, she found herself again obliged to walk with him, listen to him, and even to smile when he smiled. Being no longer able however to receive pleasure from the surrounding objects, she soon began to walk with lassitude; the General perceived it, and with a concern for her health, which seemed to reproach her for her opinion of him, was most urgent for returning with his daughter to the house. He would follow them in a quarter of an hour. Again they parted – but Eleanor was called back in half a minute to receive a strict charge against taking her friend round the Abbey till his return. This second instance of his anxiety to delay what she so much wished for, struck Catherine as very remarkable.

CHAPTER VIII

A N HOUR passed away before the General came in, spent, on the part of his young guest, in no very favourable consideration of his character. – 'This lengthened absence, these solitary rambles, did not speak a mind at ease, or a conscience void of reproach.' – At length he appeared; and, whatever might have been the gloom of his meditations, he could still smile with *them*. Miss Tilney, understanding in part her friend's curiosity to see the house, soon revived the subject; and her father being, contrary to Catherine's expectations, unprovided with any pretence for further delay, beyond that of stopping five minutes to order refreshments to be in the room by their return, was at last ready to escort them.

They set forward; and, with a grandeur of air, a dignified step, which caught the eye, but could not shake the doubts of the well-read Catherine, he led the way across the hall, through the common drawing-room and one useless anti-chamber, into a room magnificent both in size and furniture – the real drawing-room, used only with company of consequence. – It was very noble – very grand – very charming! – was all that Catherine had to say, for her indiscriminating eye scarcely discerned the colour of the satin; and all minuteness of praise, all praise that had much meaning, was supplied by the General: the costliness or elegance of any room's fitting-up could be nothing to her; she cared for no furniture of a more modern date than the fifteenth century. When the General had satisfied his own curiosity, in a close examination of every well-known ornament, they proceeded into the library, an apartment, in its way, of equal magnificence, exhibiting a collection of books, on which an humble man might have looked with pride. – Catherine heard, admired, and wondered with more genuine feeling than before – gathered all that she could from this store-house of knowledge, by running over the titles of half a shelf, and was ready to proceed. But suites of apartments did not spring up with her wishes. – Large as was the building, she had already visited the greatest part; though, on being told that, with the addition of the kitchen, the six or seven rooms she had now seen surrounded three sides of the court, she could scarcely believe it, or overcome the suspicion of there being many chambers secreted. It was some relief, however, that they were to return to the rooms in common use, by passing through a few of less importance, looking into the court, which, with occasional passages, not wholly unintricate, connected the different sides; – and she was further soothed in her progress, by being told, that she was treading what had once been a cloister, having traces of cells pointed out, and observing several doors, that were neither opened nor explained to her; – by finding herself successively in a billiard-room, and in the General's private apartment, without comprehending their connexion, or being able to turn aright when she left them; and lastly, by passing through a dark little room, owning Henry's authority, and strewed with his litter of books, guns, and great coats.

From the dining-room of which, though already seen, and always to be seen at five o'clock, the General could not forego the pleasure of pacing out the length, for the more certain information of Miss Morland, as to what she neither doubted nor cared for, they proceeded by quick communication to the kitchen – the ancient kitchen of the convent, rich in the massy walls and smoke of former days, and in the stoves and hot closets of the present. The General's improving hand had not loitered here: every modern invention to facilitate the labour of the cooks, had been adopted within this, their spacious theatre; and, when the genius of others had failed, his own had often produced the perfection wanted. His endowments of this spot alone might at any time have placed him high among the benefactors of the convent.

With the walls of the kitchen ended all the antiquity of the Abbey; the fourth side of the quadrangle having, on account of its decaying state, been removed by the General's father, and the present erected in its place. All that was venerable ceased here. The new building was not only new, but declared itself to be so; intended only for offices, and enclosed behind by stable-yards, no uniformity of architecture had been thought necessary. Catherine could have raved at the hand which had swept away what must have been beyond the value of all the rest, for the purposes of mere domestic economy; and would willingly have been spared the mortification of a walk through scenes so fallen, had the General allowed it; but if he had a vanity, it was in the arrangement of his offices; and as he was convinced, that, to a mind like Miss Morland's, a view of the accommodations and comforts, by which the labours of her inferiors were softened, must always be gratifying, he should make no apology for leading her on. They took a slight survey of all; and Catherine was impressed, beyond her expectation, by their multiplicity and their convenience. The purposes for which a few shapeless pantries and a comfortless scullery were deemed sufficient at Fullerton, were here carried on in appropriate divisions, commodious and roomy. The number of servants continually appearing, did not strike her less than the number of their offices. Wherever they went, some pattened girl stopped to curtsey, or some footman in dishabille sneaked off. Yet this was an Abbey! – How inexpressibly different in these domestic arrangements from such as she had read about – from abbeys and castles, in which, though certainly larger than Northanger, all the dirty work of the house was to be done by two pair of female hands at the utmost. How they could get through it all, had often amazed Mrs. Allen; and, when Catherine saw what was necessary here, she began to be amazed herself.

They returned to the hall, that the chief stair-case might be ascended, and the beauty of its wood, and ornaments of rich carving might be pointed out: having gained the top, they turned in an opposite direction from the gallery in which her room lay, and shortly entered one on the same plan, but superior in length and breadth. She was here shewn successively into three large bed-chambers, with their dressing-rooms, most completely and handsomely fitted up; every thing that money and taste could do, to give comfort and elegance to apartments, had been bestowed on these; and, being furnished within the last five years, they were perfect in all that would be generally pleasing, and wanting in all that could give pleasure to Catherine. As they were surveying the last, the General, after slightly naming a few of the distinguished characters, by whom they had at times been honoured, turned with a smiling countenance to Catherine, and ventured to hope, that henceforward some of their earliest tenants might be 'our friends from Fullerton.' She felt the unexpected compliment, and deeply regretted the impossibility of thinking well of a man so kindly disposed towards herself, and so full of civility to all her family.

The gallery was terminated by folding doors, which Miss Tilney, advancing, had thrown open, and passed through, and seemed on the point of doing the same by the first door to the left, in another long reach of gallery, when the General, coming forwards, called her hastily, and, as Catherine thought, rather angrily back, demanding whither she were going? – And what was there more to be seen? – Had not Miss Morland already seen all that could be worth her notice? – And did she not suppose her friend might be glad of some refreshment after so much exercise? Miss Tilney drew back directly, and the heavy doors were closed upon the mortified Catherine, who, having seen, in a momentary glance beyond them, a narrower passage, more numerous openings, and symptoms of a winding stair-case, believed herself at last within the reach of something worth her notice; and felt, as she unwillingly paced back the gallery, that she would rather be allowed to examine that end of the house, than see all the finery of all the rest. – The General's evident desire of preventing such an examination was an additional stimulant. Something was certainly to be concealed; her fancy, though it had trespassed lately once or twice, could not mislead her here; and what that something

was, a short sentence of Miss Tilney's, as they followed
the General at some distance down stairs, seemed to
point out: – 'I was going to take you into what was my
mother's room – the room in which she died —' were
all her words; but few as they were, they conveyed
pages of intelligence to Catherine. It was no wonder
that the General should shrink from the sight of such
objects as that room must contain; a room in all probability never entered by him since the dreadful scene
had passed, which released his suffering wife, and left
him to the stings of conscience.

She ventured, when next alone with Eleanor, to express her wish of being permitted to see it, as well as
all the rest of that side of the house; and Eleanor
promised to attend her there, whenever they should
have a convenient hour. Catherine understood her: –
the General must be watched from home, before that
room could be entered. 'It remains as it was, I suppose?' said she, in a tone of feeling.

'Yes, entirely.'

'And how long ago may it be that your mother
died?'

'She has been dead these nine years.' And nine years,
Catherine knew was a trifle of time, compared with
what generally elapsed after the death of an injured
wife, before her room was put to rights.

'You were with her, I suppose, to the last?'

'No,' said Miss Tilney, sighing; 'I was unfortunately
from home. – Her illness was sudden and short; and,
before I arrived it was all over.'

Catherine's blood ran cold with the horrid suggestions which naturally sprang from these words. Could
it be possible? – Could Henry's father? —— And yet how
many were the examples to justify even the blackest
suspicions! – And, when she saw him in the evening,
while she worked with her friend, slowly pacing the
drawing-room for an hour together in silent thought-

fulness, with downcast eyes and contracted brow, she felt secure from all possibility of wronging him. It was the air and attitude of a Montoni! – What could more plainly speak the gloomy workings of a mind not wholly dead to every sense of humanity, in its fearful review of past scenes of guilt? Unhappy man! – And the anxiousness of her spirits directed her eyes towards his figure so repeatedly, as to catch Miss Tilney's notice. 'My father,' she whispered, 'often walks about the room in this way; it is nothing unusual.'

'So much the worse!' thought Catherine; such ill-timed exercise was of a piece with the strange unseasonableness of his morning walks, and boded nothing good.

After an evening, the little variety and seeming length of which made her peculiarly sensible of Henry's importance among them, she was heartily glad to be dismissed; though it was a look from the General not designed for her observation which sent his daughter to the bell. When the butler would have lit his master's candle, however, he was forbidden. The latter was not going to retire. 'I have many pamphlets to finish,' said he to Catherine, 'before I can close my eyes; and perhaps may be poring over the affairs of the nation for hours after you are asleep. Can either of us be more meetly employed? *My* eyes will be blinding for the good of others; and *yours* preparing by rest for future mischief.'

But neither the business alleged, nor the magnificent compliment, could win Catherine from thinking, that some very different object must occasion so serious a delay of proper repose. To be kept up for hours, after the family were in bed, by stupid pamphlets, was not very likely. There must be some deeper cause: something was to be done which could be done only while the household slept; and the probability that Mrs. Tilney yet lived, shut up for causes unknown, and receiving from the pitiless hand of her husband a nightly supply of coarse food, was the conclusion which necessarily followed. Shocking as was the idea, it was at least better than a death unfairly hastened, as, in the natural course of things, she must ere long be released. The suddenness of her reputed illness; the absence of her daughter, and probably of her other children, at the time – all favoured the supposition of her imprisonment. – Its origin – jealousy perhaps, or wanton cruelty – was yet to be unravelled.

In revolving these matters, while she undressed, it suddenly struck her as not unlikely, that she might that morning have passed near the very spot of this unfortunate woman's confinement – might have been within a few paces of the cell in which she languished out her days; for what part of the Abbey could be more fitted for the purpose than that which yet bore the traces of monastic division? In the high-arched passage, paved with stone, which already she had trodden with peculiar awe, she well remembered the doors of which the General had given no account. To what might not those doors lead? In support of the plausibility of this conjecture, it further occurred to her, that the forbidden gallery, in which lay the apartments of the unfortunate Mrs. Tilney, must be, as certainly as her memory could guide her, exactly over this suspected range of cells, and the stair-case by the side of those apartments of which she had caught a transient glimpse, communicating by some secret means with those cells, might well have favoured the barbarous proceedings of her husband. Down that stair-case she had perhaps been conveyed in a state of well-prepared insensibility!

Catherine sometimes started at the boldness of her own surmises, and sometimes hoped or feared that she had gone too far; but they were supported by such appearances as made their dismissal impossible.

The side of the quadrangle, in which she supposed
the guilty scene to be acting, being, according to her
belief, just opposite her own, it struck her that, if judi-
ciously watched, some rays of light from the General's
lamp might glimmer through the lower windows, as he
passed to the prison of his wife; and, twice before she
stepped into bed, she stole gently from her room to the
corresponding window in the gallery, to see if it appeared; but all abroad was dark, and it must yet be too
early. The various ascending noises convinced her that
the servants must still be up. Till midnight, she supposed it would be in vain to watch; but then, when the
clock had struck twelve, and all was quiet, she would,
if not quite appalled by darkness, steal out and look
once more. The clock struck twelve — and Catherine
had been half an hour asleep.

CHAPTER IX

THE NEXT day afforded no opportunity for the
proposed examination of the mysterious apartments. It was Sunday, and the whole time between
morning and afternoon service was required by the
General in exercise abroad or eating cold meat at
home; and great as was Catherine's curiosity, her
courage was not equal to a wish of exploring them
after dinner, either by the fading light of the sky
between six and seven o'clock, or by the yet more
partial though stronger illumination of a treacherous
lamp. The day was unmarked therefore by any thing to
interest her imagination beyond the sight of a very
elegant monument to the memory of Mrs. Tilney,
which immediately fronted the family pew. By that her
eye was instantly caught and long retained; and the
perusal of the highly-strained epitaph, in which every
virtue was ascribed to her by the inconsolable husband,

who must have been in some way or other her
destroyer, affected her even to tears.

That the General, having erected such a monument,
should be able to face it, was not perhaps very strange,
and yet that he could sit so boldly collected within its
view, maintain so elevated an air, look so fearlessly
around, nay, that he should even enter the church,
seemed wonderful to Catherine. Not however that
many instances of beings equally hardened in guilt
might not be produced. She could remember dozens
who had persevered in every possible vice, going on
from crime to crime, murdering whomsoever they
chose, without any feeling of humanity or remorse; till
a violent death or a religious retirement closed their
black career. The erection of the monument itself
could not in the smallest degree affect her doubts of
Mrs. Tilney's actual decease. Were she even to descend
into the family vault where her ashes were supposed to
slumber, were she to behold the coffin in which they
were said to be enclosed – what could it avail in such
a case? Catherine had read too much not to be perfectly aware of the ease with which a waxen figure
might be introduced, and a supposititious funeral carried on.

The succeeding morning promised something better.
The General's early walk, ill-timed as it was in every
other view, was favourable here; and when she knew
him to be out of the house, she directly proposed to
Miss Tilney the accomplishment of her promise. Eleanor was ready to oblige her; and Catherine reminding
her as they went of another promise, their first visit in
consequence was to the portrait in her bed-chamber. It
represented a very lovely woman, with a mild and pens-
ive countenance, justifying, so far, the expectations of
its new observer; but they were not in every respect
answered, for Catherine had depended upon meeting
with features, air, complexion that should be the very

counterpart, the very image, if not of Henry's, of Eleanor's; — the only portraits of which she had been in the
habit of thinking, bearing always an equal resemblance
of mother and child. A face once taken was taken for
generations. But here she was obliged to look and consider and study for a likeness. She contemplated it,
however, in spite of this drawback, with much emotion; and, but for a yet stronger interest, would have
left it unwillingly.

Her agitation as they entered the great gallery was
too much for any endeavour at discourse; she could
only look at her companion. Eleanor's countenance
was dejected, yet sedate; and its composure spoke her
enured to all the gloomy objects to which they were
advancing. Again she passed through the folding-
doors, again her hand was upon the important lock,
and Catherine, hardly able to breathe, was turning to
close the former with fearful caution, when the figure,
the dreaded figure of the General himself at the further
end of the gallery, stood before her! The name of
'Eleanor' at the same moment, in his loudest tone, re-
sounded through the building, giving to his daughter
the first intimation of his presence, and to Catherine
terror upon terror. An attempt at concealment had
been her first instinctive movement on perceiving him,
yet she could scarcely hope to have escaped his eye;
and when her friend, who with an apologizing look
darted hastily by her, had joined and disappeared with
him, she ran for safety to her own room, and, locking
herself in, believed that she should never have courage
to go down again. She remained there at least an hour,
in the greatest agitation, deeply commiserating the state
of her poor friend, and expecting a summons herself from the angry General to attend him in his own
apartment. No summons however arrived; and at last,
on seeing a carriage drive up to the Abbey, she was
emboldened to descend and meet him under the

protection of visitors. The breakfast-room was gay with company; and she was named to them by the General, as the friend of his daughter, in a complimentary style, which so well concealed his resentful ire, as to make her feel secure at least of life for the present. And Eleanor, with a command of countenance which did honour to her concern for his character, taking an early occasion of saying to her, 'My father only wanted me to answer a note,' she began to hope that she had either been unseen by the General, or that from some consideration of policy she should be allowed to suppose herself so. Upon this trust she dared still to remain in his presence, after the company left them, and nothing occurred to disturb it.

In the course of this morning's reflections, she came to a resolution of making her next attempt on the forbidden door alone. It would be much better in every respect that Eleanor should know nothing of the matter. To involve her in the danger of a second detection, to court her into an apartment which must wring her heart, could not be the office of a friend. The General's utmost anger could not be to herself what it might be to a daughter; and, besides, she thought the examination itself would be more satisfactory if made without any companion. It would be impossible to explain to Eleanor the suspicions, from which the other had, in all likelihood, been hitherto happily exempt; nor could she therefore, in *her* presence, search for those proofs of the General's cruelty, which however they might yet have escaped discovery, she felt confident of somewhere drawing forth, in the shape of some fragmented journal, continued to the last gasp. Of the way to the apartment she was now perfectly mistress; and as she wished to get it over before Henry's return, who was expected on the morrow, there was no time to be lost. The day was bright, her courage high; at four o'clock, the sun was now two hours above the horizon, and it

would be only her retiring to dress half an hour earlier
than usual.

It was done; and Catherine found herself alone in
the gallery before the clocks had ceased to strike. It
was no time for thought; she hurried on, slipped with
the least possible noise through the folding-doors, and
without stopping to look or breathe, rushed forward to
the one in question. The lock yielded to her hand, and,
luckily, with no sullen sound that could alarm a human
being. On tip-toe she entered; the room was before
her; but it was some minutes before she could advance
another step. She beheld what fixed her to the spot and
agitated every feature. – She saw a large, well-proportioned apartment, an handsome dimity bed, arranged as
unoccupied with an housemaid's care, a bright Bath
stove, mahogany wardrobes and neatly-painted chairs,
on which the warm beams of a western sun gaily
poured through two sash windows! Catherine had expected to have her feelings worked, and worked they
were. Astonishment and doubt first seized them; and a
shortly succeeding ray of common sense added some
bitter emotions of shame. She could not be mistaken
as to the room; but how grossly mistaken in every
thing else! – in Miss Tilney's meaning, in her own cal-
culation! This apartment, to which she had given a date
so ancient, a position so awful, proved to be one end
of what the General's father had built. There were two
other doors in the chamber, leading probably into
dressing-closets; but she had no inclination to open
either. Would the veil in which Mrs. Tilney had last
walked, or the volume in which she had last read, remain to tell what nothing else was allowed to whisper?
No: whatever might have been the General's crimes, he
had certainly too much wit to let them sue for detection. She was sick of exploring, and desired but to be
safe in her own room, with her own heart only privy
to its folly; and she was on the point of retreating as

softly as she had entered, when the sound of footsteps, she could hardly tell where, made her pause and tremble. To be found there, even by a servant, would be unpleasant; but by the General, (and he seemed always at hand when least wanted,) much worse! – She listened – the sound had ceased; and resolving not to lose a moment, she passed through and closed the door. At that instant a door underneath was hastily opened; some one seemed with swift steps to ascend the stairs, by the head of which she had yet to pass before she could gain the gallery. She had no power to move. With a feeling of terror not very definable, she fixed her eyes on the stair-case, and in a few moments it gave Henry to her view. 'Mr. Tilney!' she exclaimed in a voice of more than common astonishment. He looked astonished too. 'Good God!' she continued, not attending to his address, 'how came you here? – how came you up that stair-case?'

'How came I up that stair-case!' he replied, greatly surprised. 'Because it is my nearest way from the stable-yard to my own chamber; and why should I not come up it?'

Catherine recollected herself, blushed deeply, and could say no more. He seemed to be looking in her countenance for that explanation which her lips did not afford. She moved on towards the gallery. 'And may I not, in my turn,' said he, as he pushed back the folding-doors, 'ask how *you* came here? – This passage is at least as extraordinary a road from the breakfast-parlour to your apartment, as that stair-case can be from the stables to mine.'

'I have been,' said Catherine, looking down, 'to see your mother's room.'

'My mother's room! – Is there any thing extraordinary to be seen there?'

'No, nothing at all. – I thought you did not mean to come back till to-morrow.'

'I did not expect to be able to return sooner, when I went away; but three hours ago I had the pleasure of finding nothing to detain me. – You look pale. – I am afraid I alarmed you by running so fast up those stairs. Perhaps you did not know – you were not aware of their leading from the offices in common use?'

'No, I was not. – You have had a very fine day for your ride.'

'Very; – and does Eleanor leave you to find your way into all the rooms in the house by yourself?'

'Oh! no; she shewed me over the greatest part on Saturday – and we were coming here to these rooms – but only – (dropping her voice) – your father was with us.'

'And that prevented you;' said Henry, earnestly regarding her. – 'Have you looked into all the rooms in that passage?'

'No, I only wanted to see —— Is not it very late? I must go and dress.'

'It is only a quarter past four, (shewing his watch) and you are not now in Bath. No theatre, no rooms to prepare for. Half an hour at Northanger must be enough.'

She could not contradict it, and therefore suffered herself to be detained, though her dread of further questions made her, for the first time in their acquaintance, wish to leave him. They walked slowly up the gallery. 'Have you had any letter from Bath since I saw you?'

'No, and I am very much surprised. Isabella promised so faithfully to write directly.'

'Promised so faithfully! – A faithful promise! – That puzzles me. – I have heard of a faithful performance. But a faithful promise – the fidelity of promising! It is a power little worth knowing however, since it can deceive and pain you. My mother's room is very commodious, is it not? Large and cheerful-looking, and the

dressing closets so well disposed! It always strikes me
as the most comfortable apartment in the house, and I
rather wonder that Eleanor should not take it for her
own. She sent you to look at it, I suppose?'

'No.'

'It has been your own doing entirely?' – Catherine
said nothing – After a short silence, during which he
had closely observed her, he added, 'As there is nothing in the room in itself to raise curiosity, this must
have proceeded from a sentiment of respect for my
mother's character, as described by Eleanor, which
does honour to her memory. The world, I believe,
never saw a better woman. But it is not often that
virtue can boast an interest such as this. The domestic,
unpretending merits of a person never known, do not
often create that kind of fervent, venerating tenderness
which would prompt a visit like yours. Eleanor, I suppose, has talked of her a great deal?'

'Yes, a great deal. That is – no, not much, but what
she did say, was very interesting. Her dying so suddenly,' (slowly, and with hesitation it was spoken,) 'and
you – none of you being at home – and your father, I
thought – perhaps had not been very fond of her.'

'And from these circumstances,' he replied, (his
quick eye fixed on her's,) 'you infer perhaps the probability of some negligence – some – (involuntarily she
shook her head) – or it may be – of something still less
pardonable.' She raised her eyes towards him more
fully than she had ever done before. 'My mother's illness,' he continued, 'the seizure which ended in her
death *was* sudden. The malady itself, one from which
she had often suffered, a bilious fever – its cause therefore constitutional. On the third day, in short as soon
as she could be prevailed on, a physician attended her,
a very respectable man, and one in whom she had always placed great confidence. Upon his opinion of her
danger, two others were called in the next day, and

remained in almost constant attendance for four-and-twenty hours. On the fifth day she died. During the progress of her disorder, Frederick and I (*we* were both at home) saw her repeatedly; and from our own observation can bear witness to her having received every possible attention which could spring from the affection of those about her, or which her situation in life could command. Poor Eleanor *was* absent, and at such a distance as to return only to see her mother in her coffin.'

'But your father,' said Catherine, 'was *he* afflicted?'

'For a time, greatly so. You have erred in supposing him not attached to her. He loved her, I am persuaded, as well as it was possible for him to – We have not all, you know, the same tenderness of disposition – and I will not pretend to say that while she lived, she might not often have had much to bear, but though his temper injured her, his judgment never did. His value of her was sincere; and, if not permanently, he was truly afflicted by her death.'

'I am very glad of it,' said Catherine, 'it would have been very shocking!' —

'If I understand you rightly, you had formed a surmise of such horror as I have hardly words to — Dear Miss Morland, consider the dreadful nature of the suspicions you have entertained. What have you been judging from? Remember the country and the age in which we live. Remember that we are English, that we are Christians. Consult your own understanding, your own sense of the probable, your own observation of what is passing around you – Does our education prepare us for such atrocities? Do our laws connive at them? Could they be perpetrated without being known, in a country like this, where social and literary intercourse is on such a footing; where every man is surrounded by a neighbourhood of voluntary spies, and where roads and newspapers lay every thing open?

Dearest Miss Morland, what ideas have you been admitting?'

They had reached the end of the gallery; and with tears of shame she ran off to her own room.

CHAPTER X

THE VISIONS of romance were over. Catherine was completely awakened. Henry's address, short as it had been, had more thoroughly opened her eyes to the extravagance of her late fancies than all their several disappointments had done. Most grievously was she humbled. Most bitterly did she cry. It was not only with herself that she was sunk – but with Henry. Her folly, which now seemed even criminal, was all exposed to him, and he must despise her for ever. The liberty which her imagination had dared to take with the character of his father, could he ever forgive it? The absurdity of her curiosity and her fears, could they ever be forgotten? She hated herself more than she could express. He had – she thought he had, once or twice before this fatal morning, shewn something like affection for her. – But now – in short, she made herself as miserable as possible for about half an hour, went down when the clock struck five, with a broken heart, and could scarcely give an intelligible answer to Eleanor's inquiry, if she was well. The formidable Henry soon followed her into the room, and the only difference in his behaviour to her, was that he paid her rather more attention than usual. Catherine had never wanted comfort more, and he looked as if he was aware of it.

The evening wore away with no abatement of this soothing politeness; and her spirits were gradually raised to a modest tranquillity. She did not learn either to forget or defend the past; but she learned to hope that it would never transpire farther, and that it might not cost her Henry's entire regard. Her thoughts being still chiefly fixed on what she had with such causeless terror felt and done, nothing could shortly be clearer, than that it had been all a voluntary, self-created delusion, each trifling circumstance receiving importance from an imagination resolved on alarm, and every thing forced to bend to one purpose by a mind which, before she entered the Abbey, had been craving to be frightened. She remembered with what feelings she had prepared for a knowledge of Northanger. She saw that the infatuation had been created, the mischief settled long before her quitting Bath, and it seemed as if the whole might be traced to the influence of that sort of reading which she had there indulged.

Charming as were all Mrs. Radcliffe's works, and charming even as were the works of all her imitators, it was not in them perhaps that human nature, at least in the midland counties of England, was to be looked for. Of the Alps and Pyrenees, with their pine forests and their vices, they might give a faithful delineation; and Italy, Switzerland, and the South of France, might be as fruitful in horrors as they were there represented. Catherine dared not doubt beyond her own country, and even of that, if hard pressed, would have yielded the northern and western extremities. But in the central part of England there was surely some security for the existence even of a wife not beloved, in the laws of the land, and the manners of the age. Murder was not tolerated, servants were not slaves, and neither poison nor sleeping potions to be procured, like rhubarb, from every druggist. Among the Alps and Pyrenees, perhaps, there were no mixed characters. There, such as were not as spotless as an angel, might have the dispositions of a fiend. But in England it was not so; among the English, she believed, in their hearts and habits, there was a general though unequal mixture of good and bad.

Upon this conviction, she would not be surprised if even in Henry and Eleanor Tilney, some slight imperfection might hereafter appear; and upon this conviction she need not fear to acknowledge some actual specks in the character of their father, who, though cleared from the grossly injurious suspicions which she must ever blush to have entertained, she did believe, upon serious consideration, to be not perfectly amiable.

Her mind made up on these several points, and her resolution formed, of always judging and acting in future with the greatest good sense, she had nothing to do but to forgive herself and be happier than ever; and the lenient hand of time did much for her by insensible gradations in the course of another day. Henry's astonishing generosity and nobleness of conduct, in never alluding in the slightest way to what had passed, was of the greatest assistance to her; and sooner than she could have supposed it possible in the beginning of her distress, her spirits became absolutely comfortable, and capable, as heretofore, of continual improvement by any thing he said. There were still some subjects indeed, under which she believed they must always tremble; – the mention of a chest or a cabinet, for instance – and she did not love the sight of japan in any shape: but even *she* could allow, that an occasional memento of past folly, however painful, might not be without use.

The anxieties of common life began soon to succeed to the alarms of romance. Her desire of hearing from Isabella grew every day greater. She was quite impatient to know how the Bath world went on, and how the Rooms were attended; and especially was she anxious to be assured of Isabella's having matched some fine netting-cotton, on which she had left her intent; and of her continuing on the best terms with James. Her only dependence for information of any kind was on Isabella. James had protested against writing to her till his return to Oxford; and Mrs. Allen had given her no hopes of a letter till she had got back to Fullerton. – But Isabella had promised and promised again; and when she promised a thing, she was so scrupulous in performing it! this made it so particularly strange!

For nine successive mornings, Catherine wondered over the repetition of a disappointment, which each morning became more severe: but, on the tenth, when she entered the breakfast-room, her first object was a letter, held out by Henry's willing hand. She thanked him as heartily as if he had written it himself. ' 'Tis only from James, however,' as she looked at the direction. She opened it; it was from Oxford; and to this purpose: –

'Dear Catherine,

'Though, God knows, with little inclination for writing, I think it my duty to tell you, that every thing is at an end between Miss Thorpe and me. – I left her and Bath yesterday, never to see either again. I shall not enter into particulars, they would only pain you more. You will soon hear enough from another quarter to know where lies the blame; and I hope will acquit your brother of every thing but the folly of too easily thinking his affection returned. Thank God! I am un-deceived in time! But it is a heavy blow! – After my father's consent had been so kindly given – but no more of this. She has made me miserable for ever! Let me soon hear from you, dear Catherine; you are my only friend; *your* love I do build upon. I wish your visit at Northanger may be over before Captain Tilney makes his engagement known, or you will be uncom-fortably circumstanced. – Poor Thorpe is in town: I dread the sight of him; his honest heart would feel so much. I have written to him and my father. Her du-plicity hurts me more than all; till the very last, if I reasoned with her, she declared herself as much at-tached to me as ever, and laughed at my fears. I am

ashamed to think how long I bore with it; but if ever
man had reason to believe himself loved, I was that
man. I cannot understand even now what she would be
at, for there could be no need of my being played off
to make her secure of Tilney. We parted at last by
mutual consent — happy for me had we never met! I
can never expect to know such another woman!
Dearest Catherine, beware how you give your heart.

'Believe me,' &c.

Catherine had not read three lines before her sudden
change of countenance, and short exclamations of sor-
rowing wonder, declared her to be receiving unpleasant
news; and Henry, earnestly watching her through the
whole letter, saw plainly that it ended no better than it
began. He was prevented, however, from even looking
his surprise by his father's entrance. They went to
breakfast directly; but Catherine could hardly eat any
thing. Tears filled her eyes, and even ran down her
cheeks as she sat. The letter was one moment in her
hand, then in her lap, and then in her pocket; and she
looked as if she knew not what she did. The General,
between his cocoa and his newspaper, had luckily no
leisure for noticing her; but to the other two her distress was equally visible. As soon as she dared leave the
table she hurried away to her own room; but the
housemaids were busy in it, and she was obliged to
come down again. She turned into the drawing-room
for privacy, but Henry and Eleanor had likewise retreated thither, and were at that moment deep in consultation about her. She drew back, trying to beg their
pardon, but was, with gentle violence, forced to return;
and the others withdrew, after Eleanor had affectionate-
ly expressed a wish of being of use or comfort to her.

After half an hour's free indulgence of grief and
reflection, Catherine felt equal to encountering her
friends; but whether she should make her distress

known to them was another consideration. Perhaps, if particularly questioned, she might just give an idea – just distantly hint at it – but not more. To expose a friend, such a friend as Isabella had been to her – and then their own brother so closely concerned in it! – She believed she must wave the subject altogether. Henry and Eleanor were by themselves in the breakfast-room; and each, as she entered it, looked at her anxiously. Catherine took her place at the table, and, after a short silence, Eleanor said, 'No bad news from Fullerton, I hope? Mr. and Mrs. Morland – your brothers and sisters – I hope they are none of them ill?'

'No, I thank you,' (sighing as she spoke,) 'they are all very well. My letter was from my brother at Oxford.'

Nothing further was said for a few minutes; and then speaking through her tears, she added, 'I do not think I shall ever wish for a letter again!'

'I am sorry,' said Henry, closing the book he had just opened; 'if I had suspected the letter of containing any thing unwelcome, I should have given it with very different feelings.'

'It contained something worse than any body could suppose! – Poor James is so unhappy! – You will soon know why.'

'To have so kind-hearted, so affectionate a sister,' replied Henry, warmly, 'must be a comfort to him under any distress.'

'I have one favour to beg,' said Catherine, shortly afterwards, in an agitated manner, 'that, if your brother should be coming here, you will give me notice of it, that I may go away.'

'Our brother! – Frederick!'

'Yes; I am sure I should be very sorry to leave you so soon, but something has happened that would make it very dreadful for me to be in the same house with Captain Tilney.'

Eleanor's work was suspended while she gazed with increasing astonishment; but Henry began to suspect the truth, and something, in which Miss Thorpe's name was included, passed his lips.

'How quick you are!' cried Catherine: 'you have guessed it, I declare! – And yet, when we talked about it in Bath, you little thought of its ending so. Isabella – no wonder now I have not heard from her – Isabella has deserted my brother, and is to marry your's! Could you have believed there had been such inconstancy and fickleness, and every thing that is bad in the world?'

'I hope, so far as concerns my brother, you are misinformed. I hope he has not had any material share in bringing on Mr. Morland's disappointment. His marrying Miss Thorpe is not probable. I think you must be deceived so far. I am very sorry for Mr. Morland – sorry that any one you love should be unhappy; but my surprise would be greater at Frederick's marrying her, than at any other part of the story.'

'It is very true, however; you shall read James's letter yourself. – Stay — there is one part — ' recollecting with a blush the last line.

'Will you take the trouble of reading to us the passages which concern my brother?'

'No, read it yourself,' cried Catherine, whose second thoughts were clearer. 'I do not know what I was thinking of,' (blushing again that she had blushed before,) – 'James only means to give me good advice.'

He gladly received the letter; and, having read it through, with close attention, returned it saying, 'Well, if it is to be so, I can only say that I am sorry for it. Frederick will not be the first man who has chosen a wife with less sense than his family expected. I do not envy his situation, either as a lover or a son.'

Miss Tilney, at Catherine's invitation, now read the letter likewise; and, having expressed also her concern and surprise, began to inquire into Miss Thorpe's connexions and fortune.

'Her mother is a very good sort of woman,' was Catherine's answer.

'What was her father?'

'A lawyer, I believe. – They live at Putney.'

'Are they a wealthy family?'

'No, not very. I do not believe Isabella has any fortune at all: but that will not signify in your family. – Your father is so very liberal! He told me the other day, that he only valued money as it allowed him to promote the happiness of his children.' The brother and sister looked at each other. 'But,' said Eleanor, after a short pause, 'would it be to promote his happiness, to enable him to marry such a girl? – She must be an unprincipled one, or she could not have used your brother so. – And how strange an infatuation on Frederick's side! A girl who, before his eyes, is violating an engagement voluntarily entered into with another man! Is not it inconceivable, Henry? Frederick too, who always wore his heart so proudly! who found no woman good enough to be loved!'

'That is the most unpromising circumstance, the strongest presumption against him. When I think of his past declarations, I give him up. – Moreover, I have too good an opinion of Miss Thorpe's prudence, to suppose that she would part with one gentleman before the other was secured. It is all over with Frederick indeed! He is a deceased man – defunct in understanding. Prepare for your sister-in-law, Eleanor, and such a sister-in-law as you must delight in! – Open, candid, artless, guileless, with affections strong but simple, forming no pretensions, and knowing no disguise.'

'Such a sister-in-law, Henry, I should delight in,' said Eleanor, with a smile.

'But perhaps,' observed Catherine, 'though she has

behaved so ill by our family, she may behave better by your's. Now she has really got the man she likes, she may be constant.'

'Indeed I am afraid she will,' replied Henry; 'I am afraid she will be very constant, unless a baronet should come in her way; that is Frederick's only chance. — I will get the Bath paper, and look over the arrivals.'

'You think it is all for ambition then? — And, upon my word, there are some things that seem very like it. I cannot forget, that, when she first knew what my father would do for them, she seemed quite disappointed that it was not more. I never was so deceived in any one's character in my life before.'

'Among all the great variety that you have known and studied.'

'My own disappointment and loss in her is very great; but, as for poor James, I suppose he will hardly ever recover it.'

'Your brother is certainly very much to be pitied at present; but we must not, in our concern for his sufferings, undervalue your's. You feel, I suppose, that, in losing Isabella, you lose half yourself: you feel a void in your heart which nothing else can occupy. Society is becoming irksome; and as for the amusements in which you were wont to share at Bath, the very idea of them without her is abhorrent. You would not, for instance, now go to a ball for the world. You feel that you have no longer any friend to whom you can speak with unreserve; on whose regard you can place dependence; or whose counsel, in any difficulty, you could rely on. You feel all this?'

'No,' said Catherine, after a few moments' reflection, 'I do not — ought I? To say the truth, though I am hurt and grieved, that I cannot still love her, that I am never to hear from her, perhaps never to see her again, I do not feel so very, very much afflicted as one would have thought.'

'You feel, as you always do, what is most to the credit of human nature. – Such feelings ought to be investigated, that they may know themselves.'

Catherine, by some chance or other, found her spirits so very much relieved by this conversation, that she could not regret her being led on, though so unaccountably, to mention the circumstance which had produced it.

CHAPTER XI

FROM THIS time, the subject was frequently canvassed by the three young people; and Catherine found, with some surprise, that her two young friends were perfectly agreed in considering Isabella's want of consequence and fortune as likely to throw great difficulties in the way of her marrying their brother. Their persuasion that the General would, upon this ground alone, independent of the objection that might be raised against her character, oppose the connexion, turned her feelings moreover with some alarm towards herself. She was as insignificant, and perhaps as portionless as Isabella; and if the heir of the Tilney property had not grandeur and wealth enough in himself, at what point of interest were the demands of his younger brother to rest? The very painful reflections to which this thought led, could only be dispersed by a dependence on the effect of that particular partiality, which, as she was given to understand by his words as well as his actions, she had from the first been so fortunate as to excite in the General; and by a recollection of some most generous and disinterested sentiments on the subject of money, which she had more than once heard him utter, and which tempted her to think his disposition in such matters misunderstood by his children.

They were so fully convinced, however, that their brother would not have the courage to apply in person for his father's consent, and so repeatedly assured her that he had never in his life been less likely to come to Northanger than at the present time, that she suffered her mind to be at ease as to the necessity of any sudden removal of her own. But as it was not to be supposed that Captain Tilney, whenever he made his application, would give his father any just idea of Isabella's conduct, it occurred to her as highly expedient that Henry should lay the whole business before him as it really was, enabling the General by that means to form a cool and impartial opinion, and prepare his objections on a fairer ground than inequality of situations. She proposed it to him accordingly; but he did not catch at the measure so eagerly as she had expected. 'No,' said he, 'my father's hands need not be strengthened, and Frederick's confession of folly need not be forestalled. He must tell his own story.'

'But he will tell only half of it.'

'A quarter would be enough.'

A day or two passed away and brought no tidings of Captain Tilney. His brother and sister knew not what to think. Sometimes it appeared to them as if his silence would be the natural result of the suspected engagement, and at others that it was wholly incompatible with it. The General, meanwhile, though offended every morning by Frederick's remissness in writing, was free from any real anxiety about him; and had no more pressing solicitude than that of making Miss Morland's time at Northanger pass pleasantly. He often expressed his uneasiness on this head, feared the sameness of every day's society and employments would disgust her with the place, wished the Lady Frasers had been in the country, talked every now and then of having a large party to dinner, and once or twice began even to calculate the number of young dancing people in the neighbourhood. But then it was such a dead time of year, no wild-fowl, no game, and the Lady Frasers were not in the country. And it all ended, at last, in his telling Henry one morning, that when he next went to Woodston, they would take him by surprise there some day or other, and eat their mutton with him. Henry was greatly honoured and very happy, and Catherine was quite delighted with the scheme. 'And when do you think, sir, I may look forward to this pleasure? – I must be at Woodston on Monday to attend the parish meeting, and shall probably be obliged to stay two or three days.'

'Well, well, we will take our chance some one of those days. There is no need to fix. You are not to put yourself at all out of your way. Whatever you may happen to have in the house will be enough. I think I can answer for the young ladies making allowance for a bachelor's table. Let me see; Monday will be a busy day with you, we will not come on Monday; and Tuesday will be a busy one with me. I expect my surveyor from Brockham with his report in the morning; and afterwards I cannot in decency fail attending the club. I really could not face my acquaintance if I staid away now; for, as I am known to be in the country, it would be taken exceedingly amiss; and it is a rule with me, Miss Morland, never to give offence to any of my neighbours, if a small sacrifice of time and attention can prevent it. They are a set of very worthy men. They have half a buck from Northanger twice a year; and I dine with them whenever I can. Tuesday, therefore, we may say is out of the question. But on Wednesday, I think, Henry, you may expect us; and we shall be with you early, that we may have time to look about us. Two hours and three quarters will carry us to Woodston, I suppose; we shall be in the carriage by ten; so, about a quarter before one on Wednesday, you may look for us.'

A ball itself could not have been more welcome to Catherine than this little excursion, so strong was her desire to be acquainted with Woodston; and her heart was still bounding with joy, when Henry, about an hour afterwards, came booted and great coated into the room where she and Eleanor were sitting, and said, 'I am come, young ladies, in a very moralizing strain, to observe that our pleasures in this world are always to be paid for, and that we often purchase them at a great disadvantage, giving ready-monied actual happiness for a draft on the future, that may not be honoured. Witness myself, at this present hour. Because I am to hope for the satisfaction of seeing you at Woodston on Wednesday, which bad weather, or twenty other causes may prevent, I must go away directly, two days before I intended it.'

'Go away!' said Catherine, with a very long face; 'and why?'

'Why! – How can you ask the question? – Because no time is to be lost in frightening my old housekeeper out of her wits, – because I must go and prepare a dinner for you to be sure.'

'Oh! not seriously!'

'Aye, and sadly too – for I had much rather stay.'

'But how can you think of such a thing, after what the General said? when he so particularly desired you not to give yourself any trouble, because *any thing* would do.'

Henry only smiled. 'I am sure it is quite unnecessary upon your sister's account and mine. You must know it to be so; and the General made such a point of your providing nothing extraordinary: – besides, if he had not said half so much as he did, he has always such an excellent dinner at home, that sitting down to a middling one for one day could not signify.'

'I wish I could reason like you, for his sake and my own. Good bye. As to-morrow is Sunday, Eleanor, I shall not return.'

He went; and, it being at any time a much simpler operation to Catherine to doubt her own judgment than Henry's, she was very soon obliged to give him credit for being right, however disagreeable to her his going. But the inexplicability of the General's conduct dwelt much on her thoughts. That he was very particular in his eating, she had, by her own unassisted observation, already discovered; but why he should say one thing so positively, and mean another all the while, was most unaccountable! How were people, at that rate, to be understood? Who but Henry could have been aware of what his father was at?

From Saturday to Wednesday, however, they were now to be without Henry. This was the sad finale of every reflection: – and Captain Tilney's letter would certainly come in his absence; and Wednesday she was very sure would be wet. The past, present, and future, were all equally in gloom. Her brother so unhappy, and her loss in Isabella so great; and Eleanor's spirits always affected by Henry's absence! What was there to interest or amuse her? She was tired of the woods and the shrubberies – always so smooth and so dry; and the Abbey in itself was no more to her now than any other house. The painful remembrance of the folly it had helped to nourish and perfect, was the only emotion which could spring from a consideration of the building. What a revolution in her ideas! she, who had so longed to be in an abbey! Now, there was nothing so charming to her imagination as the unpretending comfort of a well-connected Parsonage, something like Fullerton, but better: Fullerton had its faults, but Woodston probably had none. – If Wednesday should ever come!

It did come, and exactly when it might be reasonably looked for. It came – it was fine – and Catherine trod on air. By ten o'clock, the chaise-and-four conveyed the trio from the Abbey; and, after an agreeable drive of almost twenty miles, they entered Woodston, a large and populous village, in a situation not unpleasant. Catherine was ashamed to say how pretty she thought it, as the General seemed to think an apology necessary for the flatness of the country, and the size of the village; but in her heart she preferred it to any place she had ever been at, and looked with great admiration at every neat house above the rank of a cottage, and at all the little chandler's shops which they passed. At the further end of the village, and tolerably disengaged from the rest of it, stood the Parsonage, a new-built substantial stone house, with its semi-circular sweep and green gates; and, as they drove up to the door, Henry, with the friends of his solitude, a large New-foundland puppy and two or three terriers, was ready to receive and make much of them.

Catherine's mind was too full, as she entered the house, for her either to observe or to say a great deal; and, till called on by the General for her opinion of it, she had very little idea of the room in which she was sitting. Upon looking round it then, she perceived in a moment that it was the most comfortable room in the world; but she was too guarded to say so, and the coldness of her praise disappointed him.

'We are not calling it a good house,' said he. – 'We are not comparing it with Fullerton and Northanger – We are considering it as a mere Parsonage, small and confined, we allow, but decent perhaps, and habitable; and altogether not inferior to the generality; – or, in other words, I believe there are few country parsonages in England half so good. It may admit of improvement, however. Far be it from me to say otherwise; and any thing in reason – a bow thrown out, perhaps – though, between ourselves, if there is one thing more than another my aversion, it is a patched-on bow.'

Catherine did not hear enough of this speech to understand or be pained by it; and other subjects being studiously brought forward and supported by Henry, at the same time that a tray full of refreshments was introduced by his servant, the General was shortly restored to his complacency, and Catherine to all her usual ease of spirits.

The room in question was of a commodious, well-proportioned size, and handsomely fitted up as a dining-parlour; and on their quitting it to walk round the grounds, she was shewn, first into a smaller apartment, belonging peculiarly to the master of the house, and made unusually tidy on the occasion; and afterwards into what was to be the drawing-room, with the appearance of which, though unfurnished, Catherine was delighted enough even to satisfy the General. It was a prettily-shaped room, the windows reaching to the ground, and the view from them pleasant, though only over green meadows; and she expressed her admiration at the moment with all the honest simplicity with which she felt it. 'Oh! why do not you fit up this room, Mr. Tilney? What a pity not to have it fitted up! It is the prettiest room I ever saw; – it is the prettiest room in the world!'

'I trust,' said the General, with a most satisfied smile, 'that it will very speedily be furnished: it waits only for a lady's taste!'

'Well, if it was my house, I should never sit any where else. Oh! what a sweet little cottage there is among the trees – apple trees too! It is the prettiest cottage!' –

'You like it – you approve it as an object; – it is enough. Henry, remember that Robinson is spoken to about it. The cottage remains.'

Such a compliment recalled all Catherine's consciousness, and silenced her directly; and, though pointedly applied to by the General for her choice of the prevailing colour of the paper and hangings, nothing like an opinion on the subject could be drawn from

her. The influence of fresh objects and fresh air, however, was of great use in dissipating these embarrassing
associations; and, having reached the ornamental part
of the premises, consisting of a walk round two sides
of a meadow, on which Henry's genius had begun to
act about half a year ago, she was sufficiently recovered
to think it prettier than any pleasure-ground she had
ever been in before, though there was not a shrub in
it higher than the green bench in the corner.

A saunter into other meadows, and through part of
the village, with a visit to the stables to examine some
improvements, and a charming game of play with a
litter of puppies just able to roll about, brought them
to four o'clock, when Catherine scarcely thought it
could be three. At four they were to dine, and at six to
set off on their return. Never had any day passed so
quickly!

She could not but observe that the abundance of
the dinner did not seem to create the smallest
astonishment in the General; nay, that he was even
looking at the side-table for cold meat which was not
there. His son and daughter's observations were of a
different kind. They had seldom seen him eat so heartily at any table but his own; and never before known
him so little disconcerted by the melted butter's being
oiled.

At six o'clock, the General having taken his coffee,
the carriage again received them; and so gratifying had
been the tenor of his conduct throughout the whole
visit, so well assured was her mind on the subject of
his expectations, that, could she have felt equally confident of the wishes of his son, Catherine would have
quitted Woodston with little anxiety as to the How or
the When she might return to it.

CHAPTER XII

THE NEXT morning brought the following very unexpected letter from Isabella: –

Bath, April –

My dearest Catherine,

I received your two kind letters with the greatest delight, and have a thousand apologies to make for not answering them sooner. I really am quite ashamed of my idleness; but in this horrid place one can find time for nothing. I have had my pen in my hand to begin a letter to you almost every day since you left Bath, but have always been prevented by some silly trifler or other. Pray write to me soon, and direct to my own home. Thank God! we leave this vile place to-morrow. Since you went away, I have had no pleasure in it – the dust is beyond any thing; and every body one cares for is gone. I believe if I could see you I should not mind the rest, for you are dearer to me than any body can conceive. I am quite uneasy about your dear brother, not having heard from him since he went to Oxford; and am fearful of some misunderstanding. Your kind offices will set all right: – he is the only man I ever did or could love, and I trust you will convince him of it. The spring fashions are partly down; and the hats the most frightful you can imagine. I hope you spend your time pleasantly, but am afraid you never think of me. I will not say all that I could of the family you are with, because I would not be ungenerous, or set you against those you esteem; but it is very difficult to know whom to trust, and young men never know their minds two days together. I rejoice to say, that the young man whom, of all others, I particularly abhor, has left Bath. You will know, from this description, I must mean Captain Tilney, who, as you may remember, was amazingly disposed to follow and tease me, before you went away. Afterwards he got worse, and became quite my shadow. Many girls might have been taken in, for never were such attentions; but I knew the fickle sex too well. He went away to his regiment two days ago, and I trust I shall never be plagued with him again. He is the greatest coxcomb I ever saw, and amazingly disagreeable. The last two days he was always by the side of Charlotte Davis: I pitied his taste, but took no notice of him. The last time we met was in Bath-street, and I turned directly into a shop that he might not speak to me; – I would not even look at him. He went into the Pump-room afterwards; but I would not have followed him for all the world. Such a contrast between him and your brother! – pray send me some news of the latter – I am quite unhappy about him, he seemed so uncomfortable when he went away, with a cold, or something that affected his spirits. I would write to him myself, but have mislaid his direction; and, as I hinted above, am afraid he took something in my conduct amiss. Pray explain every thing to his satisfaction; or, if he still harbours any doubt, a line from himself to me, or a call at Putney when next in town, might set all to rights. I have not been to the Rooms this age, nor to the Play, except going in last night with the Hodges's, for a frolic, at half-price: they teased me into it; and I was determined they should not say I shut myself up because Tilney was gone. We happened to sit by the Mitchells, and they pretended to be quite surprised to see me out. I knew their spite: – at one time they could not be civil to me, but now they are all friendship; but I am not such a fool as to be taken in by them. You know I have a pretty good spirit of my own. Anne Mitchell had tried to put on a turban like mine, as I wore it the week before at the Concert, but made wretched work of it – it happened to become my odd face I believe, at least Tilney told me so at the time, and said every eye was upon me; but he is the last man whose word I would take. I wear nothing but purple now: I know I look hideous in it, but no matter – it is your dear brother's favourite colour. Lose no time, my dearest, sweetest Catherine, in writing to him and to me,

Who ever am, &c.

Such a strain of shallow artifice could not impose even upon Catherine. Its inconsistencies, contradictions, and falsehood, struck her from the very first. She was ashamed of Isabella, and ashamed of having ever loved her. Her professions of attachment were now as disgusting as her excuses were empty, and her demands impudent. 'Write to James on her behalf! – No, James should never hear Isabella's name mentioned by her again.'

On Henry's arrival from Woodston, she made known to him and Eleanor their brother's safety, congratulating them with sincerity on it, and reading aloud the most material passages of her letter with strong indignation. When she had finished it, – 'So much for Isabella,' she cried, 'and for all our intimacy! She must think me an idiot, or she could not have written so; but perhaps this has served to make her character better known to me than mine is to her. I see what she has been about. She is a vain coquette, and her tricks have not answered. I do not believe she had ever any regard either for James or for me, and I wish I had never known her.'

'It will soon be as if you never had,' said Henry.

'There is but one thing that I cannot understand. I see that she has had designs on Captain Tilney, which have not succeeded; but I do not understand what Captain Tilney has been about all this time. Why should he pay her such attentions as to make her quarrel with my brother, and then fly off himself?'

'I have very little to say for Frederick's motives,

such as I believe them to have been. He has his vanities as well as Miss Thorpe, and the chief difference is, that, having a stronger head, they have not yet injured himself. If the *effect* of his behaviour does not justify him with you, we had better not seek after the cause.'

'Then you do not suppose he ever really cared about her?'

'I am persuaded that he never did.'

'And only made believe to do so for mischief's sake?'

Henry bowed his assent.

'Well, then, I must say that I do not like him at all. Though it has turned out so well for us, I do not like him at all. As it happens, there is no great harm done, because I do not think Isabella has any heart to lose. But, suppose he had made her very much in love with him?'

'But we must first suppose Isabella to have had a heart to lose, – consequently to have been a very different creature; and, in that case, she would have met with very different treatment.'

'It is very right that you should stand by your brother.'

'And if you would stand by *your's*, you would not be much distressed by the disappointment of Miss Thorpe. But your mind is warped by an innate principle of general integrity, and therefore not accessible to the cool reasonings of family partiality, or a desire of revenge.'

Catherine was complimented out of further bitterness. Frederick could not be unpardonably guilty, while Henry made himself so agreeable. She resolved on not answering Isabella's letter; and tried to think no more of it.

CHAPTER XIII

SOON AFTER this, the General found himself obliged to go to London for a week; and he left Northanger earnestly regretting that any necessity should rob him even for an hour of Miss Morland's company, and anxiously recommending the study of her comfort and amusement to his children as their chief object in his absence. His departure gave Catherine the first experimental conviction that a loss may be sometimes a gain. The happiness with which their time now passed, every employment voluntary, every laugh indulged, every meal a scene of ease and good-humour, walking where they liked and when they liked, their hours, pleasures and fatigues at their own command, made her thoroughly sensible of the restraint which the General's presence had imposed, and most thankfully feel their present release from it. Such ease and such delights made her love the place and the people more and more every day; and had it not been for a dread of its soon becoming expedient to leave the one, and an apprehension of not being equally beloved by the other, she would at each moment of each day have been perfectly happy; but she was now in the fourth week of her visit; before the General came home, the fourth week would be turned, and perhaps it might seem an intrusion if she staid much longer. This was a painful consideration whenever it occurred; and eager to get rid of such a weight on her mind, she very soon resolved to speak to Eleanor about it at once, propose going away, and be guided in her conduct by the manner in which her proposal might be taken.

Aware that if she gave herself much time, she might feel it difficult to bring forward so unpleasant a subject, she took the first opportunity of being suddenly alone with Eleanor, and of Eleanor's being in the middle of a speech about something very different, to start forth her obligation of going away very soon. Eleanor looked and declared herself much concerned. She had 'hoped for the pleasure of her company for a much longer time – had been misled (perhaps by her wishes) to suppose that a much longer visit had been promised – and could not but think that if Mr. and Mrs. Morland were aware of the pleasure it was to her to have her there, they would be too generous to hasten her return.' – Catherine explained. – 'Oh! as to *that*, papa and mamma were in no hurry at all. As long as she was happy, they would always be satisfied.'

'Then why, might she ask, in such a hurry herself to leave them?'

'Oh! because she had been there so long.'

'Nay, if you can use such a word, I can urge you no farther. If you think it long –'

'Oh! no, I do not indeed. For my own pleasure, I could stay with you as long again.' – And it was directly settled that, till she had, her leaving them was not even to be thought of. In having this cause of uneasiness so pleasantly removed, the force of the other was likewise weakened. The kindness, the earnestness of Eleanor's manner in pressing her to stay, and Henry's gratified look on being told that her stay was determined, were such sweet proofs of her importance with them, as left her only just so much solicitude as the human mind can never do comfortably without. She did – almost always – believe that Henry loved her, and quite always that his father and sister loved and even wished her to belong to them; and believing so far, her doubts and anxieties were merely sportive irritations.

Henry was not able to obey his father's injunction of remaining wholly at Northanger in attendance on the ladies, during his absence in London; the engagements of his curate at Woodston obliging him to leave them on Saturday for a couple of nights. His loss was not now what it had been while the General was at home; it lessened their gaiety, but did not ruin their comfort; and the two girls agreeing in occupation, and improving in intimacy, found themselves so well-suffi- cient for the time to themselves, that it was eleven o'clock, rather a late hour at the Abbey, before they quitted the supper-room on the day of Henry's depar- ture. They had just reached the head of the stairs, when it seemed, as far as the thickness of the walls would allow them to judge, that a carriage was driving up to the door, and the next moment confirmed the idea by the loud noise of the house-bell. After the first pertur- bation of surprise had passed away, in a 'Good Heaven! what can be the matter?' it was quickly de- cided by Eleanor to be her eldest brother, whose ar- rival was often as sudden, if not quite so unseasonable, and accordingly she hurried down to welcome him.

Catherine walked on to her chamber, making up her mind as well as she could, to a further acquaintance with Captain Tilney, and comforting herself under the unpleasant impression his conduct had given her, and the persuasion of his being by far too fine a gentleman to approve of her, that at least they should not meet under such circumstances as would make their meeting materially painful. She trusted he would never speak of Miss Thorpe; and indeed, as he must by this time be ashamed of the part he had acted, there could be no danger of it; and as long as all mention of Bath scenes were avoided, she thought she could behave to him very civilly. In such considerations time passed away, and it was certainly in his favour that Eleanor should be so glad to see him, and have so much to say, for half an hour was almost gone since his arrival, and Eleanor did not come up.

At that moment Catherine thought she heard her step in the gallery, and listened for its continuance; but

all was silent. Scarcely, however, had she convicted her
fancy of error, when the noise of something moving
close to her door made her start; it seemed as if some
one was touching the very doorway – and in another
moment a slight motion of the lock proved that some
hand must be on it. She trembled a little at the idea of
any one's approaching so cautiously; but resolving not
to be again overcome by trivial appearances of alarm,
or misled by a raised imagination, she stepped quietly
forward, and opened the door. Eleanor, and only Eleanor, stood there. Catherine's spirits however were tran-
quillized but for an instant, for Eleanor's cheeks were
pale, and her manner greatly agitated. Though evidently
intending to come in, it seemed an effort to enter the
room, and a still greater to speak when there. Catherine, supposing some uneasiness on Captain Tilney's
account, could only express her concern by silent attention; obliged her to be seated, rubbed her temples
with lavender-water, and hung over her with affectionate solicitude. 'My dear Catherine, you must not – you
must not indeed —' were Eleanor's first connected
words. 'I am quite well. This kindness distracts me – I
cannot bear it – I come to you on such an errand!'

'Errand! – to me!'

'How shall I tell you! – Oh! how shall I tell you!'

A new idea now darted into Catherine's mind, and
turning as pale as her friend, she exclaimed, ' 'Tis a
messenger from Woodston!'

'You are mistaken, indeed,' returned Eleanor, looking at her most compassionately – 'it is no one from
Woodston. It is my father himself.' Her voice faltered,
and her eyes were turned to the ground as she mentioned his name. His unlooked-for return was enough
in itself to make Catherine's heart sink, and for a few
moments she hardly supposed there were any thing
worse to be told. She said nothing; and Eleanor endeavouring to collect herself and speak with firmness,

but with eyes still cast down, soon went on. 'You are too good, I am sure, to think the worse of me for the part I am obliged to perform. I am indeed a most unwilling messenger. After what has so lately passed, so lately been settled between us – how joyfully, how thankfully on my side! – as to your continuing here as I hoped for many, many weeks longer, how can I tell you that your kindness is not to be accepted – and that the happiness your company has hitherto given us is to be repaid by – but I must not trust myself with words. My dear Catherine, we are to part. My father has recollected an engagement that takes our whole family away on Monday. We are going to Lord Longtown's, near Hereford, for a fortnight. Explanation and apology are equally impossible. I cannot attempt either.'

'My dear Eleanor,' cried Catherine, suppressing her feelings as well as she could, 'do not be so distressed. A second engagement must give way to a first. I am very, very sorry we are to part – so soon, and so suddenly too; but I am not offended, indeed I am not. I can finish my visit here you know at any time; or I hope you will come to me. Can you, when you return from this lord's, come to Fullerton?'

'It will not be in my power, Catherine.'

'Come when you can, then.' –

Eleanor made no answer; and Catherine's thoughts recurring to something more directly interesting, she added, thinking aloud, 'Monday – so soon as Monday; – and you *all* go. Well, I am certain of — I shall be able to take leave however. I need not go till just before you do, you know. Do not be distressed, Eleanor, I can go on Monday very well. My father and mother's having no notice of it is of very little consequence. The General will send a servant with me, I dare say, half the way – and then I shall soon be at Salisbury, and then I am only nine miles from home.'

'Ah, Catherine! were it settled so, it would be

somewhat less intolerable, though in such common attentions you would have received but half what you
ought. But – how can I tell you? – To-morrow morning
is fixed for your leaving us, and not even the hour is left
to your choice; the very carriage is ordered, and will be
here at seven o'clock, and no servant will be offered you.'

Catherine sat down, breathless and speechless. 'I
could hardly believe my senses, when I heard it; – and
no displeasure, no resentment that you can feel at this
moment, however justly great, can be more than I myself — but I must not talk of what I felt. Oh! that I
could suggest any thing in extenuation! Good God!
what will your father and mother say! After courting
you from the protection of real friends to this – almost
double distance from your home, to have you driven
out of the house, without the considerations even of
decent civility! Dear, dear Catherine, in being the
bearer of such a message, I seem guilty myself of all its
insult; yet, I trust you will acquit me, for you must have
been long enough in this house to see that I am but a
nominal mistress of it, that my real power is nothing.'

'Have I offended the General?' said Catherine in a
faltering voice.

'Alas! for my feelings as a daughter, all that I know,
all that I answer for is, that you can have given him no
just cause of offence. He certainly is greatly, very greatly discomposed; I have seldom seen him more so. His
temper is not happy, and something has now occurred
to ruffle it in an uncommon degree; some disappointment, some vexation, which just at this moment seems
important; but which I can hardly suppose you to have
any concern in, for how is it possible?'

It was with pain that Catherine could speak at all;
and it was only for Eleanor's sake that she attempted
it. 'I am sure,' said she, 'I am very sorry if I have
offended him. It was the last thing I would willingly
have done. But do not be unhappy, Eleanor. An

engagement you know must be kept. I am only sorry it was not recollected sooner, that I might have written home. But it is of very little consequence.'

'I hope, I earnestly hope that to your real safety it will be of none; but to every thing else it is of the greatest consequence; to comfort, appearance, propriety, to your family, to the world. Were your friends, the Allens, still in Bath, you might go to them with comparative ease; a few hours would take you there; but a journey of seventy miles, to be taken post by you, at your age, alone, unattended!'

'Oh, the journey is nothing. Do not think about that. And if we are to part, a few hours sooner or later, you know, makes no difference. I can be ready by seven. Let me be called in time.' Eleanor saw that she wished to be alone; and believing it better for each that they should avoid any further conversation, now left her with 'I shall see you in the morning.'

Catherine's swelling heart needed relief. In Eleanor's presence friendship and pride had equally restrained her tears, but no sooner was she gone than they burst forth in torrents. Turned from the house, and in such a way! – Without any reason that could justify, any apology that could atone for the abruptness, the rudeness, nay, the insolence of it. Henry at a distance – not able even to bid him farewell. Every hope, every expectation from him suspended, at least, and who could say how long? – Who could say when they might meet again? – And all this by such a man as General Tilney, so polite, so well-bred, and heretofore so particularly fond of her! It was as incomprehensible as it was mortifying and grievous. From what it could arise, and where it would end, were considerations of equal perplexity and alarm. The manner in which it was done so grossly uncivil; hurrying her away without any reference to her own convenience, or allowing her even the appearance of choice as to the time or mode of her

travelling; of two days, the earliest fixed on, and of that
almost the earliest hour, as if resolved to have her gone
before he was stirring in the morning, that he might
not be obliged even to see her. What could all this
mean but an intentional affront? By some means or
other she must have had the misfortune to offend him.
Eleanor had wished to spare her from so painful a
notion, but Catherine could not believe it possible that
any injury or any misfortune could provoke such ill-will
against a person not connected, or, at least, not supposed to be connected with it.

Heavily past the night. Sleep, or repose that de-
served the name of sleep, was out of the question.
That room, in which her disturbed imagination had
tormented her on her first arrival, was again the scene
of agitated spirits and unquiet slumbers. Yet how
different now the source of her inquietude from what
it had been then – how mournfully superior in reality
and substance! Her anxiety had foundation in fact, her
fears in probability; and with a mind so occupied in the
contemplation of actual and natural evil, the solitude of
her situation, the darkness of her chamber, the antiquity of the building were felt and considered without
the smallest emotion; and though the wind was high,
and often produced strange and sudden noises
throughout the house, she heard it all as she lay awake,
hour after hour, without curiosity or terror.

Soon after six Eleanor entered her room, eager to
show attention or give assistance where it was possible;
but very little remained to be done. Catherine had not
loitered; she was almost dressed, and her packing almost finished. The possibility of some conciliatory
message from the General occurred to her as his
daughter appeared. What so natural, as that anger
should pass away and repentance succeed it? and she
only wanted to know how far, after what had passed,
an apology might properly be received by her. But the

knowledge would have been useless here, it was not called for; neither clemency nor dignity was put to the trial – Eleanor brought no message. Very little passed between them on meeting; each found her greatest safety in silence, and few and trivial were the sentences exchanged while they remained up stairs, Catherine in busy agitation completing her dress, and Eleanor with more good-will than experience intent upon filling the trunk. When every thing was done they left the room, Catherine lingering only half a minute behind her friend to throw a parting glance on every well-known cherished object, and went down to the breakfast-parlour, where breakfast was prepared. She tried to eat, as well to save herself from the pain of being urged, as to make her friend comfortable; but she had no appetite, and could not swallow many mouthfuls. The contrast between this and her last breakfast in that room, gave her fresh misery, and strengthened her distaste for every thing before her. It was not four-and-twenty hours ago since they had met there to the same repast, but in circumstances how different! With what cheerful ease, what happy, though false security, had she then looked around her, enjoying every thing present, and fearing little in future, beyond Henry's going to Woodston for a day! Happy, happy breakfast! for Henry had been there, Henry had sat by her and helped her. These reflections were long indulged undisturbed by any address from her companion, who sat as deep in thought as herself; and the appearance of the carriage was the first thing to startle and recall them to the present moment. Catherine's colour rose at the sight of it; and the indignity with which she was treated striking at that instant on her mind with peculiar force, made her for a short time sensible only of resentment. Eleanor seemed now impelled into resolution and speech.

'You *must* write to me, Catherine,' she cried, 'you

must let me hear from you as soon as possible. Till I
know you to be safe at home, I shall not have an hour's
comfort. For *one* letter, at all risks, all hazards, I must
entreat. Let me have the satisfaction of knowing that
you are safe at Fullerton, and have found your family
well, and then, till I can ask for your correspondence
as I ought to do, I will not expect more. Direct to me
at Lord Longtown's, and, I must ask it, under cover to
Alice.'

'No, Eleanor, if you are not allowed to receive a
letter from me, I am sure I had better not write. There
can be no doubt of my getting home safe.'

Eleanor only replied, 'I cannot wonder at your feelings. I will not importune you. I will trust to your own
kindness of heart when I am at a distance from you.'
But this, with the look of sorrow accompanying it, was
enough to melt Catherine's pride in a moment, and she
instantly said, 'Oh, Eleanor, I *will* write to you indeed.'

There was yet another point which Miss Tilney was
anxious to settle, though somewhat embarrassed in
speaking of. It had occurred to her, that after so long
an absence from home, Catherine might not be provided with money enough for the expenses of her journey, and, upon suggesting it to her with most
affectionate offers of accommodation, it proved to be
exactly the case. Catherine had never thought on the
subject till that moment; but, upon examining her
purse, was convinced that but for this kindness of her
friend, she might have been turned from the house
without even the means of getting home; and the distress in which she must have been thereby involved
filling the minds of both, scarcely another word was
said by either during the time of their remaining
together. Short, however, was that time. The carriage
was soon announced to be ready; and Catherine, instantly rising, a long and affectionate embrace supplied
the place of language in bidding each other adieu; and,

as they entered the hall, unable to leave the house without some mention of one whose name had not yet been spoken by either, she paused a moment, and with quivering lips just made it intelligible that she left 'her kind remembrance for her absent friend.' But with this approach to his name ended all possibility of restraining her feelings; and, hiding her face as well as she could with her handkerchief, she darted across the hall, jumped into the chaise, and in a moment was driven from the door.

CHAPTER XIV

CATHERINE WAS too wretched to be fearful. The journey in itself had no terrors for her; and she began it without either dreading its length, or feeling its solitariness. Leaning back in one corner of the carriage, in a violent burst of tears, she was conveyed some miles beyond the walls of the Abbey before she raised her head; and the highest point of ground within the park was almost closed from her view before she was capable of turning her eyes towards it. Unfortunately, the road she now travelled was the same which only ten days ago she had so happily passed along in going to and from Woodston; and, for fourteen miles, every bitter feeling was rendered more severe by the review of objects on which she had first looked under impressions so different. Every mile, as it brought her nearer Woodston, added to her sufferings, and when within the distance of five, she passed the turning which led to it, and thought of Henry, so near, yet so unconscious, her grief and agitation were excessive.

The day which she had spent at that place had been one of the happiest of her life. It was there, it was on that day that the General had made use of such expressions with regard to Henry and herself, had so spoken and so looked as to give her the most positive conviction of his actually wishing their marriage. Yes, only ten days ago had he elated her by his pointed regard – had he even confused her by his too significant reference! And now – what had she done, or what had she omitted to do, to merit such a change?

The only offence against him of which she could accuse herself, had been such as was scarcely possible to reach his knowledge. Henry and her own heart only were privy to the shocking suspicions which she had so idly entertained; and equally safe did she believe her secret with each. Designedly, at least, Henry could not have betrayed her. If, indeed, by any strange mischance his father should have gained intelligence of what she had dared to think and look for, of her causeless fancies and injurious examinations, she could not wonder at any degree of his indignation. If aware of her having viewed him as a murderer, she could not wonder at his even turning her from his house. But a justification so full of torture to herself, she trusted would not be in his power.

Anxious as were all her conjectures on this point, it was not, however, the one on which she dwelt most. There was a thought yet nearer, a more prevailing, more impetuous concern. How Henry would think, and feel, and look, when he returned on the morrow to Northanger and heard of her being gone, was a question of force and interest to rise over every other, to be never ceasing, alternately irritating and soothing; it sometimes suggested the dread of his calm acquiescence, and at others was answered by the sweetest confidence in his regret and resentment. To the General, of course, he would not dare to speak; but to Eleanor – what might he not say to Eleanor about her?

In this unceasing recurrence of doubts and inquiries, on any one article of which her mind was incapable of more than momentary repose, the hours passed away, and her journey advanced much faster than she looked for. The pressing anxieties of thought, which prevented her from noticing any thing before her, when once beyond the neighbourhood of Woodston, saved her at the same time from watching her progress; and though no object on the road could engage a moment's attention, she found no stage of it tedious. From this, she was preserved too by another cause, by feeling no eagerness for her journey's conclusion; for to return in such a manner to Fullerton was almost to destroy the pleasure of a meeting with those she loved best, even after an absence such as her's – an eleven weeks absence. What had she to say that would not humble herself and pain her family; that would not increase her own grief by the confession of it, extend an useless resentment, and perhaps involve the innocent with the guilty in undistinguishing ill-will? She could never do justice to Henry and Eleanor's merit; she felt it too strongly for expression; and should a dislike be taken against them, should they be thought of unfavourably, on their father's account, it would cut her to the heart.

With these feelings, she rather dreaded than sought for the first view of that well-known spire which would announce her within twenty miles of home. Salisbury she had known to be her point on leaving Northanger; but after the first stage she had been indebted to the post-masters for the names of the places which were then to conduct her to it; so great had been her ignorance of her route. She met with nothing, however, to distress or frighten her. Her youth, civil manners and liberal pay, procured her all the attention that a traveller like herself could require; and stopping only to change horses, she travelled on for about eleven hours without accident or alarm, and between six and seven o'clock in the evening found herself entering Fullerton.

A heroine returning, at the close of her career, to

her native village, in all the triumph of recovered reputation, and all the dignity of a countess, with a long train of noble relations in their several phaetons, and three waiting-maids in a travelling chaise-and-four, behind her, is an event on which the pen of the contriver may well delight to dwell; it gives credit to every conclusion, and the author must share in the glory she so liberally bestows. – But my affair is widely different; I bring back my heroine to her home in solitude and disgrace; and no sweet elation of spirits can lead me into minuteness. A heroine in a hack post-chaise, is such a blow upon sentiment, as no attempt at grandeur or pathos can withstand. Swiftly therefore shall her post-boy drive through the village, amid the gaze of Sunday groups, and speedy shall be her descent from it.

But, whatever might be the distress of Catherine's mind, as she thus advanced towards the Parsonage, and whatever the humiliation of her biographer in relating it, she was preparing enjoyment of no every-day nature for those to whom she went; first, in the appearance of her carriage – and secondly, in herself. The chaise of a traveller being a rare sight in Fullerton, the whole family were immediately at the window; and to have it stop at the sweep-gate was a pleasure to brighten every eye and occupy every fancy – a pleasure quite unlooked for by all but the two youngest children, a boy and girl of six and four years old, who expected a brother or sister in every carriage. Happy the glance that first distinguished Catherine! – Happy the voice that proclaimed the discovery! – But whether such happiness were the lawful property of George or Harriet could never be exactly understood.

Her father, mother, Sarah, George, and Harriet, all assembled at the door, to welcome her with affectionate eagerness, was a sight to awaken the best feelings of Catherine's heart; and in the embrace of each, as she stepped from the carriage, she found herself soothed beyond any thing that she had believed possible. So surrounded, so caressed, she was even happy! In the joyfulness of family love every thing for a short time was subdued, and the pleasure of seeing her, leaving them at first little leisure for calm curiosity, they were all seated round the tea-table, which Mrs. Morland had hurried for the comfort of the poor traveller, whose pale and jaded looks soon caught her notice, before any inquiry so direct as to demand a positive answer was addressed to her.

Reluctantly, and with much hesitation, did she then begin what might perhaps, at the end of half an hour, be termed by the courtesy of her hearers, an explanation; but scarcely, within that time, could they at all discover the cause, or collect the particulars of her sudden return. They were far from being an irritable race; far from any quickness in catching, or bitterness in resenting affronts: – but here, when the whole was unfolded, was an insult not to be overlooked, nor, for the first half hour, to be easily pardoned. Without suffering any romantic alarm, in the consideration of their daughter's long and lonely journey, Mr. and Mrs. Morland could not but feel that it might have been productive of much unpleasantness to her; that it was what they could never have voluntarily suffered; and that, in forcing her on such a measure, General Tilney had acted neither honourably nor feelingly – neither as a gentleman nor as a parent. Why he had done it, what could have provoked him to such a breach of hospitality, and so suddenly turned all his partial regard for their daughter into actual ill-will, was a matter which they were at least as far from divining as Catherine herself; but it did not oppress them by any means so long; and, after a due course of useless conjecture, that, 'it was a strange business, and that he must be a very strange man,' grew enough for all their indignation and wonder; though Sarah indeed still indulged in the sweets of incomprehensibility, exclaiming and conjecturing with youthful ardour. – 'My dear, you give yourself a great deal of needless trouble,' said her mother at last; 'depend upon it, it is something not at all worth understanding.'

'I can allow for his wishing Catherine away, when he recollected this engagement,' said Sarah, 'but why not do it civilly?'

'I am sorry for the young people,' returned Mrs. Morland; 'they must have a sad time of it; but as for any thing else, it is no matter now; Catherine is safe at home, and our comfort does not depend upon General Tilney.' Catherine sighed. 'Well,' continued her philosophic mother, 'I am glad I did not know of your journey at the time; but now it is all over perhaps there is no great harm done. It is always good for young people to be put upon exerting themselves; and you know, my dear Catherine, you always were a sad little shatter-brained creature; but now you must have been forced to have your wits about you, with so much changing of chaises and so forth; and I hope it will appear that you have not left any thing behind you in any of the pockets.'

Catherine hoped so too, and tried to feel an interest in her own amendment, but her spirits were quite worn down; and, to be silent and alone becoming soon her only wish, she readily agreed to her mother's next counsel of going early to bed. Her parents seeing nothing in her ill-looks and agitation but the natural consequence of mortified feelings, and of the unusual exertion and fatigue of such a journey, parted from her without any doubt of their being soon slept away; and though, when they all met the next morning, her recovery was not equal to their hopes, they were still perfectly unsuspicious of there being any deeper evil. They never once thought of her heart, which, for the parents of a young lady of seventeen, just returned from her first excursion from home, was odd enough!

As soon as breakfast was over, she sat down to fulfil her promise to Miss Tilney, whose trust in the effect of time and distance on her friend's disposition was already justified, for already did Catherine reproach herself with having parted from Eleanor coldly; with having never enough valued her merits or kindness; and never enough commiserated her for what she had been yesterday left to endure. The strength of these feelings, however, was far from assisting her pen; and never had it been harder for her to write than in addressing Eleanor Tilney. To compose a letter which might at once do justice to her sentiments and her situation, convey gratitude without servile regret, be guarded without coldness, and honest without resentment – a letter which Eleanor might not be pained by the perusal of – and, above all, which she might not blush herself, if Henry should chance to see, was an undertaking to frighten away all her powers of performance; and, after long thought and much perplexity, to be very brief was all that she could determine on with any confidence of safety. The money therefore which Eleanor had advanced was inclosed with little more than grateful thanks, and the thousand good wishes of a most affectionate heart.

'This has been a strange acquaintance,' observed Mrs. Morland, as the letter was finished; 'soon made and soon ended. – I am sorry it happens so, for Mrs. Allen thought them very pretty kind of young people; and you were sadly out of luck too in your Isabella. Ah! poor James! Well, we must live and learn; and the next new friends you make I hope will be better worth keeping.'

Catherine coloured as she warmly answered, 'No friend can be better worth keeping than Eleanor.'

'If so, my dear, I dare say you will meet again some

time or other; do not be uneasy. It is ten to one but you are thrown together again in the course of a few years; and then what a pleasure it will be!'

Mrs. Morland was not happy in her attempt at consolation. The hope of meeting again in the course of a few years could only put into Catherine's head what might happen within that time to make a meeting dreadful to her. She could never forget Henry Tilney, or think of him with less tenderness than she did at that moment; but he might forget her; and in that case to meet! — Her eyes filled with tears as she pictured her acquaintance so renewed; and her mother, perceiving her comfortable suggestions to have had no good effect, proposed, as another expedient for restoring her spirits, that they should call on Mrs. Allen.

The two houses were only a quarter of a mile apart; and, as they walked, Mrs. Morland quickly dispatched all that she felt on the score of James's disappointment. 'We are sorry for him,' said she; 'but otherwise there is no harm done in the match going off; for it could not be a desirable thing to have him engaged to a girl whom we had not the smallest acquaintance with, and who was so entirely without fortune; and now, after such behaviour, we cannot think at all well of her. Just at present it comes hard to poor James; but that will not last for ever; and I dare say he will be a discreeter man all his life, for the foolishness of his first choice.'

This was just such a summary view of the affair as Catherine could listen to; another sentence might have endangered her complaisance, and made her reply less rational; for soon were all her thinking powers swallowed up in the reflection of her own change of feelings and spirits since last she had trodden that well-known road. It was not three months ago since, wild with joyful expectation, she had there run backwards and forwards some ten times a-day, with an heart light, gay, and independent; looking forward to pleasures untasted and unalloyed, and free from the apprehension of evil as from the knowledge of it. Three months ago had seen her all this; and now, how altered a being did she return!

She was received by the Allens with all the kindness which her unlooked-for appearance, acting on a steady affection, would naturally call forth; and great was their surprise, and warm their displeasure, on hearing how she had been treated, – though Mrs. Morland's account of it was no inflated representation, no studied appeal to their passions. 'Catherine took us quite by surprise yesterday evening,' said she. 'She travelled all the way post by herself, and knew nothing of coming till Saturday night; for General Tilney, from some odd fancy or other, all of a sudden grew tired of having her there, and almost turned her out of the house. Very unfriendly, certainly; and he must be a very odd man; – but we are so glad to have her amongst us again! And it is a great comfort to find that she is not a poor helpless creature, but can shift very well for herself.'

Mr. Allen expressed himself on the occasion with the reasonable resentment of a sensible friend; and Mrs. Allen thought his expressions quite good enough to be immediately made use of again by herself. His wonder, his conjectures, and his explanations, became in succession her's, with the addition of this single remark – 'I really have not patience with the General' – to fill up every accidental pause. And, 'I really have not patience with the General,' was uttered twice after Mr. Allen left the room, without any relaxation of anger, or any material digression of thought. A more considerable degree of wandering attended the third repetition; and, after completing the fourth, she immediately added, 'Only think, my dear, of my having got that frightful great rent in my best Mechlin so charmingly mended, before I left Bath, that one can hardly see where it was. I must shew it you some day or other. Bath is a nice place, Catherine, after all. I assure you I did not above half like coming away. Mrs. Thorpe's being there was such a comfort to us, was not it? You know you and I were quite forlorn at first.'

'Yes, but *that* did not last long,' said Catherine, her eyes brightening at the recollection of what had first given spirit to her existence there.

'Very true: we soon met with Mrs. Thorpe, and then we wanted for nothing. My dear, do not you think these silk gloves wear very well? I put them on new the first time of our going to the Lower Rooms, you know, and I have worn them a great deal since. Do you remember that evening?'

'Do I! Oh! perfectly.'

'It was very agreeable, was not it? Mr. Tilney drank tea with us, and I always thought him a great addition, he is so very agreeable. I have a notion you danced with him, but am not quite sure. I remember I had my favourite gown on.'

Catherine could not answer; and, after a short trial of other subjects, Mrs. Allen again returned to – 'I really have not patience with the General! Such an agreeable, worthy man as he seemed to be! I do not suppose, Mrs. Morland, you ever saw a better-bred man in your life. His lodgings were taken the very day after he left them, Catherine. But no wonder; Milsom-street you know.' –

As they walked home again, Mrs. Morland endeavoured to impress on her daughter's mind the happiness of having such steady well-wishers as Mr. and Mrs. Allen, and the very little consideration which the neglect or unkindness of slight acquaintance like the Tilneys ought to have with her, while she could preserve the good opinion and affection of her earliest friends. There was a great deal of good sense in all this; but there are some situations of the human mind in which good sense has very little power; and Catherine's feelings contradicted almost every position her mother advanced. It was upon the behaviour of these very slight acquaintance that all her present happiness depended; and while Mrs. Morland was successfully confirming her own opinions by the justness of her own representations, Catherine was silently reflecting that *now* Henry must have arrived at Northanger; *now* he must have heard of her departure; and *now*, perhaps, they were all setting off for Hereford.

CHAPTER XV

CATHERINE'S DISPOSITION was not naturally sedentary, nor had her habits been ever very industrious; but whatever might hitherto have been her defects of that sort, her mother could not but perceive them now to be greatly increased. She could neither sit still, nor employ herself for ten minutes together, walking round the garden and orchard again and again, as if nothing but motion was voluntary; and it seemed as if she could even walk about the house rather than remain fixed for any time in the parlour. Her loss of spirits was a yet greater alteration. In her rambling and her idleness she might only be a caricature of herself; but in her silence and sadness she was the very reverse of all that she had been before.

For two days Mrs. Morland allowed it to pass even without a hint; but when a third night's rest had neither restored her cheerfulness, improved her in useful activity, nor given her a greater inclination for needle-work, she could no longer refrain from the gentle reproof of, 'My dear Catherine, I am afraid you are growing quite a fine lady. I do not know when poor Richard's cravats would be done, if he had no friend but you. Your head runs too much upon Bath; but there is a time for every thing – a time for balls and plays, and a time for work. You have had a long run of amusement, and now you must try to be useful.'

Catherine took up her work directly, saying, in a dejected voice, that 'her head did not run upon Bath – much.'

'Then you are fretting about General Tilney, and that is very simple of you; for ten to one whether you ever see him again. You should never fret about trifles.' After a short silence – 'I hope, my Catherine, you are not getting out of humour with home because it is not so grand as Northanger. That would be turning your visit into an evil indeed. Wherever you are you should always be contented, but especially at home, because there you must spend the most of your time. I did not quite like, at breakfast, to hear you talk so much about the French-bread at Northanger.'

'I am sure I do not care about the bread. It is all the same to me what I eat.'

'There is a very clever Essay in one of the books up stairs upon much such a subject, about young girl that have been spoilt for home by great acquaintance – "The Mirror," I think. I will look it out for you some day or other, because I am sure it will do you good.'

Catherine said no more, and, with an endeavour to do right, applied to her work; but, after a few minutes, sunk again, without knowing it herself, into languor and listlessness, moving herself in her chair, from the irritation of weariness, much oftener than she moved her needle. – Mrs. Morland watched the progress of this relapse; and seeing, in her daughter's absent and dissatisfied look, the full proof of that repining spirit to which she had now begun to attribute her want of cheerfulness, hastily left the room to fetch the book in question, anxious to lose no time in attacking so dreadful a malady. It was some time before she could find

what she looked for; and other family matters occurring to detain her, a quarter of an hour had elapsed ere
she returned down stairs with the volume from which
so much was hoped. Her avocations above having shut
out all noise but what she created herself, she knew not
that a visitor had arrived within the last few minutes,
till, on entering the room, the first object she beheld
was a young man whom she had never seen before.
With a look of much respect, he immediately rose, and
being introduced to her by her conscious daughter as
'Mr. Henry Tilney,' with the embarrassment of real sensibility began to apologize for his appearance there,
acknowledging that after what had passed he had little
right to expect a welcome at Fullerton, and stating his
impatience to be assured of Miss Morland's having
reached her home in safety, as the cause of his intrusion. He did not address himself to an uncandid judge
or a resentful heart. Far from comprehending him or
his sister in their father's misconduct, Mrs. Morland
had been always kindly disposed towards each, and instantly, pleased by his appearance, received him with
the simple professions of unaffected benevolence;
thanking him for such an attention to her daughter,
assuring him that the friends of her children were
always welcome there, and intreating him to say not
another word of the past.

He was not ill inclined to obey this request, for,
though his heart was greatly relieved by such unlooked-
for mildness, it was not just at that moment in his
power to say any thing to the purpose. Returning in
silence to his seat, therefore, he remained for some
minutes most civilly answering all Mrs. Morland's common remarks about the weather and roads. Catherine
meanwhile, – the anxious, agitated, happy, feverish
Catherine, – said not a word; but her glowing cheek
and brightened eye made her mother trust that this
good-natured visit would at least set her heart at ease

for a time, and gladly therefore did she lay aside the first volume of the Mirror for a future hour.

Desirous of Mr. Morland's assistance, as well in giving encouragement, as in finding conversation for her guest, whose embarrassment on his father's account she earnestly pitied, Mrs. Morland had very early dispatched one of the children to summon him; but Mr. Morland was from home – and being thus without any support, at the end of a quarter of an hour she had nothing to say. After a couple of minutes unbroken silence, Henry, turning to Catherine for the first time since her mother's entrance, asked her, with sudden alacrity, if Mr. and Mrs. Allen were now at Fullerton? and on developing, from amidst all her perplexity of words in reply, the meaning, which one short syllable would have given, immediately expressed his intention of paying his respects to them, and, with a rising colour, asked her if she would have the goodness to shew him the way. 'You may see the house from this window, sir,' was information on Sarah's side, which produced only a bow of acknowledgment from the gentleman, and a silencing nod from her mother; for Mrs. Morland, thinking it probable, as a secondary consideration in his wish of waiting on their worthy neighbours, that he might have some explanation to give of his father's behaviour, which it must be more pleasant for him to communicate only to Catherine, would not on any account prevent her accompanying him. They began their walk, and Mrs. Morland was not entirely mistaken in his object in wishing it. Some explanation on his father's account he had to give; but his first purpose was to explain himself, and before they reached Mr. Allen's grounds he had done it so well, that Catherine did not think it could ever be repeated too often. She was assured of his affection; and that heart in return was solicited, which, perhaps, they pretty equally knew was already entirely his own;

for, though Henry was now sincerely attached to her, though he felt and delighted in all the excellencies of her character and truly loved her society, I must confess that his affection originated in nothing better than gratitude, or, in other words, that a persuasion of her partiality for him had been the only cause of giving her a serious thought. It is a new circumstance in romance, I acknowledge, and dreadfully derogatory of an heroine's dignity; but if it be as new in common life, the credit of a wild imagination will at least be all my own.

A very short visit to Mrs. Allen, in which Henry talked at random, without sense or connection, and Catherine, wrapt in the contemplation of her own unutterable happiness, scarcely opened her lips, dismissed them to the extasies of another tête-à-tête; and before it was suffered to close, she was enabled to judge how far he was sanctioned by parental authority in his present application. On his return from Woodston, two days before, he had been met near the Abbey by his impatient father, hastily informed in angry terms of Miss Morland's departure, and ordered to think of her no more.

Such was the permission upon which he had now offered her his hand. The affrighted Catherine, amidst all the terrors of expectation, as she listened to this account, could not but rejoice in the kind caution with which Henry had saved her from the necessity of a conscientious rejection, by engaging her faith before he mentioned the subject; and as he proceeded to give the particulars, and explain the motives of his father's conduct, her feelings soon hardened into even a triumphant delight. The General had had nothing to accuse her of, nothing to lay to her charge, but her being the involuntary, unconscious object of a deception which his pride could not pardon, and which a better pride would have been ashamed to own. She was guilty only of being less rich than he had supposed her to be.

Under a mistaken persuasion of her possessions and claims, he had courted her acquaintance in Bath, solicited her company at Northanger, and designed her for his daughter in law. On discovering his error, to turn her from the house seemed the best, though to his feelings an inadequate proof of his resentment towards herself, and his contempt of her family.

John Thorpe had first misled him. The General, perceiving his son one night at the theatre to be paying considerable attention to Miss Morland, had accidentally inquired of Thorpe, if he knew more of her than her name. Thorpe, most happy to be on speaking terms with a man of General Tilney's importance, had been joyfully and proudly communicative; – and being at that time not only in daily expectation of Morland's engaging Isabella, but likewise pretty well resolved upon marrying Catherine himself, his vanity induced him to represent the family as yet more wealthy than his vanity and avarice had made him believe them. With whomsoever he was, or was likely to be connected, his own consequence always required that theirs should be great, and as his intimacy with any acquaintance grew, so regularly grew their fortune. The expectations of his friend Morland, therefore, from the first over-rated, had ever since his introduction to Isabella, been gradually increasing; and by merely adding twice as much for the grandeur of the moment, by doubling what he chose to think the amount of Mr. Morland's preferment, trebling his private fortune, bestowing a rich aunt, and sinking half the children, he was able to represent the whole family to the General in a most respectable light. For Catherine, however, the peculiar object of the General's curiosity, and his own speculations, he had yet something more in reserve, and the ten or fifteen thousand pounds which her father could give her, would be a pretty addition to Mr. Allen's estate. Her intimacy there had made him seriously determine on her being handsomely legacied hereafter; and to speak of her therefore as the almost acknowledged future heiress of Fullerton naturally followed. Upon such intelligence the General had proceeded; for never had it occurred to him to doubt its authority. Thorpe's interest in the family, by his sister's approaching connection with one of its members, and his own views on another, (circumstances of which he boasted with almost equal openness,) seemed sufficient vouchers for his truth; and to these were added the absolute facts of the Allens being wealthy and childless, of Miss Morland's being under their care, and – as soon as his acquaintance allowed him to judge – of their treating her with parental kindness. His resolution was soon formed. Already had he discerned a liking towards Miss Morland in the countenance of his son; and thankful for Mr. Thorpe's communication, he almost instantly determined to spare no pains in weakening his boasted interest and ruining his dearest hopes. Catherine herself could not be more ignorant at the time of all this, than his own children. Henry and Eleanor, perceiving nothing in her situation likely to engage their father's particular respect, had seen with astonishment the suddenness, continuance and extent of his attention; and though latterly, from some hints which had accompanied an almost positive command to his son of doing every thing in his power to attach her, Henry was convinced of his father's believing it to be an advantageous connection, it was not till the late explanation at Northanger that they had the smallest idea of the false calculations which had hurried him on. That they were false, the General had learnt from the very person who had suggested them, from Thorpe himself, whom he had chanced to meet again in town, and who, under the influence of exactly opposite feelings, irritated by Catherine's refusal, and yet more by the failure of a very recent endeavour to accomplish a reconciliation between Morland and Isabella, convinced that they were separated for ever, and spurning a friendship which could be no longer serviceable, hastened to contradict all that he had said before to the advantage of the Morlands; – confessed himself to have been totally mistaken in his opinion of their circumstances and character, misled by the rhodomontade of his friend to believe his father a man of substance and credit, whereas the transactions of the two or three last weeks proved him to be neither; for after coming eagerly forward on the first overture of a marriage between the families, with the most liberal proposals, he had, on being brought to the point by the shrewdness of the relator, been constrained to acknowledge himself incapable of giving the young people even a decent support. They were, in fact, a necessitous family; numerous too almost beyond example; by no means respected in their own neighbourhood, as he had lately had particular opportunities of discovering; aiming at a style of life which their fortune could not warrant; seeking to better themselves by wealthy connexions; a forward, bragging, scheming race.

The terrified General pronounced the name of Allen with an inquiring look; and here too Thorpe had learnt his error. The Allens, he believed, had lived near them too long, and he knew the young man on whom the Fullerton estate must devolve. The General needed no more. Enraged with almost every body in the world but himself, he set out the next day for the Abbey, where his performances have been seen.

I leave it to my reader's sagacity to determine how much of all this it was possible for Henry to communicate at this time to Catherine, how much of it he could have learnt from his father, in what points his own conjectures might assist him, and what portion must yet remain to be told in a letter from James. I have united for their ease what they must divide for mine.

Catherine, at any rate, heard enough to feel, that in suspecting General Tilney of either murdering or shutting up his wife, she had scarcely sinned against his character, or magnified his cruelty.

Henry, in having such things to relate of his father, was almost as pitiable as in their first avowal to himself. He blushed for the narrow-minded counsel which he was obliged to expose. The conversation between them at Northanger had been of the most unfriendly kind. Henry's indignation on hearing how Catherine had been treated, on comprehending his father's views, and being ordered to acquiesce in them, had been open and bold. The General, accustomed on every ordinary occasion to give the law in his family, prepared for no reluctance but of feeling, no opposing desire that should dare to clothe itself in words, could ill brook the opposition of his son, steady as the sanction of reason and the dictate of conscience could make it. But, in such a cause, his anger, though it must shock, could not intimidate Henry, who was sustained in his purpose by a conviction of its justice. He felt himself bound as much in honour as in affection to Miss Morland, and believing that heart to be his own which he had been directed to gain, no unworthy retraction of a tacit consent, no reversing decree of unjustifiable anger, could shake his fidelity, or influence the resolutions it prompted.

He steadily refused to accompany his father into Herefordshire, an engagement formed almost at the moment, to promote the dismissal of Catherine, and as steadily declared his intention of offering her his hand. The General was furious in his anger, and they parted in dreadful disagreement. Henry, in an agitation of mind which many solitary hours were required to compose, had returned almost instantly to Woodston; and, on the afternoon of the following day, had begun his journey to Fullerton.

CHAPTER XVI

M R. AND Mrs. Morland's surprise on being applied
to by Mr. Tilney, for their consent to his marrying their daughter, was, for a few minutes, considerable; it having never entered their heads to suspect an
attachment on either side; but as nothing, after all,
could be more natural than Catherine's being beloved,
they soon learnt to consider it with only the happy
agitation of gratified pride, and, as far as they alone
were concerned, had not a single objection to start. His
pleasing manners and good sense were self-evident
recommendations; and having never heard evil of him,
it was not their way to suppose any evil could be told.
Good-will supplying the place of experience, his character needed no attestation. 'Catherine would make a
sad heedless young housekeeper to be sure,' was her
mother's foreboding remark; but quick was the consolation of there being nothing like practice.

There was but one obstacle, in short, to be mentioned; but till that one was removed, it must be impossible for them to sanction the engagement. Their
tempers were mild, but their principles were steady,
and while his parent so expressly forbad the connexion, they could not allow themselves to encourage it.
That the General should come forward to solicit the
alliance, or that he should even very heartily approve
it, they were not refined enough to make any parading
stipulation; but the decent appearance of consent must
be yielded, and that once obtained – and their own
hearts made them trust that it could not be very long
denied – their willing approbation was instantly to follow. His *consent* was all that they wished for. They were
no more inclined than entitled to demand his *money*. Of
a very considerable fortune, his son was, by marriage

settlements, eventually secure; his present income was an income of independence and comfort, and under every pecuniary view, it was a match beyond the claims of their daughter.

The young people could not be surprised at a decision like this. They felt and they deplored – but they could not resent it; and they parted, endeavouring to hope that such a change in the General, as each believed almost impossible, might speedily take place, to unite them again in the fullness of privileged affection. Henry returned to what was now his only home, to watch over his young plantations, and extend his improvements for her sake, to whose share in them he looked anxiously forward; and Catherine remained at Fullerton to cry. Whether the torments of absence were softened by a clandestine correspondence, let us not inquire. Mr. and Mrs. Morland never did – they had been too kind to exact any promise; and whenever Catherine received a letter, as, at that time, happened pretty often, they always looked another way.

The anxiety, which in this state of their attachment must be the portion of Henry and Catherine, and of all who loved either, as to its final event, can hardly extend, I fear, to the bosom of my readers, who will see in the tell-tale compression of the pages before them, that we are all hastening together to perfect felicity. The means by which their early marriage was effected can be the only doubt; what probable circumstance could work upon a temper like the General's? The circumstance which chiefly availed, was the marriage of his daughter with a man of fortune and consequence, which took place in the course of the summer – an accession of dignity that threw him into a fit of good-humour, from which he did not recover till after Eleanor had obtained his forgiveness of Henry, and his permission for him 'to be a fool if he liked it!'

The marriage of Eleanor Tilney, her removal from

all the evils of such a home as Northanger had been
made by Henry's banishment, to the home of her
choice and the man of her choice, is an event which I
expect to give general satisfaction among all her acquaintance. My own joy on the occasion is very sincere.
I know no one more entitled, by unpretending merit,
or better prepared by habitual suffering, to receive and
enjoy felicity. Her partiality for this gentleman was not
of recent origin; and he had been long withheld only
by inferiority of situation from addressing her. His unexpected accession to title and fortune had removed all
his difficulties; and never had the General loved his
daughter so well in all her hours of companionship,
utility, and patient endurance, as when he first hailed
her, 'Your Ladyship!' Her husband was really deserving
of her; independent of his peerage, his wealth, and his
attachment, being to a precision the most charming
young man in the world. Any further definition of his
merits must be unnecessary; the most charming young
man in the world is instantly before the imagination of
us all. Concerning the one in question therefore I have
only to add – (aware that the rules of composition
forbid the introduction of a character not connected
with my fable) – that this was the very gentleman
whose negligent servant left behind him that collection
of washing-bills, resulting from a long visit at Northanger, by which my heroine was involved in one of her
most alarming adventures.

The influence of the Viscount and Viscountess in
their brother's behalf was assisted by that right understanding of Mr. Morland's circumstances which, as
soon as the General would allow himself to be informed, they were qualified to give. It taught him that
he had been scarcely more misled by Thorpe's first
boast of the family wealth, than by his subsequent
malicious overthrow of it; that in no sense of the word
were they necessitous or poor, and that Catherine

would have three thousand pounds. This was so material an amendment of his late expectations, that it greatly contributed to smooth the descent of his pride; and by no means without its effect was the private intelligence, which he was at some pains to procure, that the Fullerton estate, being entirely at the disposal of its present proprietor, was consequently open to every greedy speculation.

On the strength of this, the General, soon after Eleanor's marriage, permitted his son to return to Northanger, and thence made him the bearer of his consent, very courteously worded in a page full of empty professions to Mr. Morland. The event which it authorized soon followed: Henry and Catherine were married, the bells rang and every body smiled; and, as this took place within a twelvemonth from the first day of their meeting, it will not appear, after all the dreadful delays occasioned by the General's cruelty, that they were essentially hurt by it. To begin perfect happiness at the respective ages of twenty-six and eighteen, is to do pretty well; and professing myself moreover convinced, that the General's unjust interference, so far from being really injurious to their felicity, was perhaps rather conducive to it, by improving their knowledge of each other, and adding strength to their attachment, I leave it to be settled by whomsoever it may concern, whether the tendency of this work be altogether to recommend parental tyranny, or reward filial disobedience.

FINIS

ABOUT THE INTRODUCER

Claudia L. Johnson is Associate Professor of English at Marquette University in Milwaukee, Wisconsin and author of *Jane Austen: Women, Politics, and the Novel*, and *Equivocal Beings: Politics, Gender and Sentimentality in the 1790s*.

CHINUA ACHEBE
Things Fall Apart

THE ARABIAN NIGHTS
(tr. Husain Haddawy)

MARCUS AURELIUS
Meditations

JANE AUSTEN
Emma
Mansfield Park
Northanger Abbey
Persuasion
Pride and Prejudice
Sanditon and Other Stories
Sense and Sensibility

HONORÉ DE BALZAC
Cousin Bette
Eugénie Grandet
Old Goriot

SIMONE DE BEAUVOIR
The Second Sex

SAUL BELLOW
The Adventures of Augie March

WILLIAM BLAKE
Poems and Prophecies

JORGE LUIS BORGES
Ficciones

JAMES BOSWELL
The Life of Samuel Johnson

CHARLOTTE BRONTË
Jane Eyre
Villette

EMILY BRONTË
Wuthering Heights

MIKHAIL BULGAKOV
The Master and Margarita

SAMUEL BUTLER
The Way of all Flesh

ITALO CALVINO
If on a winter's night a traveler

ALBERT CAMUS
The Stranger

MIGUEL DE CERVANTES
Don Quixote

GEOFFREY CHAUCER
Canterbury Tales

ANTON CHEKHOV
My Life and Other Stories
The Steppe and Other Stories

KATE CHOPIN
The Awakening

CARL VON CLAUSEWITZ
On War

**SAMUEL TAYLOR
COLERIDGE**
Poems

WILKIE COLLINS
The Moonstone
The Woman in White

JOSEPH CONRAD
Heart of Darkness
Lord Jim
Nostromo
The Secret Agent
Typhoon and Other Stories
Under Western Eyes

DANTE ALIGHIERI
The Divine Comedy

DANIEL DEFOE
Moll Flanders
Robinson Crusoe

CHARLES DICKENS
Bleak House
David Copperfield
Dombey and Son
Great Expectations
Hard Times
Little Dorrit
Martin Chuzzlewit
Nicholas Nickleby
The Old Curiosity Shop
Oliver Twist
Our Mutual Friend
A Tale of Two Cities

DENIS DIDEROT
Memoirs of a Nun

JOHN DONNE
The Complete English Poems

FYODOR DOSTOEVSKY
The Brothers Karamazov
Crime and Punishment

This book is set in GARAMOND, the first typeface in
the ambitious programme of matrix production
undertaken by the Monotype Corporation
under the guidance of Stanley Morrison
in 1922. Although named after the
great French royal typographer,
Claude Garamond (1499–
1561), it owes much to
Jean Jannon of Sedan
(1580–1658).